A Most Unfortunate Woman

A MOST UNFORTUNATE WOMAN

Bruce Pippett

A Most Unfortunate Woman

Bruce Pippet

Typeset and cover design by BookPOD

Printed and bound in Australia by BookPOD

ISBN: 978-0-6451380-0-9   eISBN: 978-0-6451380-1-6

 A catalogue record for this book is available from the National Library of Australia

This novel is dedicated to the memory of
CAROLINE PIPPETT
who passed out of our world
on 21 October, 2005, aged 26

Chapter One

SOMETIMES OUR LIVES ARE PLAGUED BY AN EVENT THAT IS both extraordinary and unpredictable. It is so terrifyingly awful in its impact, that it seems clear that there is no alternative than to ring one's hands and despairingly reach out for something to clutch on to that will enable us to understand if there is a logical reason for this incomprehensible event or whether it is something that is beyond human comprehension.

Once, in my friend's life, some two years ago, there was such a calamitous occurrence. What began as just another ordinary day took a turn that left him devastated. It was so earth-shattering that I will never forget where I was and what I was doing.

At the time I was working in New York. I had a call from George the wrong side of midnight. After an evening spent with friends at dinner, my wife and I had returned home and after winding down over a nightcap had just gone to bed. "Chloe's passed away," he said, with no preliminary words other than confirming it was me he was speaking with. I was flabbergasted and found it hard to speak let alone believe what George was telling me. I heard the cry of a broken man. As his stuttering words reached my ear I gripped the telephone as if my hands were a vice. I had answered the phone sitting on the edge of the bed; his words froze me in my place. What could I say? Tears welled in my eyes as my heart went out to my best friend. He tried to tell me what happened but he was in no state to explain fully other than to say he thought Chloe had had a brain haemorrhage. "Sorry, I have to go," he finally said and...he was gone. I closed my mobile and remained glued to the edge of the bed, in a daze. Debra had been woken by the ringing and as soon as I hung up she asked me what was wrong. "It was George. Chloe's just died," I said. Debra screamed and reached over and clung to my back as tears gushed down her cheeks. I felt helpless, so many thousands of miles away, and unable to comfort and support my friend.

Debra and I immediately arranged leave from our jobs and rushed back for the funeral which was held one week later, on the following Friday. George was inconsolable. How he got through his eulogy I will never know. In the packed funeral parlour, tears flowed freely. I unashamedly cried. In her grief, Debra clung to me as if her very life depended on sticking by my side. We met George outside after Chloe's coffin was carried out and placed in the hearse for her last journey. I hugged my friend and kissed him on the cheek. Then George vanished into the black car with Michelle, his first wife, Chloe's mother, and took Chloe off to her final rest.

I was unable to take more than a few days leave so we had to fly back to New York early the next day. We had only a short time to spend at the wake that night with George and Emily, his girlfriend. Leaving George at such a momentous change in his life was gut wrenching.

Two years and a bit sped by and my contract came to an end. Debra and I returned from New York. On arriving home I immediately rang George and asked him to come over later in the day. When I opened the door in response to his knock I could see that there was still sadness in his eyes, as if the funeral had just concluded.

We had the house to ourselves. My children were now in their twenties and, just prior to our return, had left the convenience and comfort of minding the house to flat together. My wife had left an hour ago to meet up with Emily who was by now George's wife.

Immediately I opened the door and saw his face I knew I had to try and help George resurrect his deadened spirit. It was clear his pain had not been erased or much eased by the passage of time. He had, of course, given me some idea during the preceding two years of what had taken place, but I felt I was still to hear the whole story. I hoped he would tell me again, more comprehensively perhaps, what had happened to his daughter on that spring day. I thought that perhaps after he unburdened himself I could comfort him in some small way.

"Can we talk?" he asked solemnly as we shook hands. I gave him a hug.

"Of course," I said, for that was the reason I had asked him over.

"It's about Chloe," he said with a serious look on his face.

He sat down on the couch. I grabbed a couple of beers from the refrigerator, gave him one, and waited for George to tell me what he needed to say.

"Other than when we exchanged emails and we spoke on Skype I haven't had a chance to tell you, face to face, exactly what happened." He took a long draught of beer to settle his nerves and began his tale.

"My son Benny had telephoned me at work, just before eleven and told me Chloe had passed away. Naturally, I was stupefied. I could not understand the meaning of his words and how they related to me. I asked myself: How could Chloe die? It was unbelievable, almost impossible. I left the office bamboozled, flustered, and on the way to Michelle's house, picked up Emily. During the half hour or so I was driving to Michelle's I drove as if nothing was wrong with my world. It was only when we turned into the street and saw the ambulance parked outside the house next door did my mind embrace the reality of what Benny had told me.

"'Where's Chloe?' I asked a paramedic casually standing on the road adjacent to the ambulance, as if he had nothing else to do with his time but lounge around, waiting for something to happen. Somehow I was still expecting Chloe to come bouncing out of the house, full of life and energy. He nodded in the direction of the house. I rushed inside to find Michelle and her sister sitting silently and morosely at the kitchen table, heads slumped, as if in prayer. I rushed straight upstairs to Chloe's room. The door was closed. I pushed it open and saw a sight that I never want to see again. Chloe was lying on the floor, on her back, with her head slightly tilted to one side, her arms bent out in front of her as if she was reaching out for someone to hold. Later on, Michelle told me that her sister had somehow lifted Chloe out of bed and placed her on the floor in a vain attempt at resuscitation. It was clear to me that she was dead and had been for some time. I turned away and returned to the kitchen and asked the only question worth asking – what happened? At that time Michelle was giving a policewoman a list of the prescription medicines which Chloe needed to take. Apparently, if someone dies at home the police have to attend. Just to check if it is a suicide I suppose.

"Life has now, two years later, returned to some degree of normality, though I realise my life has changed forever. Yet my life is shrouded by a degree of superficiality. I imagine that people look at me and think – 'Ah, it appears as if he has finally gotten over his daughter's death.' But looks can be deceptive. And all these people's thoughts are completely adrift of the mark. Chloe is always on my mind, not only at this very moment, but all through each day...especially when I suddenly wake in the middle of the night and cannot get back to sleep. My thoughts turn to Chloe and I ask myself the same simple question that I asked two years ago – why? Why was Chloe taken from us, so early, well before her time, on the verge of a career. And she would have been a great nurse. And you know, to this very day, I have not found an answer to such a very simple question. Ever since that dreadful day, I have been depressed. I cry almost daily and frequently tear up if an emotional event occurs on TV. I even went to see a psychiatrist. She said I had a diminished interest and pleasure in activities that used to please me. Well, I thought, I know that. I go through the motions even when I appear to be giving my all. I've suffered with insomnia and I am constantly tired. Guilt grabs me and tears my heart to shreds. I ask myself: what could I have done to save her? And, in the early days, I had suicidal thoughts."

"There's no need to tell me this, George," I said, reaching out and touching his arm. To be honest, I felt a little embarrassed at these private disclosures. I felt as if it was an intrusion into his privacy. But then again, George was my friend and if he needed to disgorge his feelings and felt the better for doing so, who was I to stop him? I perceived from his demeanour that there was something else he wanted to get off his chest so I asked him to keep going.

"Just lately, something very strange has occurred while I am asleep. It's happened more than once. Not the usual mixed up, crazy type of dream based on recent events. No, these dreams are different. Chas, you are my closest friend and I need to tell you before I mention it to anyone else, even Emily, as I have to know if what I am about to tell you could actually have occurred or is it simply a figment of my tortured imagination. You have to tell me if I'm mad as well as depressed."

"Don't be silly George," I said. "You're as sane as I am," I added with a laugh. "And as for depression that is perfectly understandable seeing what you've been through." George's face carried such a serious and depressed countenance that I felt I needed to get him to lighten up. My jocularity did not improve his outlook so I asked him once more to tell me what was on his mind.

"Chloe comes and speaks to me," he said very softly, as if it was blasphemy, almost a crime to utter those words. This jolted me to my core. I sat up and listened more intently. "What do you mean?" I asked, incredulous.

"I am in a deep sleep and suddenly she appears before me, just like in a dream. When she appeared on that first night she smiled and said 'Hi Dad', as natural as could be and told me she was in the after-life and wanted to speak to me about her sudden death, her life and our relationship as father and daughter."

He stopped speaking, waiting for my reaction.

I was flabbergasted, spellbound, and in a stuttering voice told George to go on.

"She told me she had so much to say that I would be unable to take it all in at the one time. She said that every so often she would visit me while I was asleep and continue her story."

"And...has she?" I ventured, hesitating to ask the obvious question.

"Yes...twice more so far...with more to come."

"And...what has she said?" I asked. "How can you remember what Chloe says to you?"

"As soon as she has finished speaking to me, I immediately wake up. At the end of her first visit, as soon as I woke I realised I had to get all this down on paper. I rushed to my computer and typed out as much as I could remember."

"And...how much did you remember?"

"Strange to say Chas, but as soon as I began typing, her

words poured into my mind, and I continued transcribing them, verbatim, until I'd finished. And something else is associated with these visits."

"What's that?" I asked, breathlessly.

"When I wake up, I instinctively, as if I am under some form of compulsion, look at the digital clock on my side table and... guess what?"

I shook my head.

"Each time...the clock has read 3.17."

"Are you sure? It could be mere co-incidence," I suggested.

"You think so? I believe it has a deeper meaning. Maybe Chloe is telling me something?"

"Like what?" I asked

"Maybe... that's the time she died."

I looked at him. A very strange expression had taken possession of his face; it was as if it was frozen solid and he was staring down a crevasse into a never-ending abyss.

"So you have notes of what she has told you so far on your computer?"

"Yes, I do. Do you want to hear what she has told me?"

"Yes, of course," I replied, for what else could I say? I was in too deep to turn my friend away from relating his story.

George picked up a two-ringed white folder he had bought with him that lay next to him on the couch. He opened it and turned to the first page.

Chapter Two

.

HE LOOKED ME IN THE EYE.

"These notes are Chloe's words as I remember them. It wasn't a conversation as we know it; it was more in the form of a lecture. I could see her as she was speaking to me, but only above her waist. But it certainly was Chloe; of that I have no doubt. I could tell it was her because not only her face appeared before me but also the tone of her voice was exactly how I remember it. She was facing me. When she came that first night I believed I was dreaming, in a deep sleep. You may think that's all it was – a dream. But Chloe has returned twice more and continued her story as if there was no break and she was only giving me the intervening time between visits for me to digest her words, to understand her intentions in coming back...to see me. So I am convinced it is her...in some sort of spirit form. Chas, do you believe me?"

It sounded an incredible story, unbelievable. But I had known George for over thirty years and time had not evaporated the strong relationship we had formed all those years ago; it had endured. We had matured and grown to adulthood together. I had never ever suspected him of telling me an untruth. He reminded me often enough that as a lawyer he was an officer of the Court and so was bound on his oath to tell the truth. So, if he was telling me it was Chloe, well, I just had to believe him. And for George's sake I wanted to believe because he had been devastated by her sudden death. So of course I believed him! What else could I do? Tell my friend he had the symptoms of mental illness and get him off to the doctor? I had no religious beliefs but I had to accept his statement that Chloe was speaking to him from the afterlife. George certainly did not give me any reason to believe otherwise.

"Yes, I believe you," I finally said.

"Good, I'll read out my notes from this first contact." He added: "Chloe just appeared to me...and commenced speaking. All I could do was to listen passively." He took a deep breath and began his story.

Hi Dad, it's me, Chloe. I never had a chance to say goodbye before I died. To make up for that, I will come and visit you from time to time and tell you what happened to me after I died and what I have been through since. I have so much to tell you. I also want to patch up any misunderstandings we may have had during my life. When I was alive I did not turn my mind to whether there was an afterlife. Now, I know there is; even so, I certainly arrived here well before I should have. I recall being told on earth that life wasn't meant to be easy or at least there were no guarantees, so I guess that with all the bad luck that I'd had in my short life, it would just have to be me that would get here before you or Mum.

Anyway, I reckon you want to know how I got here and a bit about this place. Well, I mean, we all treasure the hope, even privately, that our existence does not fizzle out at the moment of death. That's the eternal question isn't it – what happens afterwards?

Well, for one thing, I understand now that my body was cremated after my funeral, but before that, the moment I died, my soul, my spirit, whatever you want to call it, began its journey to the afterlife. On earth, Christians call this place Heaven. But I've met people here who told me they were Buddhist or Muslim and many others who, in their brand of religion, call this place Paradise and other names, so I have decided to call this place the 'Afterlife', out of respect for these new friends of mine. I first of all found myself in a vast space; it is called the Waiting Room. It's incredibly hard to explain accurately in earthly terms; I mean, it's not exactly a room, like a living room in a house or a lobby in an hotel, but a space which from your point of view would be considered incredibly large because, as you can imagine, there are many people waiting at the one time.

Dad, this is how it all happened; although I expect by now you will have learned how I died. I went to bed one night, and after tossing and turning for a while, I must have gone to sleep. At some time during the night or early morning I thought I was in the middle of a dream. But it was only after I came here that I realised that it was my spirit on its way here. Later on, I was told I had had a seizure, a fit, and I died in my sleep. So what I thought was my dream was actually my spirit beginning its journey.

Well, I seemed to be travelling along this long corridor, a long tunnel perhaps, which seemed to have no end; it continued into the never-ending distance, much like that corridor in the novel you once told me about, 'The Trial' by Franz Kafka. I was standing up. The floor, ceiling and walls were a luminous, bright white. It appeared to me that I was being hurled at tremendous speed for what seemed a very long time, like in a spaceship, down this corridor. But I wasn't bunkered down in any flying machine. I was moving along in a vertical position as though there were a set of rails under my feet and I was able to travel at a great speed, held there by some sort of magnetic force, perhaps like a hovercraft or that magnetic levitation train in Shanghai that you travelled on. And despite appearing to be travelling very fast, I couldn't see the end. If there was one, it appeared to be covered by a mist, a fog, a dense cloud. Later, I noticed a great brightness, like the brightest of lights or the blinding glare of the sun when you directly look at it and you are momentarily blinded, and forced to shut your eyes, and by instinct you lift your hand up to protect your face from the glare.

The walls were blank. Nothing was hanging on them, no signs, absolutely nothing. As if I could have clearly noticed much anyway because I felt I was travelling at a tremendous speed. I could not measure it however because I had nothing to compare my speed with. No wind blowing back my hair. No distortion of my face like in a wind tunnel. Nothing else surrounded me except these blank walls and a floor beneath me and a roof above. And I had no idea why I was travelling in this way. I was terribly confused. I tried to put these thoughts aside. My eyes only seemed to be concentrating on this bright light in the distance. Time seemed to have stood still. It seemed like a never ending journey to an unknown, mysterious destination. And I couldn't turn around and flee from this world of white and brightness. Something held me there. It felt like I was being pushed from behind as well as dragged forward by some force. But I really believed I was dreaming, and therefore didn't care too much at the time.

Eventually I noticed that the light was beginning to glow brighter; I had a hunch I was getting closer to my destination. But I need to remind you I didn't know I was dead. I believed I was merely in the middle of another weird dream. Often we know we are in a dream; we are still asleep, on the verge of waking, but some instinct tells us we are dreaming. Sometimes people we know, friends and acquaintances, various incidents from our recent life crop up in our dreams. We recognise these people and talk to them, often in a bizarre way. Strange things happen in dreams. We can't control them. That is why when I was hurtling along this white corridor or tunnel; I was confused but I wasn't really concerned.

The light intensified to a magnitude I had never experienced before. It seemed to me like a thousand suns had exploded in some gigantic outburst I imagined the end of the universe might look like. I blinked and half-closed my eyes to protect myself from the penetrating brilliance of the light. I attempted to raise my arm to shield my face, but this force prevented me. How long this lasted I can't say because often reality is weirdly distorted. Then the blinding light began to decrease in intensity. I noticed that I'd been slowing down as if there was some connection between it and the fading of the light. Some force was bringing me to a halt.

Blocking my way was a door; it looked just like a solid, double-sized door that you see on expensive houses; it was coloured white. The knob on the door was round; it was also white. I was surrounded by a sea of white. 'What do I do now?' I thought. In a dream one can't control the sequence of events, they just unroll like a surging tide, like in a film where one scene smoothly follows another. I could think but now I wasn't able to move a muscle. Then, that force or power tugged me and pushed me forward. I was puzzled but my next step seemed so natural. For what else could I do? I'd been rushed along this long, never ending corridor, blinded by the most brilliant light, and now found myself face to face with a huge door. There was no way back. I wasn't able to turn my head around and look back to where I had come from. I attempted to move it but I couldn't turn an inch. I approached the door with some trepidation. I listened. There was no sound at all. There was only silence, a deep silence, as deep as in outer space. Perhaps like being in a desert, hundreds of miles from anywhere, in the middle of nowhere, with nothing but mangy scrub and stars for companions; maybe like somewhere in the depths of the Nullabor Plain. Remember Dad, you once told me that you and Mum were driving back from Perth. You became very tired; sometime late in the night you stopped the car to have a nap. After waking up, you got out of the car to stretch your legs. You couldn't detect the sound of any living creature; you said there were no twittering birds, no scampering rodents, no bounding kangaroos, no howling dingoes, nothing at all. You said an inky blackness enveloped you and Mum. The billions of stars in the sky provided your only connection with reality, with humanity.

I stretched out my hand and placed it on the knob. The force allowed me to move. It felt strange; the knob was there, right before me, yet I believed it wasn't. A strange mixture of something tangible and also intangible, if that doesn't seem too weird! Later on, when I knew I was dead, it came to me all in a rush. I wasn't in the physical world, so nothing existed in a solid state; it was all contained in another dimension, unknown on earth. I assumed I had to turn the knob just like on earth. In dreams things just happen so of course I expected it to turn. And it did. I slowly opened the panel of the door. It opened inwards. Because I didn't know what was behind it, I opened it a bit at a time, very hesitantly, apprehensive as to what I would find. I didn't think about not opening the door. As night follows day, everything appeared to be in order, a natural sequence of events. I felt compelled to proceed, unable to prevent myself succumbing to some irresistible temptation. What else was I to do? I was at the end of this long white corridor. An overwhelming force prevented me from turning my head with a view to retracing my steps. In my mind it was all a dream; a spooky kind of dream. Therefore I had no comprehension, no understanding of the force that had driven me, drawing me onwards towards this white door, and compelled me to open it.

After I had opened it a little way without resistance, I felt more confident. Nothing bad had happened. I gave the door a little push and it swung open. I slowly stepped across the threshold and looked straight ahead of me. A man was standing there, filling up my view. Bewildered, I stared at him. It was very strange. Still, I believed I was within the deep confines of a dream and I would suddenly wake up and shake my head in amazement.

≈

George suddenly stopped.

"That's the end of the visit on the first night," he said. "What do you think?"

I had been riveted to my seat as he read out the story of Chloe's journey to the afterlife. His ceasing reading brought me back to reality. What did I think?

What did I think? he asked me. Hell, I really didn't know what to say. I was choked with emotion. It was incredible, but as it was George telling me this, I was almost compelled to believe it. It sounded authentic, if that's the right word to use, but impossible to believe. Other people who claim to have had near death experiences write of them, but until now, I suppose I took those encounters with a pinch of salt, as perhaps personal involvement or a substantial degree of religious belief is necessary to be a believer. And to tell the truth, I was miles away from being a believer. But here I was, being dragged into an exposition of the afterlife by my best friend. And I had to believe all this was true, for George's sake.

"Do you believe me, Charles?" he asked. I had never had this sort of conversation with anyone before. It was like sex and politics; one rarely spoke of these things. Men especially stayed clear of conversation concerning the afterlife. I suppose I was one of those many people who tolerated Seventh Day Adventists and other religious organisations, even non-Christian, because as we live in a democracy we have been taught to accept, or at least tolerate, minority groups. And outspoken atheists such as Richard Dawkins whose book I had been given for a Christmas present certainly had some influence in the community. He and others looked at it from a viewpoint of lack of evidence and, in their eyes, stories of so-called miracles lacked veracity. Once dead, that was it. I suppose I hoped there may have been an afterlife but I wasn't too fussed because there was nothing I could do about it. Every one of us has to die.

But this appearance of Chloe before George in his sleep was another dimension. Was this an example of evidence sufficient to quieten down the doubters and make the atheists change their mind? Hell, I was so confused about it; I didn't know what to say to him.

"Believe in God and the afterlife?" I asked.

"I guess that's what I mean."

"You certainly have given me something to think about." Geez, surely George would pick up these stalling tactics. Like when you're a kid and your mother asks did you do something bad and you give out a denial by way of an answer that any mother can recognise as nonsense.

"Don't be vague, Chas," he said.

"I'm not trying to be but...this has come from nowhere and I need time to think about it."

"Well, I'll tell you what I think," George said boldly. "I admit that I'm no churchgoer and other than weddings and funerals I haven't been for about thirty years, but I have some belief in a supreme being. We call it God but that's just a label that religious people have pinned on it. And as I was born in a so-called Christian country and brought up in the Presbyterian Church I suppose I can be labelled as Christian. What we have as religious symbols I'm sure the Hindus, Buddhists and the Muslims have their own equivalent. I've read a little of Buddhism mainly by browsing through a few books of the Dalai Lama I've come across in bookshops. And as you know, I've been to Nepal and had conversations with Hindus and Buddhists and experienced aspects of those religions. I've visited their temples and watched their cremation ceremonies held on the banks of a river. And now...this has happened. You may call me loony but I have no doubt that it was Chloe speaking to me and nothing will ever make me change my mind."

"Listen George," I said, shifting forward in my seat, reaching out and touching his arm, "Difficult as it is to do so, I believe you when you tell me Chloe spoke to you. We have been mates for a very long time, nothing will change that. It's just that this flies in the face of what the majority of people believe, including me."

"I understand that," George said. "People often need to experience an event to believe that some event is possible. Look at the progress we have made from believing the earth was flat to planting man on the moon and undertaking incredible surgery, heart operations, separating conjoined babies and the like. All incredibly real, but previously only contemplated by people regarded as weird; what we call nutters today. Everything changes. So, from my personal experience I now know there is an afterlife...and Chloe is there."

At that very moment I heard Debra open the front door.

"Hello you two, what are you up to?" she asked, smiling at us, coming over and planting a kiss on George's cheek. "Good to see you again, George," she said, giving him a hug. "Emily went straight home if you're wondering where she is."

"George just came over for a beer and a chat."

"You two, I bet you've been talking about the good old days, how you met and all your adventures, hey Chas?" Debra replied, her voice trailing off as she wandered off into the kitchen.

"I'd better be off Chas. Emily will wonder where I am. Can you keep this quiet for a while? Wait until we've gone through all of what Chloe intends to tell me before we mention it to anyone."

"Sure George," I said. "We'll get together another day and continue the story."

"Thanks pal," he said, standing up. I stood up and followed him to the door. I don't know how it happened but by some instinct I wrapped my arms around him and gave him a big hug and kissed him on his unshaven cheek.

"See you Debra, see you soon," he yelled out, smiled at me and with his folder tucked under his arm walked down the path to the front gate. He turned, smiled and went to his car. I stood there for a long time after his car disappeared around the corner contemplating the strange world we live in.

Chapter Three

DURING THE NEXT WEEK I WAS UNSETTLED. I WENT THROUGH the motions but my mind was elsewhere. It was with George and his story. I desperately wanted to hear the next instalment. After a few days I rang him, ostensibly for a social chat. In fact, what I craved was to arrange a time for him to visit again and read what else Chloe told him. To do so without our families being involved seemed an impossible task, for we saw George and Emily socially nearly every weekend. To stop these gatherings in order for us to meet secretly would invite suspicion from both our wives who, being women, were born with a great deal of intuition. Eventually, I got myself invited to George's office for a sandwich at lunchtime. I was not hungry for food but for the story. At my urging he fetched his folder out of his briefcase.

"I'll continue from where I left off," he said, gave a little cough and began reading.

≈

The man was of an indeterminate age. He was clothed in a white gown that reached to his feet on which he wore what appeared to be slippers. He looked like a religious person; some type of minister or priest, a person endowed with maturity and wisdom. He had an appearance that took on the characteristics of a normal, solid-bodied human being, and also at the same time that of some unnatural ghost-like apparition.

He signalled to me to approach. I did so as if under a spell, hypnotised by the bewitching powers of a magician. Perhaps I was compelled to go up to him like a member of a cult or religious order must when the leader commands an audience. I quickly walked over and stopped a few feet in front of him. I had no idea of what I was supposed to do. A kindly smile radiated across his face. I didn't feel afraid although I hadn't a clue who this person was.

"Welcome, Chloe,' he said in a soft voice.

"Where am I?" I asked him.

"In the Waiting Room, in the afterlife," he replied, still smiling.

"In the afterlife!" I exclaimed in a loud voice. He said nothing.

"Why am I in the afterlife? I haven't died, have I?" I asked.

"Yes, you have," he calmly said.

"But, how..." I stammered, unable to grasp what I was hearing.

"You died from an epileptic fit caused by a brain tumour," he replied in a kindly voice.

"But I...haven't been..." and then my recent earthly life came back to me. I recalled that a week or so ago I was, once again, suffering from a severe migraine. As you well know Dad, for many years I often suffered a sudden migraine attack. You remember all those times I had a bad headache at school and the office rang you to come and get me? Mum had also told me that I appeared to have experienced a strange incident while I was on the phone. She said I stopped speaking and just stood there completely rigid. Next day, I went to see a doctor at the clinic I always attended. He was not my regular doctor as she was away, but he worked there. I took along a note Mum gave me describing what had happened to me. He read it, and then put it in my file. He said I was suffering from stress because of my university studies and this had caused my attack. For some reason he prescribed Voltaren for me as the clinic had done many times in the past. Mum was a little unsettled by this as Voltaren is used as an anti-inflammatory and neither of us thought this was what I needed. So a day later Mum made me ring and make an appointment to see my regular doctor, just to get another opinion. I never got to see her.

"Yes, we know all the details," the man said, though I had not spoken a word; it appeared he had the ability to read my every thought.

"But...dead?"

"Yes, dead," he confirmed. "You have left your earthly body, and your spirit form has arrived here for judgement."

"Judgement?" I queried, raising my voice again.

"Yes."

"By whom?" I asked, still incredulous.

"By the Supreme Being which you call God," he said. "After their death, every person must wait here in the Waiting Room until God decides if he or she can immediately be admitted to Heaven proper or to be sent away for a further period to the Half-Way Place so they can redeem themselves and make up for their errors. The other alternative is to be sent away out of the Waiting Room, not to the Half-Way Place, but to be cast out to..."

"Hell?" I quickly ventured.

"Well, living people call it that, but here we call it the 'Frozen Place'," he said. "It is the place where essentially irredeemable people are sent. People who have shown a lack of compassion and humanity towards their fellow man are those we recognise as impossible to rehabilitate. People designated as such do not live for eternity. Their life is suspended, frozen for evermore, reflecting their cold, inhumane attitude to their fellow man on earth."

I feared to ask what the people who were sent to this 'Frozen Place' had to go through, but if it was anything like I had read in the Bible or if it approached what the priests had described to us in their sermons, it was a place where I didn't wish to be sent to at all . Trembling with fear if that was to be my destination, I managed to ask him if I would be sent there.

"God will decide this later on," he continued.

At least now I knew he wasn't God; but if he wasn't...then who was he?

"Excuse me...but...who are you, exactly?" I asked. "I thought you were God!" I blurted out before he had an opportunity to respond.

"I am the gatekeeper," he solemnly replied in a calm and peaceful manner.

"The gatekeeper?" I queried.

"Yes. Your spirit left your earthly body immediately upon your death. Do you recall the long, white corridor you travelled along?"

"Yes, it seemed like a corridor," I agreed.

"And after the blinding light subsided you came upon a door?"

"Yes."

"And then you slowly opened the door and saw me standing here?"

"Yes I did," I once again agreed with him.

"Well, in earthly terminology I am called the gatekeeper because I mind the door you came through. My job is to welcome spirits to the Waiting Room." He spread his arms as if to indicate the vast area covered by this Waiting Room. "If your application is approved," he continued, "you will be admitted permanently to Heaven."

I looked around me. For some reason I couldn't see very far at all. I asked the gatekeeper why I couldn't see much past him.

"Until I finish our conversation with a spirit who has just arrived, it is best to limit vision, in case it is decided that a spirit be sent to the Half-Way Place or the Frozen Place instead of waiting here." I didn't understand what he meant so I continued my questioning.

"Where's the afterlife?" I ventured. "Isn't it here?"

"No, it's not here," he replied with a smile.

"Where is it?" I persisted.

"It's hard to explain," he said. "As I mentioned just now, you have opened the door to the Waiting Room, and you must remain here while your application is being assessed."

"And God decides?" I asked a little apprehensively.

He had a look of keen amazement on his face.

"Why, of course," he replied, as if I was a silly little girl to ask such a question, when he had not a minute ago told me that God judges every person.

I felt small again, trampled upon like I had felt many times during my earthly life. I had lost my earthly form; I existed solely in the form of a spirit yet nothing could erase from my memory the pain I had felt when I believed I had been rejected as a person, as a human being, by so-called friends who could be so icy and catty at times, or my teachers at school who cuttingly criticised me when I had trouble with a maths sum or in writing a sentence out grammatically correct. And that nun at the Catholic School in Whitehorse Road was the worst of all. Do you recall that day, Dad? After I sat for the entrance exam I went with you and Mum to an interview at the school with this nun. She had all my papers there with her, spread out over her desk. She delighted in stabbing at my answers with her crooked, arthritic finger, pointing out every error I had committed in the exam as if she was teaching a class, indicating words written on the blackboard. 'You did very badly,' she said, and she seemed to be very happy as she said this, enthusiastically rubbing it in, putting me down – and in front of you and Mum too! I was stunned and embarrassed by her personal attack and you will remember I could only stammer incoherent responses to the vicious questions to which she demanded I give her the correct answers. 'Why did you answer this question this way or that question that way?' she asked severely, vigorously thrusting her hand directly at my answers. You looked hopping mad, but you didn't say too much at the time, but as we returned to our car to drive home you told Mum, in a savage tone of voice, that even if, after all that tirade of abuse I had just endured, they offered me a place, I would never ever take one step inside the grounds of that school. 'That nun lacks compassion,' you said. And Mum, despite being brought up as a Catholic, wholeheartedly agreed with you. I was proud of you and Mum for being on my side because that school gave me the shivers and I certainly didn't want to go there. So even though I was young, I realised that bad people existed, even amongst religious people, despite their Christian upbringing, which should have trained them to be kind to their fellow man and love all living creatures.

≈

George paused. He wiped his sleeve across his eyes, the reading of that conversation and Chloe's comments about her ill-treatment too much for him to cope with. After a good minute he pulled himself together and resumed.

≈

"And when is this decision made?" I asked.

"In the future," the gatekeeper replied. "I'm like an assistant. I welcome people when they knock on the door, make them comfortable, reassure them that everything is all right, because it can be a little daunting coming to grips with one's death. Many people arrive here without any form of warning."

"Like me!" I exclaimed. "I had no idea that I was going to die. I went to bed one night and...here I am...no time for any goodbyes."

"No, none at all,' he confirmed. "Take yourself; you were asleep, and then...like a click of the fingers, you died. Your spirit immediately started out on its journey and...until you opened the door, found me standing in front of you and spoke with me, you did not know that you were dead."

"No, I didn't have a clue."

"Yet, you are here now and have begun your new life."

"How long will my spirit life last for?" I asked, feeling quite clumsy for asking such a silly question.

He smiled at me. "Why Chloe, you will be here for ever and ever," he said, once again appearing to be a little puzzled as to why I had asked a question the answer to which seemed rather obvious. I mean, all through our earthly lives we are cautioned to be kind, to undertake good works, all for the purpose of getting to the place called Heaven. We are given hope as if this lure of an everlasting life somehow compensates us for the bitter pill that most of us have to swallow to endure living on earth. And there I was – dead. Did I feel lucky? At the time I was confused – yes, I realised now that what we had been told was true – there was a life beyond the grave, and yes, I could live for evermore. On the other hand, this state of happiness was counterbalanced by the trauma I knew that you and Mum would undergo when you learnt about my death.

"Do my mum and dad know that I'm here...that I'm dead?" I asked the gatekeeper.

"Yes, they know," he announced with a solid assurance in his voice, as if he knew precisely what was going on down on earth. Well, I say 'down' because traditionally people on earth associate Heaven with being 'up there', in the sky. I was now in the Waiting Room, and yet I didn't know where it was – up, down or wherever. All I knew was that it was in another sphere of existence, although to a certain extent it resembled life on earth. The gatekeeper had an appearance similar to a human on earth. And this Waiting Room – it probably stretched out into the far distance. I say probably because I couldn't see very far past the gatekeeper. My eyes lacked the ability to see into the distance, just like the gatekeeper had told me. It had to be large I imagined, just to be able to accommodate all the people who were dying every minute of every day. Then a thought suddenly struck me. If my experience of being rushed along that white tunnel was repeated all over the world instantaneously on death for the thousands of people all over the world who die every day – how many doors must there be? How many doorkeepers are waiting expectantly for that knock on the door and the stepping inside by the spirit of another dead person? Despite me now having arrived in the spirit world, being such a newcomer and having had no previous experience of this place, I couldn't understand this aspect of the Waiting Room, and the concept of a place inhabited by spirits. My mind was totally confused; I was bewildered by my sudden transfer to a place where by definition no living person could ever be admitted. No, it was a place created for those who had passed from the physical world.

"When did...when did my mum know that I had died?" I asked

"In earthly terms, a few hours after your passing," the gatekeeper answered.

"I've lost all track of time," I replied.

"Yes, that's what happens," he said. "Time stands still, in a manner of speaking. When you came to us and pushed open the door, you could have no real idea of the earth time that had elapsed since you began your journey. There is no comparison. But I am able to tell you what has happened on earth. This knowledge has been passed on to me."

"So you are able to tell me what has happened to my mum and dad?"

"Yes, I can tell you if an event has taken place."

"Can you tell me...?" I began hesitantly.

"Chloe, that is...something I don't like to do because...it can cause distress..."

"But I'm worried about my mum!" I cried out in anguish. "How will she cope?"

"As I have just mentioned, your mother found you a few hours after your passing. At first she had no idea that you had already died; she believed you were faking, pretending to be asleep because you did not want to get up. After a few minutes she came back into your room and discovered that you had not moved and were lying there without breathing. Naturally she was stunned, shocked to the core because it was the last thing that she would have expected. She immediately rang her sister who rushed over. She rang your father. He immediately demanded that an ambulance be called. He didn't know it was too late, but it was a natural reaction. Your mother had been too shocked to understand. She couldn't comprehend that she should have called for an ambulance prior to calling your aunt. Your father, not really believing your mother would do so, also rang for an ambulance. But...I fear this is too much for you to bear."

At that point – he was right – it was all too much and I... became very emotional...because now I had lost my connection with you and Mum. I grieved for you all, especially Mum. Oh, how would she cope with living without me I wondered? And you, Dad...you loved me...I know that...in your own way. You were not overly demonstrative because after you and Mum separated you probably felt there was a gulf between us, not openly of course, but an unspoken one. Not in my eyes though. I did love you Dad and, as I said, in your own way I know you loved me. At least I could talk to you in a fashion. This story I have started to tell you is the only way I can communicate with you although I know that I will never get to hear any response you wish to make. I will be critical of you at times but all I am doing is being completely honest and putting to you certain questions that until now I haven't asked. Some will make you think deeply in regards to our relationship. Other comments will challenge what you and others believe life is all about. You will recall, I hope, that when I was lonely I often went to your house to have a cup of tea or a meal. We would discuss various things, nothing deep and meaningful, and nothing like Mum and me. That is the reason I fear for her. Except for her sister, she has no one to take my place. We were mother and daughter, but also best friends. Perhaps this was because we both experienced great difficulty in making friends. I had a couple of close friends, but other than her sister, Mum has virtually no confidante to speak to. We could chat for hours. We enjoyed analysing other people and their motives for acting as they did; people I worked with at Lort Smith, and fellow students at the university. We would dissect and analyse the behaviour of all my friends and everyone else we came into contact with. Often I had to question their very friendship and their supposed loyalty to me as a special friend. I believe that most people are confused by relationships, whether with a partner or a friend of the same sex. None of us is perfect it is said, so one must learn to tolerate an individual's particular idiosyncrasies, to regard them as a friend despite them, in our opinion, having defects in their character. And yet this is so subjective, isn't it? I'm not. I mean, on earth, I wasn't perfect. I acknowledge that. So other people, even my close friends, may have had similar thoughts about me regarding my attitude to them and my individual personality. It's only natural. Dad, you once told me to look at life from the other person's point of view. You said you read it in a book by Dale Carnegie. If you can stand in the other person's shoes he said, it is much easier to understand where they are coming from and appreciate their particular point of view. So, yes, I will miss my mum. I can only pray that she will be comforted to a certain extent by remembering the good times we enjoyed together, the occasions when we did smile and burst out laughing at the inanity of some ridiculous situation, perhaps some comedy on TV, in particular 'Seinfield', which we often watched together. One can only hope.

≈

George stopped speaking and reached for his handkerchief. He dabbed his eyes. He sniffed. How hard it must have been for him to relate such personal details to me, a mere friend. Compared with his relationship with members of his family, I was an outsider. Not a total stranger perhaps, but certainly not a blood relative. I too felt tears welling. One couldn't help being overcome with emotion. And, this story of his daughter; how wonderful he must have felt when he read what he had transcribed after Chloe had visited him. And yet how devastating at the same time.

I looked around his office and saw a jug of water and some glasses on a buffet. I rose and hurried over and poured him a drink. I had a craving for something much stronger but I put that prospect in abeyance as I had no desire to break his flow of words. He gulped the water down in one draught, looked at me and smiled, at the same time muttering some words I could not hear, for he spoke so softly. I would have loved to discuss with him Chloe's thoughts, yet I thought it best to postpone any discussion until the conclusion of her story, for I saw he had no intention of stopping and was eager to continue.

He took a deep breath and, without saying a single word turned over to the next page and began again as if he had not left off speaking.

Chapter Four

COMING OUT OF MY REVERIE I ONCE AGAIN EXAMINED THE gatekeeper's face. It beamed a smile, a loving genuine smile of kindness, unconditional love and respect for me as an individual, notwithstanding that my life on earth was not as perfect as perhaps it might have been. Love and forgiveness radiated out from him, as if now that I had died all my faults and sins had been set aside, relegated back into a time that was now past. He certainly appeared to understand and have knowledge of my inner thoughts, as if he could read my mind. I had an image of him being a clairvoyant, able to predict the events that would unfold in the future. And yet I was confused because he seemed to indicate that I had just died, but my mum found me hours later. So what was the time on earth: a few minutes after my death, or hours later? And Dad, he also told me your reaction. How could he know all this? My head was violently spinning in my attempt to comprehend these questions that saturated my mind. I had no answer. Then I recalled that he had told me that God was all knowing and this calmed me a little for then I realised that God must have somehow passed this information on to him. Still, I was a novice in this place; it was a new form of existence, so I concluded that, like the meaning of life on earth, it was something I had to accept even though I could not understand it. Perhaps when I had been here for a while, or when I was finally admitted to the afterlife I would understand.

"Yes, you are right," I finally conceded, "it is all too much... because I cannot understand why I am here...I mean...I am...I am so young..."

"That's true," the gatekeeper replied. "You were young. Why you have been called here, the reason you died, is not for us to know, even me, for I am a simple servant, a gatekeeper, a sort of receptionist," he added, with a glimmer of a smile, as if, even here, it was in order to slip in a joke or two, perhaps to make the newcomer feel at ease.

"God has His ways," he continued. "We know that on earth criticisms are made. He deliberately refrains from interfering in events unfolding on earth because, although He is all-powerful, He does not see it as His role to regulate the affairs of Man. He believes humankind, aware that there is a God, should be able to work out how to co-operate with each other so there can be peace and harmony throughout the world. So it is with illness and disease. He will not step in to perform miracles or cure defects that have cropped up. In your case, God well knew of the tumour in your brain, but in following His well-established policy He took no steps to interfere. The doctor that prescribed tablets to combat stress for you instead of sending you off to get a scan or direct to a specialist: God could not compel him to amend his diagnosis, to penetrate into his heart or soul, enter his subconscious and compel him to change his mind and refer you on to a specialist for examination. God allows nature and man to operate within the particular sphere He designed for them at the beginning of time. Mistakes are certainly made by Man, but this is the way life has been allowed to evolve. This policy, of Man being left to its own devices, also allows God's children to live within the physical world and work out the best way to conduct themselves, and having been taught the one true way to live, decide themselves which road to walk along. Unfortunately, as you well know, Man has often strayed off course. But God will not interfere despite the plaintive cries of many on earth wondering why God allows certain events to take place. This is Man's province, not God's. It is for men to work these things out."

Yes, that was exactly what I was taught on earth by the priests. But I didn't want to debate him now. I wanted to find out what was to happen next. "What happens now?" I asked, anxious to come to grips with my new form of existence.

"I have to examine you, if I can put it that way, to elicit information which I can pass on, to set out your circumstances that will assist in the making of a decision."

"But if God knows everything...why is there a need for such an examination?" I protested, not understanding why I had to undertake a process which to me at least seemed a waste of time. "I mean, the very fact that I am here in this Waiting Room, doesn't that mean that an all-knowing God would be fully aware of my life, all the good acts I have performed, all my bad thoughts and the awful deeds I have done in an endeavour to establish my place in the world, and therefore be able now, at the moment of my death and arrival here, to determine whether I am able to be immediately admitted to Heaven?"

"Yes Chloe, you are correct. God does know all about your life, but He wishes me to hear your story in your own words."

"You mean I have to give some sort of presentation in an endeavour to be admitted. I don't think..."

"It's not quite like that," the gatekeeper intervened, smiling. "No, I can assure you it is nothing like that. We hear that on earth a common saying is – 'if you can fake sincerity you've got it made' – or words to that effect. But, although this course of action may work well on earth – here it is of no consequence. God knows when a person is insincere, is being deceitful or is telling a downright lie. He can separate the wheat from the chaff, so to speak. He has knowledge of these matters. God cannot be fooled. So we don't need to ask for a presentation in your favour."

"Exactly what is it then that you, or God, require me to speak about?"

"That is in your own domain, my child," the gatekeeper replied, leaving me great scope I thought to talk about my life.

"Before I start, can I ask you a question?" I asked him.

"Certainly," he replied.

"You told me this place where we are now is called the Waiting Room."

"Yes, that's correct."

"Well, if that is true, and I do believe you...if that is true – where is everyone else who has recently died and is here, waiting?"

"An insightful question, Chloe," he responded. Without a moment's hesitation he began his answer.

"All the recently departed are here in the Waiting Room, but you haven't been given the ability to see them yet," he said. "This is the spirit world. Things are different here; it is dissimilar to life on earth. Your conceptions as to spheres of existence are still under the influence of the knowledge you accumulated on earth. As you can imagine," he said, once again glancing to his left and right, "the size of the Waiting Room exceeds what you may imagine. The breadth of it cannot be explained in human terms. Other people are here, waiting their turn, but as time operates in a different sphere, no-one is concerned. Remember that long, white corridor you travelled along?"

"Yes, of course," I answered.

"Well, the time spent travelling along the corridor cannot be calculated like earth time. So everyone waits their turn until I open the door to admit them, as I have just now admitted you. And so, people come here one by one..."

"Like Noah's Ark," I interrupted, remembering my Bible.

He smiled. "Yes, if you like, but wasn't it two by two?" he gently corrected me.

I blushed. "Well, it's sort of the same thing, don't you think?" I asked, attempting to recover my position.

"Yes," he conceded with a smile, "it's the same."

"I think I understand what you are saying," I continued, still a little unsure, but hopeful that in due course I would come to grips with this new way of existence.

I looked around me. All I could see was a hazy mist, as if a huge white wall had been lowered directly in front of my face, or I was on earth, in winter time, standing in the middle of a low-lying valley, and a dewy, misty fog had settled in this patch, waiting for the morning sun to burn it away. Here, the mist stretched up to the horizon of my vision. I could not tell how far away that horizon was. I could see nothing; no houses, buildings, roads, nor even a seat, nothing at all. I might have been on the moon or a long abandoned planet for all I could work out. And I couldn't see any other spirit. I wondered how big this place could be, bearing in mind that there were millions of people waiting for judgement.

"You look worried," the gatekeeper observed.

"Well, I was thinking over what you said about this place being the Waiting Room. All I can see is this mist, swirling around and around, in the air, covering the ground. But no people; and I can't see any evidence of any form of activity at all."

"It puzzles you, doesn't it? I merely have to remind you Chloe where you are now. Life continues here, but in a completely different form; it is a dimension to which you are not yet accustomed. All your previous notions of space and time now have to be eliminated from your way of thinking. I appreciate it is very hard for you to turn your mind to think in a way that is quite foreign to you, but you will soon begin to adjust to this new way. On earth you breathed air, you ate food, you drank liquids, and had bodily functions; all designed to allow you to operate as a living creature. Here there is no need to do any of these things. You will continue to exist in the form of your spirit. Because you have no solid body there is no need to nourish yourself by consuming food and drink. Your form as a spirit will stay exactly as it is now. I must tell you all this because you can be only truly content and at peace when you totally accept your passage to our world and leave behind your notion of a bodily existence."

"But...my parents...my..."

"Do not be concerned, Chloe," he intervened. "They grieve for you and miss you very much because they loved you. So of course it is natural for you too to miss their company. It is a normal reaction, a natural way of thinking. Once admitted however, your life will take on another aspect – it will be a beautiful life."

I realised now all that he said was true. There was no turning back. My bodily existence had terminated but yet, even existing here as a spirit could not remove from my mind the tender and loving thoughts I had of you and Mum. Mum and I were very close. I pictured her at home, resting on the couch, or sitting at the kitchen table, staring off into space, her thoughts concentrated on my sudden death. Even being religious still makes it difficult, almost impossible to truly come to grips with the loss of a loved one. Despite believing in God, the pain of a physical parting, being torn away from the joy of being with a special loved one cannot be easily overcome. There is no substitution for loss caused by death. Nothing can repair the broken relationship that I had with my mum. I died alone, without a final goodbye. That is the tragedy I now have to carry around. I don't mean I wanted a lingering death bed scene like in those soppy old movies you seem to enjoy so much, Dad. I mean an opportunity to say those things which can only be said within a close relationship. That is what tore at me – that loss of opportunity to say farewell. And I hoped that you were feeling the same way towards me. We all know that death is inevitable. Yet we all cling to the desire that it will come at a time of our own choosing or at least after the final words have been spoken. I had no desire to suffer a long, lingering death. I did not wish to end in that way. But this, this sudden wrenching apart from my life with both you and Mum I found difficult to accept. But there was nothing I could do to prevent that intense pain of internal suffering. I had to accept my death. I had to console myself that for a short time on earth I at least had you two to comfort me through all the troubles I encountered practically every day of my life. I thanked God for that small mercy. Can you understand this, Dad?

≈

George stopped, seemingly felled by Chloe's question. I asked him if that was the end of that night's visit. I wondered if he had halted because his very being was grabbed by her question.

"Yes, that was the end," he said with tears winding their way down his cheeks. I thought that Chloe had stopped at that point to give George an opportunity to ponder the question she left him with.

"What was your reaction when Chloe told you of her conversation with the gatekeeper and her realisation that she was in the afterlife for...ever?" As I spoke I realised how awkward the question must have sounded to George, but I felt at the time I couldn't put it any better than I had.

"It's virtually impossible for me to explain in words that anyone could comprehend. Chloe was right – that loss of opportunity to say goodbye that she felt also tugged at my heart, at every fibre of my being. Michelle was a wreck, naturally, for they were close, as Chloe said. I had no problem with that. We had been separated for years so I was glad for Chloe's sake that she had such a close relationship with her mother. As long as she was happy; that's all I ever wanted for Chloe."

"Fine, but this so-called 'gatekeeper'; as you know I'm pretty sceptical when it comes to religion. You know me George; I can't get my mind around the idea of a gatekeeper waiting to greet people in an afterlife."

"That puzzled me too but I have to take Chloe's words as truthful. I mean, the whole concept of being spoken to from the afterlife, let alone by your own daughter, is something that I found hard to come to grips with at first. If it wasn't Chloe speaking to me I might dismiss these visits as wild dreams, but the continuation of her story from where she had left off on her previous visit I have no doubt is evidence of its truthfulness. Have you ever experienced something like this, Chas?"

"No George, I haven't. To be honest with you, when you first mentioned it to me I was privately very sceptical. But I suspended disbelief because we've been good friends for many years and I know you wouldn't lie to me. And for your sake George I wanted to believe. I thought that if it made you a happier person then that would be a good thing. If you told all this to a psychiatrist he would be in a state of excitement examining you, getting into your psyche and trying to fathom out why you would tell such a fantastic story. And atheists would plainly call you mad and say you were suffering some sort of delusion directly resulting from Chloe's death; they would consider it a bout of wishful thinking. But don't worry about them George, I'll always be here for you."

"Thanks mate," George said.

"So how does this concept of the reality of an afterlife affect you personally?" I asked.

George leaned back in his chair and clasped his hands behind his head and gazed at the ceiling as if he was seeking inspiration from above.

"In one way it's made me a different person."

"In what way?" I asked.

"If Chloe's words are true, which I have no reason to doubt that they are, I have found the answer to what Man has been searching for since the dawn of time. There is an afterlife and one day we'll all get to where Chloe is at this very moment, no matter where we come from, what our form of organised religion is or even if there is no belief. It won't matter. We are all the same, none of us better than any other. When this is known..." he trailed off.

An incredible thought suddenly struck me. Perhaps the two of us were the only people on earth who had solid evidence of the existence of an afterlife. Surely we had, or at least George had a duty, a moral duty, to make it known all over the world. I knew that there were many documented examples of near-death experiences. Many people disregard these stories for they have not personally gone 'there' and come back. Some speak of going to Heaven for a short while and being sent back; at the direction of God they say. I had read of a man who had been severely injured in a car accident and had 'died' and returned to life. Yet in all these cases the fact was that they had returned to the land of the living, so – were they really 'dead'? Chloe had died but had not psychically returned. In fact, after the first time George had spoken to me of Chloe's visit I went to my computer and googled 'Near-Death Experiences'. There were hundreds of them. I was astonished that so many people had claimed to have died, usually as a result of an accident, gone to Heaven, had a chat with God and were then sent back. Most of the cases were laced with religious undertones so I found the stories hard to believe. It seemed so unnatural.

But Chloe's case was different. Hers was no near-death experience. She had died. So if George could make people believe him... This was the crux. How could George convince sceptics he was telling the truth? The easiest course for anyone to adopt was to disbelieve. People are sceptical until they can see, touch and feel something tangible with their own senses. Talk of a dead person speaking to a father from the afterlife, while he is asleep, can be easily dismissed. 'He was dreaming' would be a common response. 'Where's the physical evidence?' others would ask. 'Of course he would perceive a mere dream as his daughter actually speaking to him – he would wish it to be true.' I glanced at George. A more miserable and downhearted person I couldn't recall seeing in all my life. It seemed as if he no longer wished to endure the pain of living, as if he was straddling a border, the thin line between life and death, willing himself to die, thus enabling his spirit to wing its way to the afterlife to join Chloe. How he had the courage and wherewithal to relate Chloe's story to me I found it difficult to understand. I don't believe I would have been capable of doing so if I was in the circumstances in which George found himself. We took our time sipping on our hot tea that George's secretary had noiselessly brought in. George didn't say a word. He slowly brought his cup to his lips and without seeming to look at it he slowly drank from it with a glazed appearance in his eyes, his thoughts evidently many miles away. Eventually, he put down his half-finished cup.

Chapter Five

HAVING PUT DOWN HIS CUP, GEORGE RESUMED. "CHLOE'S NEXT visit came the very next night, as if she was anxious to get on with her story," he began. "It continued from where she had stopped the previous night when she had asked me if I understood what she had been telling me."

"Fine George," I said. "Please go on."

After a moment of silence, George began to read again.

≈

After a pause in my thoughts I turned towards the gatekeeper. His smile was unchanged as if he was waiting for me to refocus my thoughts; perhaps he was reading every thought that flashed through my mind. His smile was reassuring.

"What now?" I asked, for I seemed to have lost track of what he had been saying. We must have been conversing for ages, but then again I had no possible way of knowing how long it had been.

"If you are ready, you may begin your story," he said gently.

I didn't know where to begin, or what events I should describe.

Examinations had always freaked me out, Dad; I hated them and...now...this most final of all tests would determine whether I would be permitted to enter the afterlife. What if I said the wrong thing? Every word, every sentence I spoke would be analysed. How could I clearly explain my story?

"Do not be afraid my dear," the gatekeeper said. "Speak honestly. Keep in mind however that God can detect if your words are false. I have a special power to retell your story, no matter how long. I can repeat your story precisely as it rolls off your tongue, and, God will know, even by the inflection in my voice whether what you are saying is the truth."

Naturally, the gatekeeper's words increased the stress I was under, like a pole vaulter or high jumper who, having cleared a certain height might become concerned by the officials raising the height of the bar to one he or she has never successfully jumped. I had no escape route. I was trapped here, in front of this gatekeeper who I understood held the keys to the afterlife, able to admit me only when God gave him a nod of approval. Oh Dad, how I needed Mum! She would have been able to help me see things clearly, to put things the right way; she could have spoken the words I wanted to speak but couldn't. Where was she when I needed her most! My heart ached, for once again I realised that she was out of reach. I had never felt so lonely.

"I'm ready now," I determinedly said to the gatekeeper.

"Thank you Chloe, please begin your story."

And so I began.

"First, I will tell you about my mum and dad. I'll leave myself to last," I said, not wanting to give the appearance of big-noting myself or giving him the impression that I believed I was more important than you or Mum.

"My mother is a gorgeous person and I looked upon her as my rock," I commenced. "I could always count on her for support, and she always had kind and reassuring words to say to me when I was troubled. Like me, when in a crowd of people she is unfamiliar with, she kept her thoughts to herself. Yet in conversations with me or amongst the family she sparkles, just like a diamond, although I have to admit her raw emotion can burst out unexpectedly. She is caring and compassionate towards animals, ours as well as others. Perhaps that is the reason my interest in the welfare of animals was so strong; it had been passed on to me by my mother, though that is not to say that my father doesn't like animals – he does, but I'll talk about him shortly," I said.

Dad, you know all about what I'm going to say now. It's about Mum and even though you might look upon it as some sort of lecture setting out my relationship with Mum I want to tell you everything I said to the gatekeeper.

"My mother is very smart, intelligent and capable. When we were young children, she went to university and studied for a Bachelor of Arts. I believe she did it on principle because when she was a teenager her parents forced her to leave school and get a job in a typing pool in the Public Service to support her brothers' education. My father actually encouraged her to return to study, probably because my father believes he is some sort of intellectual and therefore has an interest in academic pursuits. Anyway, whatever the reason, my mother went and obtained her BA with excellent marks. She never actually used her qualification because an Arts degree doesn't allow one to do much at all, other than perhaps to become a teacher; it's more of a general degree without any specific vocation in mind. But it may have assisted her in some way because afterwards she did have some good administration type jobs. She always complained about being underpaid and overworked which to most of us women is a fairly common lament. Her greatest drawback to a happy life is her health, although how I can mention her health seeing I am the first one in our family who has died is a little strange I suppose. Thankfully she is still alive, but she has suffered from bad asthma all her life. In fact, when I was very young, only three or four, she almost died from an asthma attack. It was lucky for her that at the very moment of her attack she was sitting up in a hospital bed, having been admitted a mere five minutes previously." Remember Dad, a doctor had come to the house at 5am after you finally called in desperation because she had been wheezing all the previous day and through the night and wasn't getting any better. As Mum told the story to me, you finally came to your senses and called the doctor. She told me you had neglected her all during the day on Sunday by dashing off to a barbeque at a friend's place.

"Mum was taken by ambulance to a private hospital where subsequently she had her attack. Later she was taken by ambulance to Prince Henry's in St Kilda Road and rushed into intensive care; it was touch and go for a while, but she pulled through with the kind and loving care of the doctors and nurses. My mother came out of hospital after a week and returned home, as fit and healthy as she had ever been in her entire life. At the time I never noticed it of course because I was too young. I never thought that there was anything out of the ordinary happening. Later on, Mum told us that the dose of drugs administered to her in hospital, Ventolin, Cortisone, Becotide and others, was so high that it made her feel like a champion athlete must after shattering a world record – on top of the world. As the dosage began to be slowly decreased, as it had to be if she wasn't to turn into a hopeless addict, in the same proportion the heightened state of her health also lessened. Once she had returned to her normal dosages, a few puffs a day on her inhaler, her usual level of health, average at the best of times, once again became the norm. However, I must say that sometimes she gives the impression of using her illness as some form of crutch. When my dad used to live at home he always complained, demanding that she get up and do something. But...that's my dad.

"So all in all, my mother and I have had a lousy life, health wise. We have been drawn together because of our common problems. Despite my developing a touch of asthma at times, my bouts were nothing compared to Mum. But I was flattened by my migraines and in the end it killed me...why, I don't know."

"Later, at a more appropriate time, it will be explained to you," the gatekeeper jumped in.

"Can't you tell me right away?" I asked, a little heatedly.

Afterwards, after the time I have been describing I did find out and... but it's not something I want to talk about now... it's too painful to recall. And Dad, you know anyway, don't you?

"Sorry, I'm losing track here," I apologised.

"No need to apologise," the gatekeeper said.

"So asthma has ruined my mother's life because it turned her into a sort of invalid – well, not an actual, physically disabled person but... you understand what I mean," I said. "She was restricted in her activities – unable to play sport; no running joyfully around the park, only slow walks kicking autumn leaves around or walking slowly around the lounge room lost in her music. Dad once told me that before she had me or my brother, Mum often literally jogged around on the tips of her toes whilst she listened to her music. She hasn't been able to do that for many years. Yet the dogs we acquired not too long ago forced her to at least take them for an occasional walk, for they are very frisky dogs, and love to tear around. Mum often roped me in to accompany her when I was at home and I willingly went along, for it was at least some form of exercise which I have always felt I needed because... my weight you know... I'm sort of short and stocky and I have always had to watch what I eat though recently I had begun to lose weight. The drugs to control Mum's asthma she has been taking for forty years or more have caused her problems. Through thick and thin we stood together. Of course, she has her faults, but then again, who doesn't?" I asked.

The gatekeeper smiled, but otherwise made no response.

I allowed his smile to linger before I continued.

"We strive for perfection, don't we?" I pondered out loud, appreciating that the gatekeeper and God appeared to be like two peas in a pod and as such my thoughts would get back. For all I could make out, once the Waiting Room was reached, and subsequently the afterlife, there was no question that I would have reached a state of perfection and happiness. But I was certain that God desired that people on earth would see fit to act more kindly, with more consideration for each other and treat others as they themselves wished to be treated. It seems so simple a solution – act kindly to each other – but other forces always seem to intervene, don't they Dad? Constant warfare and poverty strangles the common person.

"Yes," the gatekeeper returned. "Man searches for perfection, and although Man understands, and has for two thousand years been taught the way to perfection, Man cannot bring itself to accept this. People know the only true avenue to happiness, but like spokes on a wheel, many roads radiate from the centre outwards in all directions and those roads that are travelled along eventually arrive at the rim, the extremity of the wheel – as far away from the centre, where God is, as one can imagine. And the result is a disaster for any traveller who has ventured out on those roads. There is a cleavage between God and those travellers that has lasted for centuries. And even the split between His followers a few hundred years ago has caused great concern here. There is only one God yet people erect different organisational structures in an attempt to claim their version is the true faith. Catholics, Protestants, Muslim, Hindu and all the other claimants to a religion are all wrong. There is no one 'correct' religion. The division of people into the various forms of practice and belief hold no sway with God. There is only one classification - Man."

I hung my head as if I was as guilty as any one of my fellow creatures. The gatekeeper had not specifically spoken about me, but his words bore into my consciousness and made me question the whole of my life.

"Don't look so glum," the gatekeeper eventually said. "Of course you may not be perfect, but then again, no one on earth is."

≈

George stopped reading.

"What a waste, don't you think?" he asked.

"Yes George, a huge waste," I replied. "But Chloe has shown so much passion, honesty and intensity; it's simply fantastic," I said.

"I am very proud of her. Of course I knew she and her mother were close and that both of them had problems with their health, but to hear it and then after I had transcribed it, read it line by line, made my heart jump and sent a shiver up my spine. I'm glad Chloe's relationship with her mum was so strong. At times I felt a complete louse for separating, but unlike in the old days, people don't stay together anymore just for the sake of the children, do they Chas?"

"No, it seems that's the way society is going. And I suppose being a lawyer, you know all this stuff."

"I do, even though family law is not my speciality. Yet Chloe came to me often when she was lonely. And I did love her dearly."

"Yes, everyone knows that George," I said.

"And this conversation – its analysis of man's desire for – how did she put it?" he asked, searching for the place in his notes.

"Yes, 'perfection', that's how she put it. And then she felt as if she had not lived a perfect life, which was Chloe putting herself down, as she tended to do."

George got up and walked around his office, staring out the window as if his mind was a million miles away.

Chapter Six

Both of us found it difficult to get together for a week or so. I went interstate a couple of times and George – well, he was up to his neck in a complex court case and literally couldn't spare a minute on anything else. As soon as George's lengthy case had finished Debra invited George and Emily over to our place for dinner on a Saturday. I hoped we might be able to get a few moments to ourselves. I planned to whisk George off into my study at a convenient time during the evening once the girls had settled into one of their lengthy gossip sessions.

"Glad to see you George," I said as he and Emily arrived. I noted George had his folder with him. I shook his hand and gave him a hug.

"Gee, you guys don't see each other for a week or so and you act like long-lost lovers!" Debra exclaimed. We all laughed.

"We're new-age men, didn't you know? I said.

"Yes, we've discovered our inner selves," George echoed.

The girls looked at each other and burst out laughing. This was understandable as neither of them were aware of our recent conversations. Of course, over the years neither of us had ever given any hint of being anything other than a man's man. George at this stage had not even told Emily of Chloe's visitations. He told me he had decided to wait for an opportune time to tell her. I didn't say anything but I wondered when that would be. After his reading of Chloe's story to me was concluded?

After dinner, the boisterous conversation subsided. While the women were in deep conversation I motioned to George to follow me to the study.

"Where are you going?" Debra asked as we began to sneak out.

"Just into the study, dear. We'll leave you girls to exchange all your gossip on your own; we'll relax in the study with a port."

"Fine, but pour us one first before you escape with the bottle, will you please."

"Okay, good idea," I said, pouring both of them a port.

"What's the matter with you two?" Emily asked, giving Debra a knowing look. "Hugging each other at the door; now they're sneaking off. I must say it's very strange behaviour. They might be jointly having their middle-age crisis!" she exclaimed to Debra, not waiting for either George or myself to respond.

"Yes," Debra agreed. "I must say Chas has been acting very weirdly lately, haven't you darling?"

"No, not really," I meekly answered. "I've been busy and work is getting out of control. Must be old age slowing me down!" I joked.

We made ourselves comfortable in the study, the Brown Bros. port neglected on my desk.

"Well George, any further visits from Chloe? I see you have brought your folder with you so I guess she's come back."

"Yes," George said. "And this time she told the gatekeeper all about me."

"Wow! What did she say?" I asked, leaning forward on my seat, eager to hear the next instalment.

George opened his folder, flicked over the pages, found his place and began.

≈

Dad, now I'm coming to the part where I told the gatekeeper about you and how you helped me. I can't be with you in person while I'm telling you this but I hope this visit is of some comfort to you. Dad, please forgive me if some of what I related to the gatekeeper is not to your liking...that's how it goes I suppose... but you know I love you...

≈

George stopped suddenly and blew heavily as if hearing his daughter tell him she loved him, notwithstanding the criticism she was apparently about to make, shook him to the core of his being. Just to hear those words. He gathered his strength and began again.

≈

"I'll tell you about my father now," I said.

"Yes, tell me about your father," the gatekeeper replied.

"He was born into a working class family. Dad had a great ambition from an early age to be a lawyer. He was very young when he got to university as he had been allowed to skip a grade at primary school because he was in a combined class and he handled the work given to the higher class with ease. After high school he went to University and studied law. You understand that all this took place well before I was born so I am only passing on what information I have been supplied with by my parents, and of course my grandparents."

"Of course, I understand that," the gatekeeper responded with a smile. "Man must invariably rely on various facts he has been told or what he reads of in books, gleaned from the internet or sees on film to gain knowledge of the past. We experience personally only a very small percentage of the knowledge that we acquire."

"Yes," I answered, "now that I think about it that is true. That is why many people continue their education after their formal schooling is finished – they keep studying in an attempt to find the key to it all, the meaning of life as it is sometimes put; it is such a mystery. People want an answer to the eternal question – why am I here?"

"Many ask that question, Chloe," the gatekeeper said, "but very few find the answer."

Do you understand, Dad? After hearing all that I will say to you, perhaps you will be able to look at life in a different way. Until I met the gatekeeper I was uncertain about the meaning of life, I mean – the reason for our lives on earth. On earth I bumbled along, following the flow of life, trudging sheep-like after the crowd, agreeing with my peers because...who was I to take a stand and adopt some other position? It took my death for me to realise there is a contrary position, and my visits to you are some sort of plea I guess, to you and others to whom you tell my story, that the majority of people live lives that are devoid of the real essence of life. Sorry Dad for sounding as if I am lecturing you or telling you off, but it's what I now believe and understand. Now I'll return to my conversation with the gatekeeper.

"Mum told me she met Dad when she was a secretary. Dad was a lawyer and worked at some big firm in town. Well, a few months after they met, they married. But after being married to Mum for a very long time and having had my brother and me he had a kind of mid-life crisis. He met another woman and eventually left us, his real family. He told me and my brother about it one night. I remember it very clearly as if it was yesterday. I was hurt, but for some reason I didn't shed a tear. I don't know why – it seemed so unreal that my father would just walk out the door and never spend another night with us under the same roof. Perhaps I was too dumbfounded, too shocked by the suddenness of his impending departure to be able to respond at the time in any other way. Admittedly I was young, about thirteen or so, and not as confident as I became later on once I had grown up and experienced life a bit more. Even now, many years later, I believe that the whole scene was unbelievable and unfathomable. Of course I realise that many marriages and relationships end in this way, but usually these tragic events seem to occur elsewhere than in your own family, like something you read about in a magazine or see in some television soap opera or film. It doesn't affect you personally. But it happened in our family...and we were probably never quite the same ever again. Dad often came to see me at home; he would take me to ballet on Saturday mornings. And I understand he supported me financially as much as he could, though I had to leave my school and go to another one where the fees were lower. Yet to Dad's credit, a couple of years after he left he paid for me to return to the Methodist Ladies' College, MLC as it's called, to do Year 12. I said earlier that Dad went through a mid-life crisis. He certainly did, but I believe his crisis has continued to this very day. He gives off the appearance that he is happy, but every time I saw him he seemed to have the world on his shoulders, as if some gigantic problem was weighing him down. I'm probably not the best person to say this because I often was depressed myself, but even I noticed a state of depression hanging over him that in my younger days I couldn't pick up. Perhaps I was too young to detect anything. I don't know really... all I know is that despite Dad constantly being in a relationship with a woman after he left us, he never looked entirely happy, even after he remarried. Oh, when I was lonely I would ring him and he would do his best to comfort me, but I still detected unhappiness in his voice and in his general demeanour.

"Dad is different," I continued. "Sometimes he is like a child playing silly games; often he can be more like an aggressive tyrant because he can lose his temper very quickly and raise the roof with his screaming. He doesn't tolerate idleness at all. If he came around to see me at home and found me and Mum quietly sitting on the couch enjoying a program on TV, in a strident voice he would demand to know: 'What are you watching that rubbish for?' And he would complain about our dogs barking and running around the house at break-neck speed. However, despite all that, I would dutifully get up from the couch and make him a cup of tea and attempt to divert his mind elsewhere by asking him various questions as to what he was doing. I must say, however, he was very interested in my studies as a nurse and when I began to have interviews for jobs he told me that he entered all the times for my interviews with the various hospitals in the calendar on his computer. He would ring me that night or the next day to find out how my interview went. Yes, he was very encouraging and supportive but..."

Dad, I couldn't say any more because once again, realising I was dead, my thoughts immediately returned to the sheer waste of it all...my life was nipped in the bud just as it was beginning to bloom...And I hope you don't believe I was too critical of you. Maybe you believe I was but being in a good relationship means both parties should be able to tolerate the truth. Whatever you did I supported you as I know you supported me. That was all I could ask for; your love and total support.

"Thank you Chloe," the gatekeeper finally said, comprehending that I was temporarily speechless. "Thank you for telling us about your father...I can feel the love that flowed between you. You loved your father, and he loved you, despite each of you being aware of the other's weaknesses and various mistakes that each of you made."

"Yes, we all make mistakes, don't we?" I wondered out loud,

"otherwise we wouldn't be human. Human beings are frail creatures, but each of us does our best..."

"But if humans followed God's way then the world would be a much better place, don't you think?" the gatekeeper posed.

What could I say in reply but meekly agree?

I felt that what the gatekeeper had said was the undeniable truth. Of course the world would be a better place. Everybody knows that. But I really believe it is impossible. Various nations and groups attack other nations or defend themselves calling on the name of God. So if God is invoked, and killing is willingly undertaken in His name, what hope does humanity have?

≈

While my brain was digesting Chloe's words 'what hope does humanity have?' George closed his folder of notes. Yes I thought, it's a world seemingly torn to shreds when various groups call on the name of their God to embark upon killing another group of human beings also claiming God is on their side. Contemplating God's warriors in all their different cloaks was one thing; how George regarded Chloe's words was another.

George had not said a word. While I waited for his reaction I took the opportunity to go over Chloe's words. She had told her father to look at life from a different perspective, to seek the real meaning of life. And she believed he would tell other people of this experience of having a connection with the afterlife; but tell them what? Chloe's story; who would believe it? The notes George was reading to me sounded like a script from a sci-fi film or a stream of consciousness outpouring of a father's grief. This is what the herd of sceptics would come out with. The trouble was that Chloe's story as told to George could not be corroborated by anyone. I could not do so because I was a mere listener to this tale. Yes, I may have believed but I would be accused of bias; I was his best friend so how on earth could I be independent? Of course I would back him; that's what friends are for, isn't it?

And her criticisms of George; how would he take that? Most people resent being told the truth or that they have acted childishly or stupidly. George's separation from Michelle, Chloe believed, led to George sinking into a depressed state and a change in his general mood. She might be right; she had the opportunity to observe him more closely than I ever did.

Her reference to George acting like an aggressive tyrant was news to me. I had always regarded George as fairly mild in temperament, as most people believe a lawyer should be. Then again, it's well known that families are capable of hiding their secrets from the outside world.

I had shivered inside when Chloe said her life had been nipped in the bud. She recognised it; we all did. Thinking too much about it could drive a man insane. So if George developed depression due to his separation – how much more the loss of his daughter would have driven him deeper and deeper into depression is easy to imagine.

As these thoughts whirled around inside my mind George lifted his head.

"What did you think of that?" he asked me.

I felt like a boxer, pinned to the ropes with no hope of escaping the volley of blows about to descend. Men are often reluctant to talk of these things to another man. The situation was surreal and yet I forced my mind back to where it had begun – that my best friend George was narrating a story which he indicated was true. If it was painful for me to endure, how much more must it have been for George to tell it?

"It certainly focused my mind, that's for sure," I said.

"Chloe certainly understood me," George said.

"In what sense?" I asked, attempting to draw him out. I

wanted him to react to his daughter's words, yes, even to her criticisms, mild as they appeared to be.

"Well, she referred to my mid-life crisis. It happens so regularly to men I guess there is some truth in it. Whether a change in outlook, adopting a different attitude to your own place in the universe can be considered a crisis, I can't say for sure. All I know is that people talk of some event that springs out of nowhere as evidence of that man having a mid-life crisis. What caused mine is something I haven't turned my mind to. Separating from Michelle; yes, that was a catastrophic event, pretty explosive at the time. I've told you what happened, Chas...a long time ago. Whether it was the other woman syndrome brought about by some degree of dissatisfaction with my marriage which caused me to seek out other company as a form of compensation for myself, I frankly don't know. It's hard to put into words. Do you understand me, Chas?" he asked.

I believe I did. He seemed to be recognising the separation had monumentally changed things, his life, and consequently that of Chloe's. Chloe saw it. She said he seemed to have the world on his shoulders, as if he was full of regret.

"Your separation, George," I cautiously began, "Chloe believes it was the start of a...battle with depression...that you have always been unhappy since...that you may have regretted leaving home?"

George thought for a moment. I had no idea what his answer would be.

"Hindsight is a wonderful thing, don't you think? Of course, we all have regrets. I reckon even you, Chas," he said with a grudging smile on his face.

"Yes, I have regretted it," he went on. "Of course I have; not only for my sake, but also for Chloe and her brother as well as Michelle. It affected them badly. It cut me up too, and as Chloe implied, I believed I was the perfect separated father, making up for the guilt I carried around for tearing the family apart. But I did it, even though I probably did not want to. All of our lives were changed for ever. On the other hand, I would be completely crazy if I retreated from life and sat in my own private cave somewhere and meditated solely on the fact I might have stuffed up my life. Tomorrow the sun will rise as it did today and life has to go on. I can't change the fact that Chloe died. Nothing will bring her back to us here on earth. It'll only be in the afterlife we meet again. Therefore, I am very grateful for her in telling me her story. Who else has had that opportunity of contact with a loved one in this way? No, I am still alive and so I can't sit on my backside and weep for twenty or thirty years. I'm not Miss Havisham you know!" he said giving a little laugh. "Chloe is right. I go in and out of depression regularly. Sometimes it's because of her – I mean if I talk to people too much about her...I crack up..."

George stopped speaking and raised the back of his right hand up against his nose as if to stem a flood of tears that were about to fall. I could see his watery eyes. What could I do to help? We were men and here we were, on the verge of descending into a couple of weepers. I leaned forward in my chair and lightly touched him on the arm by way of support.

"Thanks Chas," he mumbled. He sniffed back tears and dabbed his eyes with his handkerchief.

"Had you reached the end of that visit?" I asked him as gently as I could.

"Yes," he said in a croaky voice.

"Let's go and join the girls," I said. I stood up and went over to him and helped him out of his chair.

"Dry those eyes, George," I said. "Otherwise they will wonder what we've been up to."

He took a deep breath and composed himself. I gave him a hug and we went out to face our wives.

Chapter Seven

"WHAT HAVE YOU TWO BEEN UP TO?" DEBRA ASKED AS WE entered the living room.

George and I exchanged glances as if we were two young schoolkids caught out by a teacher smoking behind the shelter sheds.

"And what's with the white folder?" Emily asked her husband.

George seemed to be clinging to it like a mother with a new born baby, fearful of losing possession of a long sought after treasure.

"Oh, just some material Chas and I have been discussing," George replied in a somewhat dismissive manner.

"What kind of material?" Debra asked in a sharpish, suspicious tone.

Some people say that on certain occasions it is legitimate to lie to your spouse. Others suggest it is best to be always truthful and allow all your secrets to be disclosed. That way, nothing festers. George and I were pinned against the wall. The alternatives were to tell an outrageous lie or come clean. What a dilemma confronting us! Yet I felt our situation was different to others. George was now faced with the proposition of revealing that his deceased daughter was speaking to him from the afterlife. Even among loved ones there would be a sense of incredulity. But on the other hand, after initially being sceptical, I believed every word George had told me. So why not his wife; why not my wife? Couldn't they also believe? And Chloe wanted us to tell others. Her story had to be told. I had no idea of how much more George had to disclose or even if he would be able to. Everything depended on Chloe's visits continuing. George had no idea when they would end. Further, he might not even be told if there was more to come. Chloe might not return to visit him; she might just fade away along with people's memory of her.

"What do you think, George?" I asked.

George seemed to be struck dumb, as if he had been hit by a bolt of lightning. As far as George was aware, Chloe did not visit anyone else, not even her mother. So this was a personal matter between George and Chloe. Yet I regarded Chloe's visits as serving a wider purpose. There was of course her desire to communicate with her father but perhaps, through him, the whole world. Why Chloe had been chosen to communicate with her father from the afterlife I did not understand. To my knowledge this had never happened before. Examples of near-death experiences abound but this was different. The scope of this ambition to eventually tell the world was impossible to comprehend, as if on a black night you are standing on a mountain top in the middle of the desert and your only companions are the billions of stars beaming their light from unimaginable distances and from time long past. Gazing at the stars is, in reality, looking back in time, back to the time the universe began. A human mind has no way of understanding the process behind this. Were these visits by Chloe merely another aspect of an existence our limited intelligence could not comprehend? Is that how it could be explained?

While these conundrums ran through my addled brain there was a silence that was so unnatural it was almost frightening. We all were waiting for George to speak. Because I realised it was George alone that could decide to open up his story to others I wanted to speak to him without our wives being present. I could not find the fortitude to ask George if he wanted a minute with me to discuss what we should do. That really would have caused our wives to become suspicious. Perhaps their thoughts might race to one of us having committed an act of infidelity. Pressed to express an opinion as to what was contained in George's folder their answer could not possibly be that the folder contained a transcription of a story from the afterlife.

I tried to push George into opening up. "It'll come out one day," I said which, on reflection was a pretty dumb thing to say. I instantly thought our wives would become even more suspicious and kicked myself for being so stupid. "Do you want me to say something, George?" I asked him, avoiding eye contact with Debra. At that moment I could feel her eyes drilling into me. I was too afraid to catch her eye so I assiduously avoided it.

"If you could," George said very quietly, so softly I could hardly make out what he said as he maintained his gaze on the floor.

We had been standing all this time. I motioned George to sit down. He did so as if I was his personal carer and he needed my constant assistance to live. I indicated to Debra and Emily to sit down on the lounge suite facing George. I sat down beside George and, in general terms, began to unfold to our wives Chloe's story.

Other than my ragged voice, not a sound could be heard. George sat back, head drooping and eyes closed. At first Debra and Emily looked at ease, each of them lightly holding a glass of red. But as I proceeded to tell them what part of Chloe's story I could remember, their interest accelerated and within a minute or so they had both put their glass down and were sitting on the edge of their seats listening to the story. When I had finished they continued to sit, in silence, stunned, and incapable of speech. I looked at Debra; she had a disbelieving expression splashed over her face; her mouth ajar as if she was on the verge of speaking but lacked the wherewithal to get the words out. Emily was shaking her head from side to side as if she found it impossible to accept the veracity of what she had heard. Being George's second wife she was a step removed from Chloe. Whether her reaction would have been the same if she was Chloe's mother I am unable to say. All I know is that both of them had a countenance that combined shock and disbelief.

"Well?" I finally asked out loud. The silence was killing me; I needed some reaction from them. I did not care what it was – whether they believed Chloe's story or not; this did not unduly concern me. I desperately needed some response.

"George," Debra eventually said, "is this true?"

Emily repeated Debra's question.

Heads turned towards George. I expected him to answer immediately but his gaze remained fixed on the floor.

"George?" I quietly said. "Tell them it's true; tell them I have faithfully related what you told me."

George picked up the folder.

"Yes, it's true. Look at this," he said, thrusting the folder in their direction. As if it was rehearsed, both of them reached out to claim the white folder. They grasped it at the same time and, sitting close together, gingerly opened it and began reading.

"Oh my God, George, what is this?" Debra asked.

"It's a transcription of each of Chloe's visits," I answered for him. "After each visit from Chloe concludes, for some unknown reason, he wakes up, gets out of bed and goes straight to his computer and transcribes every word that Chloe has said."

"And you can remember all this?" Emily asked in astonishment, flicking through the folder, page after page.

"Yes, that's right," George said.

"Now, I indicated to George that despite not having any religious beliefs, I do believe every word of his story because..."

"You're his best friend," Debra completed my sentence.

"Yes, we all know that," Emily said.

For the next twenty minutes or so Debra and Emily pored over each page of George's folder with a mind-numbing intensity. I had never previously seen such devoted concentration on a task from either of them, as if their very lives depended on being able, if asked, to recite the script back to George and myself verbatim. I sat back and observed them as they silently read the contents of the folder. I believed my job was done. George's secret, Chloe's story, was out in the open. As individuals, Debra and Emily each had a choice: to believe it or not. Of course they had to believe that George had typed this script out on his computer. They held it tightly in their hands. Whether they believed George's assertion that the transcription was of Chloe speaking from the afterlife was another matter. Perhaps they would conclude it was all a dream, something created by George, some event in his mind, mere wishful thinking; a method of suspending belief in Chloe's death and continuing to believe she was still alive. Alternatively, they might consider George was mentally ill and in desperate need of help. And one of them might believe; the other not. I waited expectantly for one of them to say something.

"Why didn't you let me in on this before, George?" Emily asked him.

George shrugged his shoulders. "At first I was unsure myself where all this was leading. But I had this feeling, even after the initial contact that it was not a dream; it was actually Chloe speaking directly to me. Some impulse made me leap out of bed and type what she had told me on that first night. I was wide awake and had this experience, something surging through my body as if I was, at least for the moment, in a state of...how can I put it...like I was in the throes of an out of body experience; I felt a clarity in my mind that I could not explain. The words flowed through my mind and I transcribed them as if I was copy typing. It was as if I had been given some power, an ability to undertake this task that in other circumstances I would have no hope of emulating."

"Oh George!" Emily exclaimed and went over to him and clasped him to her breast. He buried his head in her. His shoulders heaved as he, almost violently, let loose his emotion. It appeared that the strain of losing Chloe, and now being confronted with her visits, typing out her words from the afterlife and then narrating his transcripts to me and this further release of the whole thing to our wives, had finally pierced him, worn him down and caused his pent up feelings to explode.

I looked at Debra. She had tears trickling down her cheeks; whether in happiness or sadness I could not say. All I knew was that the atmosphere was choked with passion and intoxication; a fever of excitement I had never experienced before filled the room. Chloe's words had seemed to have dried up our capacity for speech. It was so incomprehensible that, in any event, speech was useless.

Debra went and made the ubiquitous cup of tea for us, as if this would give us the strength to speak.

"I don't know why, but I believe you George," Debra said as she put his cup of tea down in front of him, giving me a side-ways glance. She had not previously looked at me for guidance as to what she should say. She wanted George to be aware of her own opinion, independent of me. George already knew I believed him. But belief by his closest friends might have been taken for granted. After all, what are friends for? Friends do believe each other; they trust them to speak the truth. The real test lay ahead, in the future, to the time when George believed it was providential to spread his story far and wide. Cynics of course would sneer at the story as being ludicrous. Atheists would surely laugh it off as the wild dreams of a devastated father, unwilling to accept the inevitable – that death brings finality to existence, even to his daughter.

"What happens now?" Emily asked to no one in particular.

"There is nothing to do but wait, I guess," I said. "It is all in Chloe's hands. She may visit George again tonight; on the other hand it may be days or weeks away. Isn't that so, George?"

"Yes. I have no idea when she will reappear. I do believe she will come back because I have a feeling her story is nowhere near finished. I feel there is a much more for her to say about her conversation with the gatekeeper, a whole lot more."

Conversation eventually drifted away from Chloe. I'm sure George's revelations were at the back of Debra's and Emily's minds; they certainly pervaded my thoughts. How much more so for Debra and Emily who had only tonight learnt of this story? Though we were inseparable as friends the remainder of the night continued as though a façade, a wall, had been erected between Chloe in the afterlife and us. The conversation became stilted. I suppose we had had to erect a barrier for our own sanity. Perhaps it was our version of a wake after a funeral when conversation invariably turns to matters other than the morbid talk of death; anything other than death. But Chloe's spirit lingered in the air, despite the barrier we had erected. We could impose our own barriers but we could not prevent her spirit penetrating our hearts. Other words might escape our lips and be taken hold of, but our inner thoughts were filled with Chloe.

Chapter Eight

OUR WIVES WERE SO INTRIGUED BY GEORGE'S REVELATION OF Chloe's visits that they insisted on George revealing further instalments only in their presence. I would have preferred to be the first to hear these instalments because I believed I had some proprietary interest; George had turned to me first to tell Chloe's tale. However, George succumbed to the combined entreaties of Debra and Emily and gave his word that they would be included in further disclosures.

We therefore agreed that on the evening following each visit we would meet and listen to George read out his typed up notes. Naturally, I assumed a discussion by the four of us would follow. We planned to alternate the place of meeting between our respective homes. I had my doubts this regimented plan would be successful. It seemed to me to be too calculating; I didn't want these meetings turned into a ghoulish circus by elevating it to a form of entertainment for the night. Instead of attending the cinema or going out to dinner we were to sit around and listen to George. Our wives didn't see it that way. They regarded Chloe's story as so important that rather than see our meetings as entertainment they considered them akin to world shattering events, as if Chloe's visits, once revealed by George to the outside world, would be seen as more important than the Dead Sea scrolls and cause an utter sensation. I was not as optimistic, but rather than engage in heated debate with our wives, George and I privately agreed to go along with them, at least for the present.

A week or so after our revelation, Chloe came back. George had feared that upon wakening and getting to his computer Emily would know what he was doing and get up and want to look over his shoulder as he typed. George and I had earlier discussed this possibility and we agreed that, as forcibly as possible, without reverting to any form of abuse, he would tell Emily that there could be no interference with his procedure as it might hinder his ability to transcribe Chloe's words. George confided to me that cross words had been exchanged but Emily had eventually realised how serious George was and, reluctantly it seems, conceded the point.

The following Saturday we went to George's and after one of our quickest dinners that I could ever remember we gathered in the spacious lounge room. George began reading from his notes.

≈

Hi Dad, it's me again. I'll continue with my conversation with the gatekeeper.

Dad, I hung my head slightly and thought of all my loved family and friends who I would never see again.

After a time I lifted my head and found the gatekeeper looking at me in the same manner as when I had opened the door and first laid eyes on him. His countenance showed a radiant, loving and understanding smile, and I wondered what thoughts occupied him as he met my apprehensive face. Instinctively, I realised I must have shown a face of utter despair with an aura of deep despondency surrounding me – so why was he smiling so resplendently at me?

"You look down in spirit," the gatekeeper remarked.

"Do I?" I responded. "Perhaps it's because I have been

permanently separated from my mum and dad. It crossed my mind that I won't ever feel happy again."

The gatekeeper just smiled. But his smile did not annoy me as a smile of insincerity might have done on earth. I could not detect any evidence of smugness or contempt; nothing of the sort. It was a smile of unreserved, unconditional love; total sympathy for my position.

I forced a smile in his direction. In response, his own smile grew in intensity.

"Are you ready to tell me a little about yourself?" he ventured cautiously, as if he thought that I might need more time to pull myself into shape so I could speak coherently about myself. I felt I had no other option than to speak.

"Yes, I'm ready now," I said. I looked around me; I don't know why really; perhaps I subconsciously was looking for somewhere to sit down. He picked up my anxiety and gently guided me by the arm to a nearby place. As we walked the necessary few short steps, the mist seemed to instantaneously part, something like the opening of the Red Sea must have felt to Moses, and I suddenly found myself seated beside him. How can I describe where we sat? It was an octagonal shaped gazebo, built as if of wood with seats hugging the internal circumference, surrounded by grassed areas and a small pond that wound itself around areas of rocks and large boulders, with trees and bushes, and various grasses and reeds standing around the winding edge. I could see these things in close proximity to where I was, but my horizon was still very limited.

Dad, you must know that describing scenes has never been my forte; on reflection however I must say this area was much like a university campus or certain parts of the Botanic Gardens you often dragged me to when I was young. You and Mum certainly appeared to thoroughly enjoy walking around inspecting all the plants and shrubs, but sometimes I felt that you tended to forget how short my legs were. The constant walking and general rambling around, up and down dale tired me much faster than it did you. However, I believe my brief description might allow you to draw a picture of it in your mind. But a cautionary word – at that point of time...but I've wandered off, I was about to tell you what I went on to say to the gatekeeper.

"Begin whenever you feel settled, Chloe," the gatekeeper said.

"I have few specific memories of my early years," I began. "I do remember though that on my first day at school I cried because I did not know many kids. There were only a couple of children from the day care centre I went to which was conveniently located opposite the school. Otherwise, I did not know a single child. Some of the older kids seemed to me to be very tall and many of them would run crazily around and around the school yard, often in a threatening and frightening manner, bullying the younger ones. I hated school actually, and though I had one close friend, it was typical of the bad luck that continually seemed to haunt me that she eventually shifted away from the school way out further in the eastern suburbs. After a few visits to her new home we lost touch with each other. At the back of my mind was the thought that her mother influenced her into believing that for some reason I was not a suitable companion. Why the mother had such inclinations I could not start to guess.

"When I went to secondary school at MLC I had two close friends, but after the first year they abandoned me and became exclusively engrossed in each other, just like sticky glue, and did not really care about me or developing or maintaining any other relationships. Both of them avoided me and totally ignored me as if I did not exist. I never found out why – perhaps it was just a natural part of growing up, a way of leaving childhood behind and allocating it to a distant past. One of them was originally like a sister to me; we were virtually inseparable, but often this same friend would disappear from my life for lengthy periods, as if our friendship meant nothing to her at all. This hurt me immensely for I felt that I was being used – good enough to hang around with at one moment, the next not even eligible to clean her boots.

"My life altered course dramatically when Dad left home. I had to change schools because, well I don't really know why, but I suspect it had to do with money, or lack of it might be the real reason. I think something had happened that caused Dad to lose a lot of money. Coincidentally, my friend also had to leave the school and, consequently, when we started at our new school in Year 9 neither of us knew anyone at all. The girls were rather cold and did not really want to develop a friendship with us. Relationships are difficult to establish, and even harder to maintain, so for my own personal development my change of schools was not a big plus in my life.

"While all these disruptions to my school life were taking place and messing up my life, my ambition to become a dancer was being thwarted by my insane body development. Ballet dancers traditionally are very thin, waifish even, in appearance, and lo and behold, here I was sprouting breasts at a rapid, seemingly unnatural rate. In normal circumstances, young girls crave full-sized breasts because, when they are young and fanciful, they reckon they can be used to lure boys to...oh, sorry, perhaps I shouldn't talk like that here," I said, suddenly recalling where I was.

"Chloe, there is no need to feel any embarrassment here," the gatekeeper said.

"Thank you," I said, relieved that such remarks would not be held against me. "And my dad shortly after paid for my breast reduction...and took me to the hospital to get it done...

for which I was eternally grateful. Looking back now I consider it strange that I needed the operation because I was quite young. By that stage and after a period of soul-searching I had stopped doing ballet. I found it hard to accept at first for I loved nothing more than attending my classes and rehearsing for, and performing in, our annual concerts. I had become extremely self-conscious about my size. The final concert I performed in was terribly embarrassing for me. Shortly afterwards we all agreed that I needed an operation for my own health and to help my psychological development, for I underwent one crisis after another in my mind in regard to what I considered my personal case of deformity. Perhaps if my height had towered over six feet I might have been able to get away with it, but being relatively short I had no chance.

"After the operation I felt a sense of renewal, as if I had been born again; I believed a stigma had been removed. Funny isn't it, when so many women willingly undertake surgery to increase the size of their breasts to make them feel more attractive and appealing to men, here I was, reducing mine to avoid stares and whispers which I am certain dogged me everywhere.

"Ballet was only one of my creative outlets. At primary school I also began to learn classical piano. My parents even went so far as to purchase a piano that I could practise on at home between lessons. My teacher was young and inexperienced as a teacher, but he had a singular flair combined with a certain degree of seriousness. He must have possessed some faith in my ability for he entered me in the examinations that were held every so often. I apparently took his teaching to heart for as the years rolled by I began to breeze through one grade after another. My hands are rather small, so I had no vision of ending up as a classical concert pianist. Far from it – my ambition only stretched to the point where I could be confident of my capability to perhaps impress the family or hopefully demonstrate to some young guy who might have been a little interested in me, that I had more to offer than a pleasant appearance. Where I received this artistic bent from I have no idea, but I tend to favour my Mum's side of the family being my musical ancestors as she could sing and play the guitar quite well, and her father was reputed to have been an excellent violinist when young. Unfortunately, he had been forced to stop playing during the Depression when lack of a job and associated hunger forced him, and thousands of others, on to the country roads with the aim of finding a rabbit or two, just to survive.

"As I mentioned, when I was young I found it difficult to make friends. Really, one could say I didn't know how to. I was too sensitive I believe, and failed to ignore remarks made by people; perhaps I took everything too personally and spent far too much energy minutely analysing every word that was said to me, fearful that I would miss an intended slight."

≈

Dad, you often said this was the reason why Mum could not gather a host of friends around her. Maybe I took after her? Instead of taking a deep breath, relaxing and allowing most words from an acquaintance to be brushed aside as a mere nothing, unless of course it was patently obvious that an insult or put-down had been attempted, I followed Mum's example and examined each person I came across for hidden dangers before I could allow them to be my friend.

≈

"I suppose it could be said that I never really adapted my life to playing the rules of society well at all – even my dad is a little like me in that regard, although to an outsider he gives off an image of being part of the winners' circle. Inside, in his own heart, he most likely feels like I do nearly all the time – a loser in the game of life, despite being a lawyer. Certain skills are required to be able to mix it socially with one's peers. I didn't have an ability to converse knowledgeably on any subject that came up, plus I had little or no innate desire to be at the centre of, or even near the action. Attending social functions is a necessary requirement to hone your skills, but I was terrified at the prospect of doing so, much like some people are scared of visiting the dentist. It was as if I froze at the very thought of having to speak to anyone I didn't know. My degree of self-confidence was low; I had no belief in my ability to match it with any other person, and I was always afraid that someone else would get the 'better' of me. As I matured as a person I became more confident, but it took a considerable amount of time, much more than should have been the case."

"You are very hard on yourself, Chloe," the gatekeeper jumped in.

"Maybe I am," I replied, "but this is how I felt as I was growing up."

"You are not confusing popularity with 'success', are you?" he asked.

"What do you mean?" was my response.

"You read the Bible when you were a child?"

"Yes, of course, at school," I replied.

"You are familiar then with the saying – 'Blessed are the meek...'?"

"Yes, I am."

"Well, if you live your life in accordance with the scriptures and the word of God, then what have you to fear? The message is very clear. God is not interested in the rich man, the highly successful business man, the boasting man or the articulate man who weaves a picture that is meant to deceive. Rather, He has His eye out for the meek and mild people spread across all the nations on earth, salt of the earth people as it has been termed. We hope that eventually the meek and mild will inherit the earth. As you have undoubtedly read, it is far easier for the meek and mild person to enter Heaven than those other types. You should be happy that you are different to them. They are not your peers. For it is a person such as you that benefit in the long run. There was no need to be concerned with those people. They may believe they are winners, in first place, but I can say to you that they already occupy last position. Their conduct is directed at temporary, temporal matters, without a second's thought for the moral and the spiritual. You felt down in spirit on earth because you felt deprived of the level of success as measured by those types of people, but, I say again, there was no need for you to compare yourself with them. I believe that by your conduct you demonstrated a love for your fellow creatures which exceeded by far the attitude of those people who sought an advantage which, in the end, is totally illusory. They confuse wealth, power, and social success with the true reason for the existence of humanity as exampled by those who love their neighbour as much as themselves, and who would prefer to help out their fellow man than deliberately take advantage of a person less fortunate than themselves. For is it not the purpose of Man to seek out and find, and then assist, those people who find themselves in a much less advantageous position to ourselves, the sick in mind and body and spirit, those people who due to varying circumstances cannot adequately fend for themselves?"

He spoke in a mesmerizing way. I felt rooted to the spot, amazed at the words that flowed like a thunderous stream from his mouth, and yet I still felt it was necessary to chide myself for I thought – why should I feel surprised, for I was on the afterlife's doorstep and from the moment I had become aware of where I was and what had happened to me, all the mystery of that eternal question – what is the meaning of life? – was instantly unlocked.

Dad, I will not bore you with details of my conversation with the gatekeeper concerning my arts degree at the university, for you are very familiar with my study there. Nor my Certificate of Animal Nursing which enabled me to work at the Lort Smith Animal Hospital. I merely recited the facts, and as you surely appreciate, bare facts are somewhat uninteresting, aren't they? It's the little things, the gossip maybe, those intriguing, apparently minor, events that humans seem to delight in discussing amongst themselves, tit-bits of information that allows the cracks to be filled in, so to speak. Psychological insights into human behaviour are of much greater source of interest; I mean we all want to know what happened and so ask the question – why? Until we unravel the facts and subsequently find out the reason for a particular act or occurrence we are left in the dark, and confused and puzzled as to why some person said this, or query why another person did that.

So, in general, I explained my reasons for committing myself to finding a job looking after animals; I told him that I expected that it was my 'soft' side breaking through. As you will no doubt remember, various strays have regularly found a place they could call home at our house. Do you remember our cat, Hamlet? I was still young when he was hit by a car in front of our house, and died. You had to pick him up with a shovel, put him in a plastic bag, and then bury him in a hole you dug for him in the back yard. I remember how you lessened my grief with concern and understanding. I loved you for that. We made a small white cross out of some pieces of old wood we found and erected it on the tiny grave under the trees. We stood over his grave for a moment of silence and I said a little prayer for poor Hamlet. I was so sad, and I recall I cried my heart out and had to run next door to be comforted by our elderly, kind neighbours. Yes, perhaps all that history of being involved with the troubles of our own animals led me to believe that I could make a difference to some fragile animal's existence.

At Lort Smith we treated them all, the sick, the unwanted; often dumped somewhere by a cruel person, left to die, perhaps tied up in a bag of some description. Oh, and of course there were so many we often had no other alternative than to put those unloved creatures to sleep. Forlorn expressions looking up at me when the time had come often caused me to shed tears. I earnestly believe that their individual look of despair demonstrated knowledge of their impending demise. As I am telling you this I imagine that you have Fuzzy on your mind, Dad. You told Mum and me that you didn't believe it was right to have poor Fuzzy put down, but really Dad, he was very sick. Just because you saw him hop onto the chair in the kitchen did not mean he was not in pain; he was Dad, he was unquestionably suffering. He could hardly walk. Dad, I worked with animals, I got to intimately understand their nature and it was quite clear to me that Fuzzy had had enough of living. Cruelty to animals is immoral, not forgetting the illegality of it, and I believe it is worse than an act of evil by one human towards another. It is a demonstration of an uncaring, almost sadistic, nature, something I have never agreed with. I am not criticising you Dad, but from where I stood at the time, my decision, or I should say, my joint decision with Mum to take Fuzzy to work to have him put down was an act of kindness. In normal circumstances nobody wants to die – and if anybody knows that is true it is me – but when the body has broken down and the degree of pain is increasing, no more humane decision can be made than to alleviate the suffering felt by an animal, and Dad, I can assure you that Fuzzy was in pain. His lamentable moaning and cries demonstrated that life was getting all too much for him. I had no option than to end that pain. You might be relieved to know that I didn't do it myself – I couldn't bring myself to do that – one of the vets did.

You often asked me during the time I worked full-time at Lort Smith why I didn't attempt 'human' nursing as you put it. At the time I believed I did not have the capability, or the intellectual requirements to become a nurse in a hospital. I envisaged long hours of study, of classes, which I imagined would go right over my head. Don't get me wrong, even in those early days my sympathy for humans in need was strong; it was just that I considered I was far better suited caring for animals. What made me change my mind and decide to do 'human' nursing I cannot accurately pinpoint. Perhaps it stemmed from the time Grandma was sick in hospital. Do you remember, Dad? I expect you do because it was your own mother. You picked me up one day to go and visit her. When we arrived she burst out crying as she believed that you had totally forgotten her because you had not been to visit her. Her increasing dementia blocked her remembering that you had told her you were very busy with some cases. Your protestations that you had come to the hospital as soon as you had a chance to visit her fell on deaf ears. She demanded that she be allowed to leave hospital as she had to return home to care for your brother. Later, you complimented me on a remark I had made to Grandma while we were attempting to calm her down. At the time I did not feel that I had said anything out of the ordinary, but you seemed to be quite taken by it and showered me with praise. I believe that I said something to the effect – 'you've been looking after people for years now Grandma, it's time someone looked after you.' Of course I was referring to the nurses at the hospital. Your mother had expended so much energy in devoting her time to the service of others with her work for the Red Cross and taking care of your brother that, to me at least, it was perfectly natural, that at her age, eighty-two or three wasn't it?, she should for once in her life relax and allow the nurses to take care of all her needs. After all, she was sufficiently sick enough to be in hospital. Afterwards, I began to toss a change of vocation around inside my head. Happy as I was with my career as a veterinary nurse I began to speculate on whether a change to a 'human' nurse would be a better way for me to contribute to the well-being of society. I was not attempting to devalue my role as a veterinary nurse; rather it was a nagging thought in my head that caring for sick humans might give me greater satisfaction in the long run. But this idea took a great deal of time to develop. Life continued to rush by me while the idea lay dormant in my brain. As you well know, it was at least a good two years after your mother died that I finally decided to give 'human' nursing a shot.

The gatekeeper was pleased when I reached the point of telling him of my decision to switch from animals to humans. He said it was to my credit or words to that effect. Dad, you know me, don't you? I am not a boastful person, or a braggart or show-off, but I must say the gatekeeper's words brought a smile to my face. Then somehow, I just couldn't help myself and, practically in a loud shout asked him: 'Then why did I have to die if what I intended to do, be a nurse, would have been so beneficial to the community?'

He merely looked at me and smiled kindly.

"I have no answer to your question, Chloe," he said, "for that is entirely within the province of God. Only He has knowledge of such mysterious things. When you speak to Him later, perhaps you may care to ask Him that very same question."

I made no answer, yet the gatekeeper continued to smile at me.

"So I returned to La Trobe University to do my Bachelor of

Nursing. I was familiar with the campus as I had graduated in Arts from there." You will recall the details, won't you, Dad? By far the part I liked best was the practical aspect – working in the hospitals, doing useful things such as assisting in caring for the patients. I believe I was very good at the clinical side of the course. In fact, I was personally involved in a dramatic incident on the very first day I undertook a clinical day at the Royal Women's Hospital. A pregnant woman in her early thirties had collapsed at home and was rushed into the emergency department. When she was wheeled in she had white skin, almost tinged with yellow. She was slumped on the trolley and rushed into the resuscitation room with a MICA officer executing CPR. Before I could think, announcements were calmly being broadcast even though we were in the middle of a desperate situation. Female obstetric registrars and three anaesthetic registrars, theatre scrub and various other nurses rushed in. I was asked to get 21 gauge needles and syringes and various other equipment for the anaesthetic staff. One of the anaesthetic registrars was trying to get intravenous access in the woman's neck. It appeared to me that nothing else existed in the minds of all the staff than to save this woman's life. The woman looked sallow. No sparkle was present in her eyes, her pupils were fixed and dilated; there was no flush of colour in her cheeks. She was limp and lifeless. Grunting sounds flew from her mouth through the bag and mask as oxygen was artificially pumped in and out of her lungs.

"ECG electrodes were thrust into my hand. I panicked. Which colour goes where I mumbled to myself? Eventually I worked everything out but there was no cardiac electrical activity. It was barely 15 minutes since this woman had arrived. Nothing we had done worked. All we could do was to try and save her 32 week foetus. It was born and connected to the ventilator. However, when his brain function was recorded it showed no activity. He was brain dead. The father, after consultation with the paediatricians, agreed to withdraw treatment. He died being held in his father's arms. The last entry in his history by a paediatric consultant read: 'No heart rate, no blood pressure, no respiratory rate, no signs of life. RIP'. That was my first day. It had been so busy. I was exhausted. Does this happen every day I wondered as I wandered out into the afternoon sunshine? It had been upsetting to have a woman and her unborn child die on my first morning, but I guessed this was what nursing was all about. As I made my way home I felt very humble."

And as you realise Dad, I was no hot-shot academic and I constantly struggled to come up with adequate responses to all our assignments. Fellow students often confirmed my opinion that the academic part of the course was not, to us at least, what we regarded as important to the profession of nursing. Perhaps if any one of us had wanted to gain skills in order to become an academic or involved in administration I could see a point to it, but, for example, having to read a difficult research paper by some highly qualified doctor and then comment on the paper was to me a waste of time. How much better would it have been if additional hours had been spent in the hospitals themselves, learning on the job, assisting the qualified doctors and nurses in caring for sick people? It's fine to be academically trained and have a high degree of theoretical knowledge, but nursing I considered to be a hands-on profession. It was the care you devoted to a patient that was important, not whether you could impress a lecturer with a piece of writing.

Dad, you must recall that time I showed you a research paper and asked you to read it, to see if you could help me. Even you found it nearly incomprehensible, though I admit that after you had read it a second time you were able to explain it to me very clearly. So if you and Mum, who had also read it, had some difficulty coming to grips with the complexity of the paper, how was I to cope? Somehow I did and scraped through first year. Yes, it was difficult, but my stints in the hospital made up for it. Now I am here and unable to help a single person. I didn't even get to complete my degree; just one more assignment was due to be handed in. Clinical work at the hospitals had concluded and I was applying for nursing positions at various hospitals. Dad, you used to telephone me the day after every interview and asked me how it went. I appreciated your enthusiasm because I felt that you were taking an interest in me. Being loved and respected was always very important to me. Mum of course has constantly loved me, although from time to time we have had terrible rows, particularly regarding my study habits. You too, Dad, often chided me for staying away from home on the weekends at my boyfriend's place and not devoting sufficient time to study. But I was studying Dad, I really was, though probably not in a manner that you believed was worthwhile. We all regarded you as a bit of a fanatic Dad, whether it was your running, or your pedantic tendency for being early wherever you had to visit, business or pleasure; whatever you had an interest in you went full bore, as though you were obsessed. Your stories of getting up at 5am to study when you were at university made no impression on me or Mum I am sorry to say.

While I was telling the gatekeeper of my career in nursing, at one point I wondered out loud whether I actually received an offer for any of those jobs I had applied for, because I had died before I had heard from any of the hospitals. So I asked the gatekeeper a direct question.

"Yes Chloe, you did receive job offers after you died," he said calmly.

I trembled inside, because it once again brought home to

me the fact that my life had been cut off prematurely, and I was prevented from entering the nursing profession.

"Your mother took telephone calls from two hospitals."

"Which ones were they?" I asked anxiously.

"I believe they were the Alfred and Box Hill Hospitals," he answered.

Grief and happiness overpowered me simultaneously. Grief, because I was not able to take up either of the positions, and happiness because it surely was a sign of recognition at last; at least two hospitals believed I had the ability to be a nurse. Someone outside my family at least believed in me, judged that I had sufficient knowledge and skill to be allowed to care for people when they were at their lowest ebb, vulnerable, sick, perhaps edging towards their own death. Oh, of course I was not fully experienced or capable as yet, but I had enough brains to realise that being accepted to commence work as a nurse would have been only the beginning, but at least it would have been a start on my journey. Dad, I expect you know all this, and I believe that you too would have felt exactly the same as I did when the gatekeeper told me. I know you would have been proud of me. Were you, Dad? Were you proud of your little girl for achieving her goal? I hope so.

≈

George reached for the glass of water Emily had placed within his reach. He gulped down two huge mouthfuls as if he was attempting to drown his sorrow. I must admit that I had to swallow hard to prevent breaking down. Of course he would have been extremely proud of Chloe; what kind of father would he have to have been not to be proud? But to hear those words and then see those words that he had faithfully typed out must have surely been an emotional moment for him. And now, to reach that point in his recollection of her words surely caused his heart to skip a beat. He said sorry to us, but what was there to be sorry about? Hell, his daughter had died so tragically; he had nothing to apologize for. He took some deep breaths to steady himself before he could speak.

"Chloe asked me whether I was proud of her. I had no means of responding to her plea, her entreaty. No wonder her visit finished at that point. Her face seemed anguished, begging almost in desperation as if she was fearful of my answer, even though she knew she would not be able to hear my answer. How could she fear my response? Perhaps it demonstrated some insecurity as even if I said I was proud of her she yet still might not believe me. And not being able to reassure her personally: that was agony. I had never loved her more than at that moment, but it was all too late to tell her. Even if I shouted my love to the heavens I had no idea whether she would hear me. These visits were the only method of communication we had but it was all one way. That is why I am so eager to type out each episode immediately it occurs because...I have to have some record that would last...in perpetuity so to speak. Something I could read when I felt loneliness descend on to my shoulders and I had to reach out for some connection with her, some reassurance that her life had not been without value."

George stopped. Emily rushed over and clung to him. I looked at Debra and shrugged my shoulders as if to suggest – what is there to say? I believed no words could convey our sorrow and sympathy at the inner pain George was enduring. The visits did not appear to dissipate his grief; he accepted them of course, but the fact that Chloe was no longer with him could not be eradicated from his mind.

Emily sat down. Her eyes were red, rimmed with tears. She gave off a wan smile. George looked at me. Our eyes were locked together; it appeared that this was our vehicle of communication with each other, making speech unnecessary.

"Her life came vividly back to me after this visit," he suddenly began. "She was telling the gatekeeper, but in a sense I feel she was reminding me of all her trials and tribulations. She felt unloved by the outside world believing so-called friends were ambiguous in their words, in their actions. Often she would discuss these concerns with me though more often with her mother. We loved her; nothing was more certain but I'm afraid Chloe was one of those timid creatures who were created too soft, too sensitive to prosper in a rough and tough world. Of course I regarded her as succeeding in ways that other people had no prospect of emulating. Her love of animals was a classic example; her switch to nursing another. What a tragedy that the nursing profession was robbed of such a lovely and caring person before she could do more good! And I was never more proud of her than on the night she was awarded her Bachelor of Nursing posthumously by the University. All the other students received their certificates personally from the Vice-Chancellor. At the conclusion of the handing out of these certificates the Vice-Chancellor walked down the steps to where Michelle and I were sitting in the front row of guests and handed us Chloe's certificate. Not only that, but the whole body of students on the other side of the auditorium stood up and applauded our Chloe for what seemed like five minutes. Every time I recall that moment I... "

George's voice had reached a stage where I thought he might crack under the emotional strain he inevitably was under. I understood his situation and realised I had to act quickly to calm his emotional state. Oh, how I wish I could have been there with George and Michelle to witness such an event! But we were in New York and couldn't get back.

"George," I said, "it's obvious that you loved Chloe; we all know that; the whole world knows that. Your eulogy at the funeral proved it. There is no need to beat yourself up as if you were covering up some guilt you may have over Chloe's death. You have done nothing wrong. You have a right to be proud of her; you have a lot to be proud of."

"Thanks Chas. It's just that her physical absence is so hard to bear. With an elderly parent there is sorrow of course but you know the parent has lived a life as long as expected, the three score and ten rule; but when your own child leaves you at such a young age, on the verge of doing so much good...it guts you to the bone."

"Of course it's tragic, George," Debra broke in, "but as Chas said you should be proud of how much Chloe did accomplish in her life. Her studies, her ballet, her piano, her care of animals, her nursing...so much George...she was such a good girl," Debra concluded, dabbing her eyes with a tissue.

George nodded his head vigorously, fighting back tears. The presence of other people did nothing to smother his emotion. George and I could deal with this on a different level. We were males, supposedly made with a higher tolerance level to showings of grief. Perhaps we had made a mistake in allowing our wives to hear all this. Now it was far too late to back-track. What was done was done; our wives were involved; nothing could alter that. I worried about George's health. Not his physical health, but his mental welfare. Being a lawyer he was naturally already inundated by stress on a daily basis, having to deal not only with his many clients but with his partners as well. But this tragedy – how much more unneeded stress could he take? I glanced at Debra and attempted to indicate this conversation had to be brought to an end.

"How about I make us all a cup of tea or coffee, George?" Debra asked, much to my relief.

"Good idea!" snapped Emily.

Our wives rose in unison and trundled off to the kitchen to play their part in this continuing drama. I was left alone with my friend. We sat in silence, lost in our own thoughts. There was no need to speak. The silence said it all.

Chapter Nine

ANOTHER TWO WEEKS ELAPSED. CHLOE HAD NOT RETURNED. George began to worry.

"What if she doesn't come back?" he asked me in desperation when he phoned me one Thursday afternoon.

"I am sure she will," I replied, laughing as I spoke in an attempt to reassure him. Then a terrible thought crossed my mind. Her last visit had ended with that penetrating question: 'Were you proud of your little girl?' How could she know his answer? I shivered inwardly as my mind contemplated this conundrum.

"I'm not so sure," George said.

We talked of other things. Then I mentioned we would come over on the following Saturday night irrespective of whether Chloe had come back. Our meetings had not been arranged merely to allow George to read out his notes. We were all close friends and were used to getting together. George and Emily had come over the previous Saturday although Chloe had not reappeared.

"So we'll see you on Saturday, George," I said. I slowly replaced the receiver and leaned back in my chair; I swivelled around to gaze out over the bay. The water was flat and peaceful; a bright sheen radiated off it. Light white clouds hung high in the sky. The absence of wind allowed the clouds to remain stationary as if they had fallen asleep, lulled to laziness by the bright sun and blue sky. My thoughts turned to Chloe. Her story as told to

George disturbed me. How many millennia had passed since the evolution of man and the first humans had asked themselves – what happens after I die? How many religious people of myriad persuasions, how many philosophers, how many thinking people: indeed, how many of the ordinary, salt of the earth people, had posed the same question since the beginning of time? Perhaps it was like querying the size of the universe and wondering whether it was expanding or contracting; it was an aspect of existence that was beyond the reach of Man; far in excess of the extent of our limited comprehension. It was something that one just had to accept as a done deal if one was to remain sane. Poor Chloe; her sudden death had effected us all. Every day I wondered how George, not to forget Chloe's mother, had the wherewithal to cope. Chloe's death was against the nature of things; it was a contortion, a deformity of the accepted order. By whose command did any child die before its parents? However, I kept these thoughts to myself. My role was primarily to help George overcome his grief, not to occupy the field with wild theories on the meaning of life. These theories that were spinning around in my mind had to be put to one side.

Saturday night came. I knocked on the front door with a bad feeling that Chloe's story had petered out.

"Chas!" George exclaimed as he opened the door. "Debra!" Debra and I exchanged glances. He seemed very happy.

"You all right, George?" I asked as we made our way into the lounge. Emily dashed out of the kitchen and almost fell into my arms; her excitement was palpable. She hugged Debra and kissed her cheek.

George joined us, rubbing his hands together with a huge smile spread across his face.

"Guess what?" he asked.

Overpowered by the welcome we had received I let him answer, though I felt I knew what he was about to say.

"She came back!" George exclaimed putting his arm around Emily's waist.

"Fantastic!" was all I could say.

"Yes, she came back," he repeated.

"And you've typed it out?" I asked, adding "When?" before he could answer.

"Last night," George said. "Come on, let's start," which seemed to be the answer to my question as to whether he had typed it out. He was so excited I wondered how he was able to contain himself and refrain from calling me during the day.

"What about some drinks first?" Emily asked.

"Okay Emily, but hurry up," he said.

And so we sat down with our drinks and watched in anticipation as George excitedly opened his folder and began the next episode of Chloe's story.

"She told me she had finished speaking with the gatekeeper about herself. This is how she went on," George said.

≈

"It's time for me to leave you now, Chloe," the gatekeeper said, bringing me out of my reverie. To tell you the truth Dad, I felt quite apprehensive, scared even, and I asked myself: what was to happen to me now that the friendly gatekeeper was going to leave me all alone?

"Where are you going?" I demanded to know in a voice that, unusually for me, hovered on the aggressive. This forceful question did not seem to faze him.

"Why Chloe," he said with a smile, bordering on a grin, "I am going off to see God to discuss you."

I emitted a huge sigh of relief.

"But how long will you be?" I asked. "I mean, do I have to wait here on my own, without any company?"

"My dear Chloe," he replied, reaching over and touching me gently on the shoulder in a demonstration of empathy. "Do not be afraid. Immediately I leave you, you will have the ability to see all that lies before you. You will be able to partake in the joy of making the acquaintance of others who are also waiting for judgement."

"I expect there are so many waiting here with me that I guess my waiting time will be quite long," I observed.

"Well," the gatekeeper said with a lavish smile, "we'll see. God is mysterious and who knows when any one will be called. The length of time a spirit spends here in the Waiting Room does not determine the order of entry into Heaven."

I hung my head a little for I felt very bewildered. When I looked up again the gatekeeper had disappeared, almost like a magician in a puff of smoke. It took me some time for me to recover from the shock of his sudden departure, but as I gazed around in the vain hope of catching a final glimpse of him I noticed that the horizon was now very far away, as if a laser had removed cataracts from my eyes allowing me for the first time in my life to have the gift of sight. Dad, I must tell you that when my eyes had adjusted to this phenomenon I believed I had never seen such a beautiful sight. Stretching out to the far horizon I saw vast areas of rolling, deep green grasslands, spotted here and there with oasis-like patches of what at this distance appeared to be small, tranquil ponds, around which sat men, women with babies in their arms and children at their feet, chatting amiably as though they did not have a care in the world. I looked upwards and now I saw a sight that could never be seen on earth. Far away, I could see a ball of fire which I took to be our sun; I saw the blue oceans of our earth and the clear shape of the continents; I saw our moon as well as stars of the brightest magnitude, yet there seemed to be sky interspersed with the stars of these far-flung galaxies, the Milky Way and others, billions of stars it seemed. My eyes had been given a power of sight unimaginable on earth as if I had the power of sight almost equal to the most powerful telescope. This place appeared to have a different perspective from any other that I had come across. I could see objects in the sky that were far away whereas if I had been on earth I am certain that I wouldn't have had any means of catching even a slightest glimpse.

The inhabitants I saw in this Waiting Room intrigued me. In appearance they matched the gatekeeper. Despite being in the spirit form, I could see what seemed to be a mixture of races, white people, black people and various colour permutations happily talking together. I gazed past the group closest to me and took in the magnificence of the scenery behind them. It had the appearance of a beautiful manicured golf course, one without trees or perhaps even that of a peaceful cemetery. Yet other than the few seats I observed scattered here and there, I could not see any other structures.

I had not moved an inch since the time I began my conversation with the gatekeeper. I felt that I was becoming used to my surroundings; my confidence had improved sufficiently to allow me to go over and meet these people as I had no clue as to when the gatekeeper might return. I did not know how long these people had been waiting; it could have been a very long time. Naturally, I believed that I was in the queue behind them, despite what the gatekeeper had just told me. I determined to seek out one of this group and attempt to gain greater knowledge of this Waiting Room and the circumstances that led to their death. With a great degree of apprehension, I took my first small step forward in my future life.

The first person I came across was seated on his own. I detected that the passage of time perhaps had not treated him kindly and had prematurely worn him out, though I guessed by his countenance that death had at least had the decency of alleviating his troubles to some extent, leaving him with a more contented appearance. I approached him tentatively, for at this moment I had no idea whether I could converse with him in English as I had been able to do with the gatekeeper. When I was first able to see I had spotted him in conversation with some others who it now appeared had wandered off elsewhere.

I stood in front of him and with the kindest smile I could put together looked at him. He lifted his head and returned my smile.

"Hello," he said, "my Gaelic name is Seamus, but I'm usually James or Jimmy to my friends."

"Hello, I'm Chloe," I returned. I was a little nervous so I hesitated in extending my hand in friendship. After a few seconds he grasped my hand within both of his as if he was greeting a long lost friend. But in my mind I was certain that I had never laid eyes on him during my life. His grip was strong, but not the same as the handshake of any person on earth. Dad, it is impossible to describe it as you would not understand. We had no physical body, remember. There was a no solid texture to his hand that could be felt. His accent hinted at his being Irish.

"What did you die of my dear?" he asked with a certain precision, as if death was the only thing we had in common. I could only recite to him what the gatekeeper had told me.

"Oh, yes, you are a most unfortunate woman," he murmured. Of course, I had to agree with him; the death of any person is unfortunate at any time but when it is you that has died, well, that is doubly unfortunate.

"And what did you die of, Seamus?" I ventured to ask him. A shade of embarrassment overtook his face.

"Self-inflicted, my dear," he rolled out, "and call me Jimmy please," he added.

"Not suicide!" I gasped.

"Not exactly, my dear. In a peculiar sort of way you could say I drowned."

"In the sea, was it?" I asked.

"No, I drowned myself by drinking myself to death," he said, with an exaggerated shrug of his shoulders as if he was saying – well, I knew the dangers of excessive drinking and totally ignored them.

"Oh," I said, "I'm sorry."

"It can't be helped now, can it?" He scanned my face to ascertain my attitude. Dad, you know I am a soft and caring person (at least I always tried to be). I've nursed sick animals as well as people hospitalized for one of any number of reasons, so how could I register disapproval of any person whose life was overtaken by the need to drown his sorrows in drink? Dad, you know I don't mind a drink. I suspect that every one of us have succumbed to the temptation of drinking to excess occasionally by deliberately getting drunk. Catherine and I did, but I'll tell you about her later. It's all a part of being considered normal, don't you think?

"Would you like to tell me all about it?" I asked.

Jimmy looked taken aback.

"You mean you wish to hear all about my alcoholism?"

Well, of course I did. I had time on my hands waiting for the gatekeeper to come back; indeed, it seemed I had a whole eternity in front of me. So I asked him very politely to tell me his story.

Jimmy smiled.

"Yes, we do have an eternity," he muttered to himself, as if he had read my thoughts. "I'm waiting too," he said, "but I'm not very confident that I will pass the test, taking into account the life I led on earth, and how I died. You know," he continued, "I never put a foot inside a church from the day I was married until they carried me out in a coffin on the day of my funeral. Being an alcoholic who drank himself to death doesn't help either," he concluded with a dreaded resignation to his fate ringing through his voice.

"But won't you be forgiven?" I put to him.

"Perhaps, but I never went to church because, despite born a Catholic, and brought up by my parents as one, I wasn't a believer," he dolefully went on.

"Well, if you show remorse and are genuinely sorry for the grief and misery you caused to your family, and sincerely regret your past conduct I am certain that you will be forgiven, despite not being a believer."

"But, I've been waiting for what seems like ages since I spoke with the gatekeeper. I know he explained the procedure to me, still, I'm worried."

"Let us put that aside, Jimmy," I attempted to placate him. "You have told your story to the gatekeeper, and after God hears your story...well...I'm sure that...you will be successful in the end."

Dad, I didn't think I would be able to persuade him as, you know, I never had the ability to persuasively argue a case much, not being a forceful talker, unlike you Dad with your legal training and your brains. He glanced at me and I picked up that his countenance was beginning to change.

Wanting to turn his attention away from his anxiety, I pressed him to begin his story.

"I lived in Ireland," he began, "all my life. I was born a Catholic at a time when we had a great deal of trouble with the Protestants. Battles were fought throughout much of the country with the

British soldiers and even when I was quite young my mother would tell me off for getting into scraps, throwing rocks at the soldiers then running like hell when they fired rubber bullets or shot water cannons at us. Mother was scared I would be on the receiving end of a real bullet. Secretly though, I think she was proud of me, fighting for our independence and all. My dad was a clerk in a small exporting company and my mum, when she wasn't minding me and my brothers, often worked part-time in a bakery shop."

He looked at me to see if I was listening, for while he was speaking his eyes had remained fixed on the ground.

"Go on," I quickly said, to reassure him that I was listening intently to his story.

"I'll skip a bit because it's not all that interesting and I don't want to bore you."

"Whatever you wish," I replied.

"When I was in my twenties, a long time ago now," he commenced, with a hint of a twinkle in his eye, "I met a lass one day on one of the many protest marches I marched in. Her name was Mary, and a real jolly lass she was too; curly brown hair, blue eyes and a broad smile. She had one little feature on her face, a little black spot on her left cheek, a beauty spot she used to call it. She was indeed a beauty, oh my, she was, and I was the envy of all the lads in the neighbourhood for becoming attached to such a stunner. After walking out together for a couple of years we married, and over the following few years we were blessed with two beautiful girls, Kathy and Rebecca my Mary decided to call them, and who was I to disagree?"

"What type of work did you do?" I asked him. Dad, I was thinking of those old films, the ones about miners working underground, facing danger every moment of the day and generally working for a pittance. Perhaps the work was so hard that a miner was forced to have a drink after work to wash the dust out of his lungs, and one drink led to another and...

"I did have a job," he said, interrupting my runaway thoughts. "I followed my father into the manufacturing company he worked for. The company made pots and pans of various types and sizes and lots of things useful to a handyman. At first I was an odd-jobs kind of clerk, running here and there, and picking up parcels from customers, collecting and delivering or posting the mail. I began to rise through the ranks until eventually I had an office of my own and a job as accounts manager, responsible for paying all the bills and chasing up debtors. A further promotion gave me the title of Sales Manager. As part of promoting our company, I sometimes had to meet directors and sales representatives of our customers and the hearty fellows amongst them often arranged a drink at the pub to celebrate an order or contract which had gone through or generally any excuse that came to their imagination.

"Drinking one beer with a customer spread to two, and then three, four...I even began to drink on my own on the days my regular customers couldn't join me. At first, Mary was completely unaware of my drinking as I was easily able to convince her that I had meetings with important clients after work or with the boss. By this time my father had died unexpectedly from a heart attack so there was no big wig at work to keep an eye on my comings and goings. Mary herself was becoming more involved in her own activities, joining a book club and a women's organisation advocating equality for women or some sort of political reform. I had lost interest in politics by then. I could see no end to the bickering and fighting and although by the time I died most of the antipathy and fighting had died down, the rights and wrongs of the issue were no longer of concern to me. All I was interested in was keeping my job to earn money to support the family and my drinking habits."

"You thought of your family? That's unusual," I quickly continued, "because my understanding of an alcoholic is that their entire thought process is concerned with getting that next drink; they live to drink you could say."

"Yes, there's an element of truth in what you say," he said, "but you may be getting ahead of yourself. Certainly that is the end result with most alcoholics, as it was for me. I'm talking about the very beginning, that period when I did not realise I had progressed from a social drinker to a rampant alcoholic. What did I read somewhere? More than four drinks a day and by definition one is classified as an alcoholic?"

"So you drank every day?"

"Oh yes, even on the weekends I would sneak away and have a few sly ones while Mary was doing something or other. I could also camouflage my problem when we mixed socially. I was able to openly drink in front of Mary and our friends because it was socially acceptable I suppose people would say; everyone gets a little tipsy occasionally."

"Yes, you're right," I agreed. "But did you have advertisements on TV warning of the danger of drinking and driving like we have?"

"Yes we did, but that was nothing to me you must realise," he said. "I became accustomed to the taste, as I continued, day after day, hiding my affliction as best I could; it was like a disease. Something inside of me had grabbed me by...whatever...I can't really explain...I ain't too good at speaking," he said, quietly dropping his voice.

"Oh, don't put yourself down," I said. "To me, you speak very well, better than I can."

"No lass, you're wrong. I can speak the Queen's English but I ramble on here as I did on earth. All I can speak of is my drinking...because that was my life...in the end..."

"What eventually happened?" I asked.

"In the end it became a sort of an open secret at work," he explained. "I became paranoid because whenever I came across people at work talking together they would quickly disperse as I approached them. I overheard their whispered conversations, catching a phrase now and again. It was always about me. I know it was. 'What else could it be?' I asked myself. It was me alright; they were discussing my drinking. While I was signing up new customers, additional accounts that made the company lots of money I was still okay, but eventually things began to fall apart. Now, when I rang to make an appointment with an established customer, the way they spoke to me made me realise they were putting me off. Excuses began to be made – they hadn't sold their last order, business was a bit slow, cash flow problems – you know the litany of excuses people come out with."

I didn't really, never having been in business or in this man's situation, but I held my tongue as I desperately wanted to hear the rest of his story.

"I became depressed as orders began to fall dramatically," he continued. "The manager who took over after my father died called me into his office and, in an angry voice, demanded to know why my sales were disappearing at a rapid rate. 'Pull yourself together, Jimmy my lad,' he said, warning me that he would have to let me go as it was costing the company money to keep me on and, without sales...'"

"Did he realise you were drinking as much as you were?" I asked.

"Well, of course. He had originally actively encouraged me to entertain the customers. The traditional long business lunch or a quick one after work was done with for the day was fine with him, as long as it resulted in increased sales. He might have known but he didn't say anything...because I was important to the company; I was the best salesman we had by far. You know, us Irish can drink even more than..."

"...us Australians?"

"I thought you came from Australia!" he exclaimed.

"How did you figure that out?"

"Perhaps it's your accent, lass. I've heard it in Ireland and more so in London, and on TV."

I had detected an accent when he first spoke to me...and he said he was from Ireland, so this reinforced my realisation I would find here people from all over the world. As you know Dad, I had travelled to various places in the world such as Hawaii, China and Europe, so I was aware of the diversity of people who make up the world. Remember, I gave you a book of sayings I bought in Paris about fathers and a clock from Hawaii. Now that I was here, I had an eternity to meet people from every nation and from all walks of life and, if I made it into the afterlife, I was certain that I would encounter the same cross-section of nationalities that I would meet in the Waiting Room. I wasn't the best scholar or conversationalist in the world, but I was interested in people. I believed that the spirit world would contain none of the banalities of life on earth. People would be free of stress and relaxed because there was no work to do and no need to rush around in a hurry in an endeavour to 'get somewhere'. So I took it for granted that conversations with people would be the only activity to occupy our time.

Another problem then crossed my mind. This man, Seamus, Jimmy I called him, was Irish and spoke with an accent of sufficient mildness for me to clearly understand him, but how would I cope when I came across a person who could not speak English; what would happen then? My thoughts returned to the gatekeeper: he spoke English. How could non-English speakers tell him their story? This puzzled me. Was there some miracle behind all this? The answer came to me by some process of deduction – if I was in the spirit world, as I was, then, necessarily, there must be a God, because the gatekeeper had told me so. Surely this was a tremendous miracle. If the transfer of my spirit from my body to the spirit world could take place, then it is easy to assume that the gatekeeper and all the inhabitants of the spirit world would instantly be able to communicate with each other without the requirement of interpreters. I'd never previously turned my mind to this situation. I wondered whether I would be the one to sometimes speak in a foreign language or would it be the other way round? I concluded that eventually I would find out and therefore I should remain calm and let time sort out this conundrum.

Jimmy seemed to have waited for me to finish my silent analysis, for when I glanced at him he was sitting quietly, smiling at me.

"Sorry," I said, "I interrupted your story."

"No my dear, there is no need to apologise. I have plenty of time," he continued, which I gathered was a common answer here. Plenty of time certainly, but those in the Waiting Room hadn't had their personal interview with God and one could never be certain on being sent on to the afterlife; there was always the possibility of being sent to the Frozen Place. And it dawned on me that Jimmy could be in some danger, for I assumed that his love of drinking and the misery it could cause, though he had not as yet reached that point in his story, might lead God to decide that perhaps a little stay in the Waiting Room or even in the Frozen Place might be a suitable punishment. But I brought myself up quickly because I realised that I was assuming God's mantle, trespassing on His exclusive reserve, and rushing to judgement before all the facts were disclosed. And I remember you, Dad, many times telling us not to rely on what the papers said was the evidence given in court cases. 'It's only part of the evidence,' you would say, 'I can't give you my opinion about this case because I wasn't in court listening to the proceedings'. Yes, that's what you consistently said to us whenever a notorious case hit the papers. From a legalistic point of view you were probably correct, but the public doesn't look at things like you do Dad, do they? They are not lawyers, Dad. People love to gossip, and what is better to gossip about than some juicy dramatic case, such as that dingo case. Everyone jumped to the conclusion that the mother had murdered her baby daughter, didn't they? And even you broke your own golden rule by telling us she killed her baby and a dingo had nothing to do with it. Yes, there were lengthy excerpts from the case in the newspapers and you still regarded her as guilty, didn't you Dad? And look what happened in the end. It took a while I grant you, but eventually she was proved to be innocent and released, wasn't she Dad?

≈

Once again George came to an abrupt halt. I gathered that his daughter's words had touched a raw nerve.

"Are you okay, George?" I asked him.

"Just thinking...poor Chloe. I mean, in this long story from her...she is saying all these things to me. And, I will never again be in a position to talk to her...father and daughter because...she is gone."

I nearly cracked. I too then realised how precious my family was to me and how so little time is spent communicating with our loved ones. We all act as if we have plenty of time. Our lives are too consumed I guess with getting on with life to sit back, relax, and let our minds wander over the one thing that really matters in our lives, our family. For George and Chloe, all this was over. He would have to rely on his memories of Chloe because that was all that was left for him, and this story which he was relating to us. This was difficult because I was a man and it is so unusual I thought to have this sort of conversation with another man, even if he is your best friend. I could imagine such a conversation with a woman. They have a greater degree of perception to analyse, to interpret and minutely discuss a situation and conclude who is right and who is wrong. Perhaps George originally decided to unload his burden on me because I was a father. He had lost a daughter; Debra and I had children too. Maybe he thought we would understand. I did and I'm sure Debra did as well, but I had no idea how we would react if we were ever in the position that George and his family found themselves in. And frankly, I never wanted to find out.

Emily refilled his glass and we waited for him to continue.

≈

"I had drifted off again so I told Jimmy to resume his story."

"My problem was that I was unable to limit my drinking to the odd social occasion. The disease grabbed hold of me and wouldn't let go. I knew that I was losing customers at a rapid rate. I knew my boss and my fellow workmates had their concerns. I knew my family were aware of my problem. Advice was poured into my ear, day after day, but I just could not drag myself out of the mire, the big bog I had sunk into. I was eventually sent to Coventry, figuratively you understand," he added with a sly smile, quite unnecessarily I thought as even stupid me was aware of the saying. "Yes," he continued, "I was shunned by all and sundry, my workmates and even my family.

"My boss eventually gave me one week to get my head together: stop drinking or else I'll send you packing he said to me rather heatedly. One week, one month – what did it matter to me? It was all the same, it could have been one year; it wouldn't have made one iota of difference."

I shook my head slowly, as much as in sadness as in disbelief. I mean Dad, this man's job was on the line and he couldn't, or wouldn't, do a thing about it. Shouldn't he have gone to AA? I put this to him.

"Hah, hah!" he laughed. "Of course I tried that, but I was too far gone. I had all the best intentions not to touch another drop at the close of each meeting, but as I walked home a feeling, an overwhelming, overpowering feeling of desperation for a drink smacked me, hard and unforgiving. If a pub happened to pass me by as I dawdled home I could not resist the temptation to walk through the door and order a brandy, even if the publican was about to close the door. How many I downed I couldn't say, sufficient I guess to have the tag 'alcoholic' still stick; more than enough for my wife to abuse me when I finally battered on the front door, which I had to do because in my drunken state and surrounded by darkness, I could never find the key hole. She would be berating me even before she opened the door. 'Drunk again I see,' was her usual sarcastic remark. Her voice would be bathed in contempt, hatred, without any sense of caring, sympathy, empathy or whatever is the correct word. Perhaps the time for compassion had long gone. Yet in my drunken state I never expressed any dissent, never disputed her right to be angry. Her words penetrated my brain like a spear. I knew I could not argue with her. All I could do was mumble 'sorry'. It seemed to be my favourite word, as though I was a small child and, having discovered how to pronounce a new word, I kept on repeating it whatever the circumstances were. From the moment I stumbled across the threshold until I crashed on to the sofa and lay there, dishevelled. I was unable to say any word other than 'sorry'. I must have sounded like a broken record, stuck in the same place, the same groove, until a gentle push moved the needle on."

He hung his head between his knees and started blubbering. Now, when it was far too late, he regretted his inability to pull himself out of the hole into which he had descended. A mountaineer who has fallen into the depths of a crevasse high up on a mountain could not have felt as helpless.

Gradually his sobs turned to a sniffle and he lifted his head. I saw no tears. Evidently we could outwardly imitate a state of sadness here but the physical outpourings of tears could not be replicated.

"Sorry," he said, and gave out a meek smile. He was doing it again; that must have been his inner thoughts.

"If only my wife could see me now," he took up again. He was remorseful, but his chance had gone, like a cloud flowing across the sky aided by a roaring wind quickly disappears over the horizon; too late by far for him to regret his inability to change his ways. And Dad, I immediately thought of our lives on earth. We take on a certain role; we conduct ourselves in a particular manner, and it is only years' later do we come to regret some past action. Some may regret not studying as diligently as they could have; husbands and wives regret lost opportunities to patch up strained or broken relationships. Have you ever regretted anything, Dad? I suppose you must because you too are only human. Of course, I too regret some events in my life, short as it was. Then again, I am in no position now to change my ways, to apologize to a friend I might have offended, to undertake a different course of action – whatever one can think of – it is too late for me. Dad, I'm now in a position to offer you, and I guess people in general, some advice. Please live your life showing respect for every living creature, human or animal, for eventually every human will find themselves here in the Waiting

Room. Life should be lived according to the guiding principle of showing concern for every living thing you come across. Think about your life as you continue your travels through it; don't wait until the opportunities to alter your course have vanished into thin air.

≈

George once again came to a sudden halt in his narrative. This is very powerful stuff I thought. His daughter was right. We are always rushing on to the next point in our lives, often forgetting to stop and smell the flowers as it is said, disregarding the world around us, concerned only for our own welfare, enmeshed in our own self-interest. George lifted his head and looked at me as if he was going to say something as commentary, but not a sound came out of his open mouth, as if his vocal chords were clogged with some substance that choked the emission of any sound. Rare is the opportunity when our mind is sufficiently clear to grasp the meaning of what is being put to us. I was beginning to be convinced by the message of his daughter's story. I knew George already was. That was natural enough I suppose, looking back now and remembering that first day George came to see me, for he was Chloe's father and he had to believe; he had to have faith, for to what else could he cling? He was staring at the wall, as if he was under some hypnotic spell, when he suddenly began to continue Chloe's story, without a word of explanation as to what caused him to have stopped.

≈

"Yes," I said, "your wife would be proud of your expression of regret for your conduct, but can you proceed with your story?

I'm afraid with my wandering mind and interfering questions I have interrupted you far too much."

"My lass, it is indeed a pleasure to talk to you, so don't give your meanderings or questions a second thought," he said.

He steadied himself before continuing.

"Of course, I was eventually let go. I guess the boss had no other alternative; naturally his primary concern was for the company and its reputation. I had to be dispensed with before I could inflict any more damage. I accepted his decision rather meekly at the time because in my heart I realised he was right. He had given me an opportunity to get back on track but I brazenly rejected the chance to do so. I was sneaking off to find a drink, missing appointments left right and centre, and anyway, those I did keep turned out to be a disaster; a real shambles, because I was often still drunk. Though I personally attended my customers' premises, excuses came thick and fast as to why they couldn't give me an order. How long this situation lasted I have no clear recollection. It may have been days or weeks or months. At the time I was beyond care and I was unable to be reformed; the damage I had done to myself was irreparable.

"So I was dismissed. Unless I overcame my addiction to the demon drink there was precious little prospect of finding an alternative job. Life at home became a battlefield. Not only had I lost my job but Mary became violent and abusive towards me. I often was in no condition to respond. I defended myself as best I could before passing out. Many a time I felt a brutal kick from her as she careered around the house yelling out abuse; she called me every name you can think of, and would often kick me in the ribs with the points of her shoes as I lay prostrate on the floor.

"As soon as I sobered up, I would gather together whatever money I could lay my hands on and stumble out the door, and head for the nearest pub. Usually I would drink on my own, for often I had descended on the pub as soon as the publican opened the door. I would sit on a stool at the bar drinking a beer or Guinness one after another until the publican would give me an intense stare with his penetrating eyes and shake his head from side to side. His meaning was clear – I was drunk and he therefore had no intention of serving me anymore that day. I would graciously accept this because although I knew I was an alcoholic, and would always be one, yet I had to rely on the publican to tell me I'd had enough. If he forgot about me for some reason or other I would continue to pour drinks down my throat until I could take no more. My head would slump down on the bar and I would pass out, unconscious. After I woke up I was invariably guided to the door and pushed outside on to the footpath. Despite my condition I always was able to find my way to the liquor shop and purchase a few more bottles if I hadn't run out of money. At the pub I usually drank beer or Guinness, but once my head was caressed by fresh air I was somehow attracted to spirits and therefore branched out and bought a large bottle of brandy, whiskey, vodka or whatever I felt the urge to drink on that particular day. Not too far away was a park with a spread of trees, garden beds of various flowers whose names I can't remember, seats sprinkled here and there and a children's playground that had seen better days. Making my way to a vacant seat I would sit there while I gazed pensively about me, all the while gulping down huge mouthfuls directly out of the bottle, oblivious to the people passing nearby. Often I would drape myself along the seat, and fall into a state of oblivion. When I finally woke it would be late afternoon; the sun would be descending behind the trees and, no matter the weather, I would be engulfed by a fit of the shivers. Time to go home I would tell myself. A sort of in-built radar would somehow get me to the front door as if I was a homing pigeon. Mary was often out. I wouldn't have a clue where she was. My children too were nowhere to be seen. Sometimes I would go to sleep on the front door step while I waited for her to arrive home. Mary would eventually drag me inside. My girls would then mysteriously appear. I could barely scrape a word together to speak to them. Not surprisingly, they treated me as if I was afflicted with leprosy. They were afraid to touch me lest their limbs began to fall off. Supper often went untouched. This is a very hazy time for me to recall accurately. I may have eaten; I may not have. It was really all the same to me. Food no longer concerned me. It was alcohol I was intent on chasing. 'Intent' may be too soft a word – I was patently desperate for the stuff! By now I was no longer sleeping with Mary. She had well and truly kicked me out of our bedroom. At the time I did not blame her. I still don't. I know a marriage should be 'in sickness and in health', all that wedding vow stuff you know, but why should I expect my wife to forgive me my perpetual drunkenness? I was indeed sick, but any attempt I did make to get out of the situation was lukewarm at the best. I was my own worst enemy I believe and had no right to demand anything from her. Why should I have imposed such an intolerable burden on her?" he asked me, not expecting me to respond.

All this time he had not once looked in my direction. His gaze was immediately ahead of him into the distance, as if he was in a trance. From time to time I too turned my gaze into the distance in an effort to catch a glimpse of whatever he seemed to be resolutely staring at. Far off, I could vaguely make out other groups of people moving slowly across the horizon. His tale had by now taken on a pathetic nature. I was certain he regretted his past misdemeanours because they had destroyed his most valuable asset, his family, and led him ultimately to where he was now.

He stopped for a brief moment and slowly turned his head towards me to gauge my reaction.

"Go on," I said as gently as I could, for I genuinely sympathised with him.

"Well, Mary asked me to leave," he began. "I had to agree because I had no viable choice. She found me a room in a small two story boarding house owned by a widowed lady, Mrs Fitzherbert, her name was. I was given a small room which contained only a worn out single bed, a dilapidated wardrobe and a wobbly side table. There was a large common dining room where we ate our meals and a small, dark parlour with wallpaper peeling off the walls where an old TV was available if one was so inclined. Mary told me she would pay the rent, for she had no faith in my ability to find the money to pay it when it became due. I knew that, deep down in her heart, she still loved me but the alcoholic lifestyle I had adopted and imposed on her sank her obligation to put up with me for better or for worse, and inevitably clashed with the happy family situation she required. Meals were included in the rent and for a while I generally ate at the dinner table with the other lodgers. Nods and muted greetings were all that passed between us at meals, as if each lodger had a secret hidden deep inside their chest, yet had no intention in divulging it to another living soul. I am quite comfortable speaking to you, but back then I wanted to literally turn my face to the wall and hide myself away from these people. I had no desire to hear stories of their awful lives, and certainly I had no wish to embarrass myself and tell my story of how I had dragged myself down. Having no job, I had ample spare time to continue my drinking unaffected by the inconvenience of breaking off my drinking time to front up at a job. This situation continued for months, I think. Well, to be quite frank, I have no idea of how long it was because one day seemed to effortlessly blend in with the day before and the day after. Mrs Fitzherbert, sensibly I now realise, had a rule prohibiting drinking alcohol in our rooms. Being able to drink in my room could have been a total catastrophe for me as I would have been able to slink back carrying all the bottles of spirits I could buy with whatever funds I happened not to have already spent, and drink myself to sleep every night. However, she did allow each lodger a choice of one glass of beer or a sweet sherry with the evening meal. One beer! What was that to me? Not enough to wash the dust from my throat! There's a proverb isn't there – never look a gift horse in the mouth? How could I resist a free glass of beer when it was offered to me? I couldn't, and didn't. Mary also gave me an allowance each week which I spent almost entirely on drink, although it was intended to pay for clothes and toiletries and small things like that. I felt a heel, for I was a kept man. Yet the stupor I had fallen into could not be reversed. I tried cold turkey. It lasted barely a day. Once again, I tramped off to AA in an attempt to get myself back on the right road, but it was useless. Oh, I attended meeting after meeting, but as my drinking didn't decrease by more than a beer or so a day, I effectively had no prospect of permanently stopping. You are supposed to stop cold turkey but I couldn't, I just couldn't. I was a broken man, my life continuing from one day to the next without variation."

"Did you see your children?" I ventured.

"Yes. Mary allowed me to come over to home for an hour or so on the weekend on the strict condition I was sober which, in her eyes, meant I hadn't had a drink at all that day. To avoid embarrassment, I usually went to visit the girls early on Saturday morning before the pub opened. On every visit there was a degree of nervousness on the girls' part, and on mine as well. My alcoholism was an unspoken topic we could not touch. During the week I missed them desperately and so did everything I could to ensure my visit didn't upset them. It felt as if I was back in the old days of courting because I had to be on my best behaviour to be allowed to see the girls. After an hour or so, Mary would hustle me away citing some particular reason why no further time could be allowed. I guessed that she too was anxious each week because for the two of us nothing could possibly be worse than to have a bitter argument in front of the children. The door closing with a bang behind me allowed me to sigh with relief. Another milestone had been passed, yet I could not see any improvement in my situation. My visits were invariably of roughly the same length; there were long periods of silence until one of us was forced to ask some bland question to restart the conversation. Of course, the girls had their school activities to report on and they did so in a brief fashion, devoid of animation. I had no job and so was restricted to telling them short versions of the very few conversations I'd had or overheard at the boarding house during the previous week. Sometimes I described each of the other lodgers and their peculiar habits and individual idiosyncrasies. The girls would laugh at my descriptions as often I gave out little performances as in a pantomime. Morning tea would be served. I felt like a long lost relative or family friend who had unexpectedly turned up after a spell in the jungles of Africa. It was like a high afternoon tea you see in the movies, everything prim and proper. It went on week after week despite us all being totally unaccustomed to acting in that way. Then something totally unexpected happened."

"What was that?" I asked anxiously.

"My lifestyle was unchanged; drinking; no job and nothing in sight. I had even begun to sleep outside at night, even though I had a bed to go to. It was summer and many a time I found myself in the morning stretched out on a park bench, having not moved an inch from where I had crashed the previous evening. If it had been winter, who knows what would have happened to me. As it was, I felt I was beginning to succumb. I often felt decidedly unwell and could hardly open my eyes in the morning. Only the thought of my two girls kept me going. The prospect of not seeing them forced me to limit my drinking to some extent every Friday so that Saturday morning I would be sufficiently sober to pass Mary's strict examination and meet with the girls for one single hour, this magic hour, this treasured hour of existence; my only reason to stay alive from one day to the next, from one week to the next."

"But what exactly happened?" I asked, beginning to be exasperated at his long windiness and with a tinge of impatience in my voice.

"I can't really say from personal knowledge, but I will tell you what the gatekeeper told me when I arrived."

Exactly the same scenario as me I thought. I realised then that for people who have no forewarning of their impending death, it is the gatekeeper who describes the circumstances leading to that person's death.

"This is what he told me," Jimmy commenced.

"I had been drinking at the pub all afternoon. I had gulped down lunch at home, that is, at the boarding house, at around one o'clock and then rushed back to the pub. At six I left the pub intending to return back to the boarding house to have my supper. I'd discovered that if I ate regular meals every day it allowed me to continue drinking. I'd a feeling that this is what I intended to do and the gatekeeper reinforced this by revealing to me my thought process. Naturally, I was tipsy when I pushed my way through the pub doors. Apparently I was staggering along the footpath as drunks are apt to do, but I must have been drunker than normal for I lurched on to the road. Not in to the centre, but along the gutter, staggering along as best I could with the flow of the traffic. Cars were parked along the street and to avoid me colliding into them I would give them a wide berth, veering around each one in an exaggerated half circle, darting back to the gutter at the end of each car or line of cars. I expect I was pretty unscientific in my walking, lurching around each obstacle, each car, as if it was a bomb that would explode if I even dared to touch it. It was still light at this stage and I was confident of finding my way back to the boarding house. Lass, I have to remind you again that these recollections I am filling you in with come entirely from the gatekeeper; I have no recollection of what occurred next.

"I had veered around a car he told me when, without being aware of it, I was hit violently from behind by a motor cycle; I was thrown in the air and fell with a thud, hitting my head on the road, like a diver diving into water, except that I had tanked this dive and lead with my head. I was rushed to the hospital having already lapsed into a coma from the very force of my collision with the hard. I lingered on for three days, never regaining consciousness. And then I found myself here, as you did I expect, at a door, and came face to face with the gatekeeper. I asked him how my wife and two girls were. He told me that immediately they heard of my accident they had rushed to the hospital and maintained a constant watch at my bedside until I passed away. I knew nothing of this as I was in a coma. You hear about happy endings where people lay in a coma for months and even years, and suddenly wake up, perhaps because the constant noise and words of encouragement by visiting family sinks into the patient's subconscious; sounds are heard which penetrate the brain, and, by some miracle which no doubt even a doctor cannot sufficiently explain, the patient suddenly opens his eyes and stares at the ceiling, wondering where he is and what has happened to him. In my case it was not meant to be. So now, like you," he said, "I am here, waiting judgement."

"For all your troubles it is obvious your family still loved you," I said, hoping to instil something positive into his situation.

"Yes...yes, when trouble comes...it is the time when you discover who your true friends are it is said, and in my case, it demonstrated that my wife and two girls, deep down in their hearts, still loved me."

"I believe there is a moral to your story," I suggested.

"What's that?" he asked.

"Well, it is that on earth the door is always open for disputing parties to communicate with each other, whether they are nations or simply regular human beings like the two of us once were. The opportunity for patching up differences always exists. I've always held the view (and this is my own personal opinion mind you) that even seemingly destroyed relationships might be able to be put back together by a recognition that what the other person actually says may not, for some reason, truly represent their heart-felt opinion. We need more understanding and compassion towards our fellow man. Only then will there be genuine peace. Even in the short time I've been here I have come to realise that the never ending fighting between nations and various groups of people within one nation, has no place here because there is nothing contentious happening. There is a saying that men are born equal; this may be true, but I believe a truer statement is that every individual dies equal to everyone else. No greater truism exists. But the time between birth and death needs to be worked on, don't you think?"

Jimmy rose from his seat. I too rose.

"Chloe," he said, "it has been a pleasure to meet you." Before I had the opportunity to respond he smiled broadly and quickly moved away as if he had an urgent appointment or he was commencing a search for something he had lost. I was left alone again, wondering whose path I would cross next in my wandering around the Waiting Room.

Dad, before I describe my next conversation, I wonder what your reaction was to Jimmy, the alcoholic. I often thought you had a very strict attitude to people who broke the law; you never seemed to have a kind word for them: anti-social behaviour you called it. You seemed to regard any digression from the law as a valid reason for the authorities to stamp a heavy foot on the offender. I assume you would treat alcoholism as anti-social behaviour, a lack of moral fibre perhaps rather than some form of disease. Is compassion lacking in your heart? We never seemed to find the time to discuss this subject fully or even at all it seems to me now. Once again, it is far too late. I wonder what your reaction will be to the very next person I encountered.

≈

George stopped his reading.

"Do I lack compassion?" he asked me with an ashen complexion.

"I wouldn't have thought so," I answered rather hesitantly, although I knew George had strong views which he often expressed in an angry, explosive manner from time to time. And, in any event, I thought – what has a lawyer to do with a subjective concept such as compassion? I was also a corporate man and realised that compassion was the last thing on the mind of most high-flying executives. Lawyers are not regarded as the most understanding and compassionate of people. When it came to their work, especially in commercial law which I understood was George's forte, any expression of compassion for people other than your own client seemed to disappear; it was a no-go area. George had in the past hammered the point that he acted entirely on his clients' instructions. He often told me that his individual thoughts of the morality of a transaction were not relevant and of no concern to him. So I quickly came to appreciate how his daughter's questioning his lack of compassion for people guilty of what she referred to as 'anti-social behaviour' cut George to the quick.

"Chloe's right you know," he suddenly said with a solid determination. "That's the way we were trained, to act for a particular client and disregard all other considerations, even morality. As long as your client came up trumps, that was the main thing; nothing else mattered. And we worked with the law; we didn't make it of course, but once it was on the books then it was up to us to use our knowledge of the law, of the system, to crush our client's opponents, at whatever cost. Younger lawyers of course now hold a different view, as they would; they have been brought up in a different environment."

He sat back and slowly sipped his drink. I could practically see his mind ticking over; it was so obvious. He was questioning himself, his philosophy, his whole attitude to life itself. I wouldn't say it had the quality or attributes of a religious experience, but I perceived his internal suffering, as Chloe's words sank deeper and deeper into his consciousness. He may have been walking along his own personal road to Damascus. His internal suffering certainly made me think about the more serious side of life; about life itself, and what it meant to live on earth as a human being. It seemed the penny had dropped for Chloe and her narrative seemed to be some sort of attempt to get George to grasp her point of view.

Chapter Ten

LIFE CONTINUED, ONE DAY GIVING WAY TO THE NEXT. I went interstate for a business meeting; George was in the Supreme Court fighting some huge commercial case. Debra undertook her domestic duties with her usual diligence. Our children, Daniel and Andy, having sought their independence, had their own problems to deal with.

Emily endeavoured to keep George level-headed. She told Debra he was apt to engage in temper tantrums over what she regarded as unimportant matters. She believed it was his choice to plunge himself into his work, not only handling the most complex of cases but also by taking on less important ones that he could have quite easily delegated to a junior lawyer. It was his way of coping she believed. Emily related how his anger rose exponentially with each day that passed without a visit from Chloe. I too did my utmost to help him by ringing him almost every day and grabbing a quick lunch with him when we both had time. Sometimes I just made time, regardless of my work situation. I knew I had to prevent his mind slipping back to his total occupation with Chloe's story.

Another three weeks passed. I detected his anxiety; consternation clearly showed on his face.

"I wish she'd hurry up," he said one day on the phone.

"She will come back soon, George," was all I could say. I regarded such a response as lame, but what else could I say?

Eventually, Chloe returned late the following Friday night; more accurately, during the early hours of the Saturday morning. George rang to tell me while we were having breakfast. Chloe had spoken of someone else she had met, a young woman called Jessie. It was our turn to host a Saturday night. I had no need to ask George to come over that night with Emily; it was imprinted on our minds.

There were few formalities when they arrived. Debra had the usual drinks on the kitchen bench, lined up like soldiers, so it was merely a matter of grabbing a glass and settling into our accustomed seats and waiting for George to open his folder and begin.

"This is how she began," George said.

≈

She told me her name was Jessie. Whether that was her real name I couldn't say. Her chosen profession I gathered was rife with false names. I had wandered for a little while after James walked off, enjoying the absolute stillness and admiring the scenery when I suddenly came face to face with her on a pathway. Now I could engage another person in conversation. We exchanged greetings. I noticed that she was taller than I was, and her face carried features that men would classify as classically beautiful. This, of course, meant nothing to me. Not too far away was a small area where people could sit down. We went over and sat down side by side.

I gave her my name and some details of what the gatekeeper had told me about my death. I cut my story much shorter than when I had spoken with James because I foresaw that my own story would, on constant repetition, become terribly boring to me if I repeated it in detail to every person that I came across.

After I'd finished, I asked her to tell me everything she could of herself.

Jessie hesitated, as if she was reluctant to disclose even the simplest of details.

"Are you certain you want to hear about my life?" she asked, unable to mask her apprehension. Perhaps she was hiding a dark secret I thought – but does it really matter I wondered, now that we were both dead? I had by this time realised that in the spirit world there would be much less of the underhand goings-on or deliberate withholding of 'secrets' that occupied the lives of many living people.

"Of course I do. Why wouldn't I?" I asked her in as bright a voice that I could muster. "We are all equal now, aren't we, waiting here? Whatever you tell me can't affect anything any more; your relationship with people on earth has come to an end. There is no longer anything to fear."

Hearing me say this she became a little more cheerful.

"Yes, how silly of me," she remarked.

"My parents were well-off," she commenced, "and sent me, when I was barely six, to an exclusive girls' school. I had to board at the school because my parents' owned a large sheep farm in the Western District."

"You're from Victoria!" I exclaimed.

"Yes, I am," she replied.

"So am I," I gleefully told her. As she began to speak, I had detected a flat, monotone voice, in contrast to James' lilting Irish accent, and realised she could only have been an Australian.

"I hated it," she continued. "The school was tightly controlled by an awful clique of teachers, though some of them were not so bad. They were severe, imposing a very strict regime. Punishment was handed out frequently and freely if a girl's homework wasn't finished or she got a poor mark in one of the numerous tests they forced on us. The end of a term could not come around quick enough for me; the long train journey home was the only occasion I was truly happy during each and every year that I went to this school. A few of the boarders did befriend me during term but after we all left for the holidays I had no contact with them until the next term came along. And at home I had few friends because I did not attend the local high school. Kids who I might otherwise have been friends with had made solid friendships with their own schoolmates so I had no hope of being admitted to their circle. I kept to myself, and rarely bothered to leave my room once it had been firmly established in my mind that there was no prospect of establishing any close relationships in town. I was an only child and though my parents had brothers and sisters, they lived far from us, and therefore I hardly ever saw my cousins.

"This accursed life extended for ten long years. Of course, there must have been an occasional time when I was sufficiently happy to play with an acquaintance. In general however, I regarded life as rather miserable. As I approached the finish of my school days I had become so apathetic and lazy I suppose my interest in my studies dropped off rapidly. What physical or psychological punishment the teachers saw fit to hand out to me did not worry me. As far as I was concerned they could rant and rave as much as they liked; it made no difference to my state of mind. 'Idleness leads to depravity' was the cautionary expression they blasted me with. 'It's bad to be lazy' and other like expressions they conjured up in their minds were forced down my throat. 'You'll end up in the gutter!' one of the vicious ones threatened me with. What did I care then? It was not a religious school but what little religious faith I had to begin with slowly disappeared as the years went by. In the end, I could not stand their pseudo religious preaching. Isn't it ironic? Now what do I find? In a way they were right."

"What did the gatekeeper say when you told him all this?" I asked, concerned by her self-deprecation.

"He listened patiently while I told him everything, even the bad bits. He always had a smile on his face and constantly spoke to me in a way I had rarely come across on earth; it was as though he regarded me as a real person and not someone's plaything, to be tossed around and abused at leisure. I couldn't believe it; I knew I was in another dimension and it certainly shocked me when I realised I was here, in this Waiting Room."

"I agree," I said. "The gatekeeper impressed me too. Pity that he couldn't spend some time on earth," I added, "what a sensation that would be!"

"He might even be able to cure many of the world's problems," Jessie optimistically suggested.

My experience of my time on earth convinced me that it would take much more than the presence and example of the gatekeeper's words to rid the world of all that is wrong with it, don't you agree Dad?

≈

George laughed.

"Of course, after all that has happened, I have to agree, but didn't this take place two thousand years ago?" he put to me.

"You mean...Jesus?" I asked.

"Yes, I suppose so. What good did that do? Chloe, like all young people I guess, was extremely idealistic and being where she was, and coming under the influence of this 'gatekeeper' as I assume she did, it is easy for her to believe that the world's problems can be fixed by a few home-spun tales. And yet, this is what some religious groups are waiting for: another Messiah to come along and right all the wrongs."

"That's what the Jews have been saying for two thousand years. They are waiting for a Messiah, but I don't know George. It is a problem that has plagued humanity for aeons so why would this 'gatekeeper' be able to achieve what many peaceful orientated people such as Ghandi and Martin Luther King have failed to achieve?"

"We can talk after," Debra butted in. "Let George finish."

George maintained a stiff stare. Perhaps he too was bamboozled by this conundrum? He let it slide and after looking at each one of us, continued.

≈

I wanted to get Jessie back on track so I asked her what she did after she left school.

"I returned home after finishing school, but quickly left to seek my fortune you could say. I had no intention of staying on the farm. Furthermore, the nearest town held very little interest to me, so I decided to try my luck in the city where I had been to school. I had money; that was no problem, plenty in fact. My parents, although they regretted me leaving, had no hesitation in giving me enough money to last for quite a while. I briefly contemplated sharing with another girl or even a boy, but in the end I decided I would be better off on my own, in case my chosen flatmate turned out to be a dud. I wanted to make my own way in the world, be independent, without having to exist on hand-outs. A swish unit in Toorak or South Yarra was well within my reach, but instead I chose a small place in a run down apartment block in St Kilda. You know, I was just seventeen, naïve perhaps, wanting to grow up fast, gain some experience of life and eventually make a mark. I needed to be a 'somebody', just like Rocky who wanted to be a 'contender'. Unfortunately, I had no qualifications as I had left that dreadful school after Year 11 and had nothing to fall back on. Because people had told me so, I fancied I was attractive and had all the necessary attributes to be a model. I was tall, had a traditional hourglass figure and had a wholesome look about me. The good ones earned packets according to the gossip that I had heard, and from what I had read in the magazines; there is the glamorous lifestyle as well which certainly attracted me. If others could do it, there was no reason why I couldn't also. I made some enquiries. Then I went to see an agent who arranged for me to go and visit a photographer to put together a portfolio. The photographer was Italian with long, slicked back hair and a three day growth, the epitome of trendy. Within a very short time of starting the session it was obvious he was more interested in my body than taking photographs. He was as bad as the agent who more or less suggested that I had to sleep with him if he wanted me to be actively promoted and become a success in the industry. He hinted that every aspiring model eventually found her way to the 'casting couch'. Believe it or not, but at the time I was still a virgin. I had been a boarder and lived a lonely life, leaving me virtually no opportunity to meet a boy even if I wanted to, which at the time I never really did. The photographer made me pose provocatively, in a way that oozed sex; sometimes I was practically naked; a bit over the top for a fashion model I thought. The photographic session was barely a cover for his attempt to seduce me.

"Hardly a job came along although the agent assured me that he was working flat out on my case, as he put it. I privately wondered whether another agency would be able to look after me better than he was. I went to a group interview at a large and well known agency. There must have been a hundred hopefuls waiting in this large room. After we completed an individual parade, in which we all attempted to give off a classy and professional image, we had our 5 minute personal interview after which I was told: 'We'll call you'. I was never called. I was becoming quite desperate. As I said, it wasn't the lack of money. Rather, it was the dent to my already low self-esteem, which really started on that fateful day I stepped through the gates of that boarding school. Life was rushing past me. I had to find something to do, and quickly, to fast-track my career; I did not want it to be over before it had even started. Reluctantly, I decided to have sex with the agent," she whispered, as if she didn't want anyone to overhear a reference to sex here. "Although I was still a virgin, my interest in sex had begun to develop as I got older, and though I realised it wasn't an ideal situation for me I...He wasn't the most handsome man I ever encountered in my life, but at least he was on the proper side of ugly," she said with a laugh.

"And so, you had sex?" I asked tentatively, as if we were entering into discussion on a subject regarded as taboo.

"Well, I didn't just go up to him and openly propose we do it; I was way more subtle than that," she confided in a confident manner. "At this time I was getting the odd job from him. One time he placed me at a lunchtime fashion parade at a major department store, Myer it might have been, and, as usual, he came along to run his eyes over everyone. After it was over, he came up to me as he always did and congratulated me on my walk, my poise, my attitude, how I had shown the clothes to best effect and so on; all the typical encouraging, hypocritical prattle that people in the industry go on with. Finally, he asked me to celebrate such a great show by sharing a late lunch with him. This was my chance. For quite some time, various plans had been running through my mind of how best I could get him to that position where he would think that he had finally conquered me; another fashion model he could notch on his belt. Little did he know that no matter in what circumstance it came about, it was all going to happen entirely at the time of my choosing. To me, it was just the first step I had to take to get anywhere in the industry or in my life for that matter. He certainly was correct in that aspect because I often overheard conversations in various dressing rooms of girls complaining or boasting, depending on their particular leanings I suppose, of having been obliged to sleep with some important figure that might be able to enhance her career.

"We went to a fancy restaurant in South Yarra, Lynch's. He certainly did not spare any expense, ordering the best of everything, particularly wine. He was fired up, acting as though he had struck a certainty, throwing down glass after glass, talking loudly, as if his life depended on it. I was aware his tactics were to get me drunk so he could more easily seduce me, but I was awake to that trick. Instead, I turned the tables on him, continuously plying him with champagne, giggling and laughing as if I was having the time of my life, pretending I was drinking as much as he was. I made an effort to ensure that he saw my glass at my lips so he would assume I was falling into his trap. The table was eventually cleared. We skipped the offered coffee and continued to drink. He switched to spirits but I told him I preferred something more sparkling than a whiskey, and anyway, I whispered in his ear, it was only champagne that turned me on. He reacted exactly as I thought he would. He broke out in a huge smile and started smarming up to me even more, calling me every affectionate name under the sun he could pull out of his bag of tricks. He grabbed my hand and squeezed it; he ran his fingers up and down my arm, like raindrops, all in an effort to make me want him. As soon as he had drained a glass, I would signal the waiter to hurry over with another. I don't know what the waiter was thinking, but I am sure he had seen this sort of thing many a time. This game continued until very late in the afternoon when I hit him with: 'Aren't you going to invite me back to your place?' I had a notion he lived nearby. I knew that he was divorced and lived on his own – he had made that plain early on, almost on the first day we met.

"As it was, his apartment was only 5 minutes by car away. He could not contain himself on the way, running his left hand up and down my thighs while he steered with his right. He certainly had had more than enough to drink to blow more than .05, but somehow, from prior experience no doubt, we got back to his place unscathed. Thinking back, it was foolhardy of me to allow him to have driven home, but my mind was focused on other matters.

"Hardly were we through the door than he began to throw his clothes off, scattering them willy-nilly around the room. Then, stark naked, he grabbed me by the hand and dragged me in the direction of his bedroom. No turning back now I thought as he propelled me on to his bed.

"And there wasn't. We became lovers and my modelling career blossomed as never before. Jobs came in from him thick and fast; I was in such demand he doubled my daily fee. He got me jobs wearing famous designers' latest fashions. I believed I had made it to the big time, especially when top magazines vied with each other to use me for their covers. Overseas trips followed, one after another. New York, Paris, you name it. All I had to do was to keep on having sex with him, and act the perfectly satisfied lover, and my career would continue expanding at a rapid rate. I had to fend off other agents who kept baiting me with so-called better offers to work for them, but with the unstated requirement to be a good time girl with them on the side. As it was, I had begun to enjoy the sex a lot more because...well, you know, I was getting used to it...and it ensured I retained my lifestyle and earning capacity. I was bringing in serious money and so I bought myself an apartment not very far from Geoff's place; oh sorry, I forgot to tell you, the agent's name was Geoff. It was very luxurious, art deco style, and I made sure I got contents to match. He wanted me to move in with him instead of buying my own place, but I had enough sense to ensure I retained my independence. If I was working at some other career, in an office perhaps, and Geoff was a big wheel somewhere, if I had loved him, I wouldn't have hesitated in moving in with him. But I did not love him. To me, it was all business. Sleeping with him I saw as a pre-requisite to advancing my career. It wasn't for love; it was purely for the purpose of getting me higher up the ladder. Not only did I look after my own interests by sleeping with him, but I also worked out at a gym to keep in shape. I believed that nothing could be worse than losing jobs because you had put on weight or wrinkles were spreading like wildfire over your face. I hardly touched alcohol and naturally I stayed away from gorging myself on fast food. Then it all went wrong."

"Did you have a falling out with him?" I asked.

"Well, not in the beginning, but...in the end..."

"What happened?"

"My work schedule was punishing. Often I would have a photo shoot for a national magazine at the break of dawn, followed by a fashion parade in the morning, morning tea functions for the social set raising money for charity; perhaps again at lunchtime or in the afternoon, and then something would invariably follow at night. Sometimes it would be another job or some industry function or cocktail party that Geoff would drag me off to. By the time I got to bed I was totally exhausted. Mixing this hectic work schedule with the constant travel eventually started to wear me out. I found it difficult to get to gym as I just had no time and so I was forced to rely on a starvation diet to maintain my weight.

Limiting my eating to ensure I did not balloon out left me feeling rather weak. One day, a girl I was sitting next to in the dressing room while I was checking my makeup, commented that I didn't look healthy; she said I looked drained and devoid of energy. I told her what was happening in my life. Unfazed by all that I told her, she said: 'I've got something to help you'. She pulled out a packet of pills and handed them to me. I asked her what they were for. 'Oh, just some uppers and these,' she said, producing another packet from her bag, 'are downers'".

"Did you take them?" I asked, intrigued at how her story was panning out.

"Yes I did, I started immediately. It certainly made an impact. Suddenly, I had a bucket load of energy and I seemed to bounce from one job to the next without feeling tired at all. I was on an artificial high, but I didn't really care as the uppers ensured I was able to keep up my frenzied work load. Geoff was amazed at the difference he saw in me. 'I'm sleeping better,' I fibbed, and this was true to some extent but not for the reason he would be thinking of. Though the use of pills appeared to be widespread amongst the girls I just couldn't admit to him that I was taking anything as I didn't know what his reaction would be as we had never discussed the subject. I wasn't willing to take a chance. I kept popping more and more pills. Sometimes, I was so excited at night I didn't want to go to bed and catch up on sleep. All I wanted to do was go out and have fun. I worked Geoff over pretty good and he would be so exhausted he would fall asleep immediately; not me though, I could never tire myself out. I was living a maniacal way of life, always buoyant, laughing, giggling, talking loudly, effervescent; a real wild cat. To calm myself down I was forced to gulp down more downers, especially to get to sleep. For months I was alternately up and down, all day and night. Often my mind went blank and I would have no idea how many tablets I had taken, or when, so to remove any doubt I would pop in a few more, just to be sure. Over time my downers kept me asleep for longer and longer periods. I was waking up later and later every morning. This eventually became a problem as I had jobs scheduled nearly every day. Then one day, Geoff had to ring me to wake me up because I had not turned up for some magazine shoot. I stumbled out of bed feeling as if I'd had no sleep at all. To put some energy into me, I threw down some uppers and raced out to meet him for the shoot, without even stopping for a coffee. Gradually, these uppers and downers took control of my life. I was hooked on them and couldn't get off the roundabout I had initially willingly jumped on. After a while, Geoff realised what I was doing to myself and blasted me unmercifully because, from his point of view, I was a fantastic meal ticket, and he certainly didn't need his favourite star to self-destruct. He had other girls on his books but, in my opinion, none of them had any chance of reaching the star status that I'd obtained.

"One day I couldn't get out of bed at all; I lay there all day virtually unable to open my eyes. I missed two jobs. Geoff was livid. He fronted up at my place later in the day and shook me senseless; he seemed to be trying to shake out whatever devil had possession of me. 'Go cold turkey,' he demanded, shouting in my ear and yanking my shoulders backwards and forwards. I agreed at first, but after two days I couldn't cope and I was reaching out for those pills again. 'Unreliable' he labelled me, and started to cut back my bookings, especially the morning ones, as he reckoned there was no guarantee that I would arrive on time. Rumours began circulating that I had lost the plot. I started to ignore the girls because I didn't want to get involved in any sort of heavy conversation with them that might turn bitchy. Yet no one had any genuine sympathy for me. Modelling, like most industries or professions, I guess, is a dog eat dog world and my downfall would elevate another model to fame and fortune. To be fair, Geoff did attempt to persuade me to give the pills away after his cold turkey solution bit the dust, but I believe it was only his self-interest that kept him concerned for a while. There was no empathy, no concern for me as a person suffering from a disease. No, he and all the rest of them, the clients I mean, looked at me from an investment point of view. Their thinking was focused on what was in it for them."

"How did all this mess you were in eventually work out?" I wanted to know.

"I was in a delicate situation; my life was in a real stew," she began. "Jobs dried up as if a sudden drought had overtaken the land, as Geoff banned me from working for him, period: no work at all. We had a contract but he had stitched me up right from the beginning. He said: 'Don't try to take me to court as your stupid conduct is a breach of contract.' I contacted some other agents but the word had spread that I was an addict, popping pills all day, and could not be relied upon to be in a fit state to perform as a model should. My appearance became haggard. I was not eating properly; I began to lose weight, which is funny I suppose for a model to say because most of us are very slim to start with; some are on the verge of anorexia. I was never as bad as that because I was never ultra-slim to start with. Certainly my looks fell away; I didn't look healthy. Money was not an issue; I didn't need it, not straight away at least. Of course, Geoff and I broke up; after all, it was purely a business arrangement, and now he could impose his will on some other young naïve starlet that undoubtedly would come along and impress him."

"Did you get another job?"

"Not at first; I lounged around during the day, sleeping most of the time, before heading out at night to rev up my otherwise dull and boring life. Somehow I eventually ditched the pills because I had no need of them to help me with a busy work schedule. I could sleep in to my heart's content. No one had any call on me. I began eating and returned to gym. It wasn't as difficult as I imagined it would be. I suppose I had the willpower to do it. Most lonely people do have some sort of instinct to overcome obstacles, if they want to.

"I was still young, in my early twenties, and had no intention of lying around at home all day and all night. I got to know all the nightspots around St Kilda as well as in town. Soon I became fairly well known at most places. Boys would try and pick me up and occasionally if I was in the mood I would take one home to give me some pleasure for an hour or so. Most of them were so drunk by the early hours of the morning that it would have been difficult for them to notice my appearance, and even if they had noticed, what was it to them? They were being taken away by me for a good time so I reasoned they wouldn't complain. It was a rarity to take home the same guy more than once. I preferred a new challenge or should I say a new guy because (and this is not boasting) I would be lying if I said it was a challenge. To me it was like doing the weekly shopping at the supermarket. There were rows and rows of goods on display from which I could choose. Other women might select a packet on the shelf that I had no interest in, while I would calmly pick another one that I wanted. A smile was usually sufficient to bring them to heel; they would approach me like a puppy dog rushing up to its master with its tongue hanging out for a pat of approval. They would big note themselves in front of their mates and walk over, often with an exaggerated sway of their hips, and commence their inane drivel. I would pretend to be enthralled by their charm and would fall into a conversation with the guy as though I was interested. But of course I wasn't. Before long the most expensive drink I could think of found its way to my hand and we would ensconce ourselves in a dark corner chatting away as if we had known each other for years. Their words would rush in one ear and, as quickly, be expelled out the other. Week after week the stories had the same dimension. It was a game to me because I had no long term interest in them; I only needed a playmate for a few hours.

"Month after month rolled by; life was once again becoming boring. I reckoned I needed another challenge. Having sex with men I momentarily fancied no longer had any real appeal. I started taking pills again to help me make it through each day but I also started out on some harder stuff – drugs of every description. You name it – I experimented with it at least once. Unusually for me, I wasn't taken in by the supposed thrill or ecstatic feeling of taking these drugs. Smoking a joint or injecting myself didn't turn me into an addict. Every drug crossed my path; even so I remained, luckily for me, just a recreational user.

"One day I was flicking through the classifieds in the paper keeping an eye out with the faintest of interest in the jobs. I was restless as I said, and smoking pot and popping pills and the odd bit of sex no longer gave me much satisfaction.

"An ad for an escort agency jumped out before my eyes. 'Girls wanted,' it said. Naturally I had heard about the brothels and escort agencies that were springing up everywhere from the time brothels had been legalised. At some time in the past I had even given a fleeting thought of becoming involved, you know, just for the money because, as I understood it, the industry was cash based and I'd heard stories of escorts and prostitutes who worked in the brothels becoming very wealthy. But the nitty gritty of what was involved concerned me more than the prospect of making heaps of money which I didn't really need. Working at a brothel, taking on anyone who came in the door, whether they were fat or thin, handsome or ugly, clean bodied or hairy sent a shiver up my spine. I didn't want to have sex with a total stranger; and after all, the men I chose in the clubs I at least knew something about by having had a drink and a chat with them prior to me whisking them away. On a few occasions, rare I must admit, I decided not to take someone home after spending time talking because I sensed that I would not be happy with the result. I would give out some excuse and disappear quickly, leaving them wondering what they had done wrong.

"But escort work seemed to be to be quite different although I needed to check out the procedure to ensure that I wouldn't be getting involved in a de facto brothel decked out in the façade of an escort agency. The end result might be the same, but to me, being an escort had an element of an agreement, a transaction, and a situation that didn't entirely involve sex. I rang the number listed in the paper. A very well spoken woman answered. Having to deal with probably a different class of man than those who exclusively visited brothels, I wasn't really surprised at the velvet tone of her voice. She explained the procedure to me. I would come in for an interview, leave them a photograph, and depending on my interests, age, attributes etc I would get a call a few hours in advance if I was required to escort anyone. I asked her what type of functions I would be expected to attend and what sort of man would I escort.

"'Oh, you'd be surprised,' the woman said. 'In your case, being fairly young we would most likely match you with a gentleman in his late twenties or early thirties who might need an escort to attend a business dinner or function with colleagues; there may be an overseas or interstate visitor who might merely need a companion for dinner or the theatre; it all depends on the gentleman.'

"'How would I get paid,' I asked the woman.

"'Well, there is a minimum booking fee of three hours; you get a percentage of that. After the booked time is finished, well... then...it's your business is the best way I could describe it,' she told me.

"In other words, if I could persuade the so-called gentleman to part with a few extra dollars in return for ending the night with some sex; that was a private matter for me and him."

Dad, here I will interrupt my telling of her tale because, while she was proceeding with the finer details, I wondered where all this would end and her fate. So far I had not discovered any hint of redemption, for it appeared to me that if her life continued in the same way there was little possibility she would get beyond the Waiting Room. Then I recalled where I was and the fact that, although encouraging, the gatekeeper had not given any iron-clad guarantee that I would be one of the lucky ones, one of the chosen few. I also had to admit that I hadn't heard the whole of her story and as she appeared to be approximately the same age as me, she did not have much time to turn around her life. I had, of course, never led the sort of life she was describing. What she was telling me was completely foreign to me. We all have our faults, but at this point in her story I must say I didn't hold out much hope for her, which was a real pity because, otherwise, she was a rather likeable person. Do I make myself clear, Dad? I hope so. I wouldn't want you to think that my relatively few interruptions to her story meant that I agreed with her conduct. Far from it: I was so engrossed that I believed it was better not to interfere with the torrent of words that flowed out of her mouth.

"So, after your conversation with the agency, what did you do?" I asked, attempting to get her to come to the point quickly.

"The next day I went and saw them, dressed up to kill," she resumed. "I had a collection of my best photos from my modelling portfolio with me to show them that I was no slouch and could act in a manner that would satisfy the most fussy of tastes. The woman was taken aback when she initially cast eyes upon me. I gathered that although all the escorts could do themselves up to look the part, she had not seen anyone like me for a while. Although I had touched up my face a little, I don't want to brag, but I naturally had a very soft face, without any observable blemish; I guess you could say nature bestowed me with the right looks.

"I filled in an information form that asked for all the usual particulars. When I came to the part where I had to write a sentence about the type of person I wished to escort I was at first stumped for an answer, but then it dawned on me that I didn't want to pitch myself too low, so I wrote: 'A first-class gentleman, handsome looks, of impeccable manners and an articulate conversationalist.' The woman raised her eyebrows when she read this. 'We can all dream I suppose,' she said, 'but I know what you mean,' she concluded with a forced smile. I returned the smile as if to say: 'Well, if you've got nothing on your books that fit that description, perhaps I need to go elsewhere!'

"'I must admit,' the woman said again, 'most of our clients act in a certain manner in an attempt to convince you that they belong in that category.'

"'Men do like to big note themselves, don't they?' I replied."

"When did you get your first escort?" I asked impatiently, disregarding her reply to that woman.

"Within a few days," she replied. "It was a businessman, in town for a conference. I expect he was lonely, bored to death sitting in his hotel room. He was probably thinking a bit of female companionship would take his mind off his loneliness. The agency had contacted me some time during the day. It was a Friday and, come to think of it now, I believe his conference was scheduled to finish late that afternoon and instead of flying home that night he decided to stay and return the next day."

"So it was a proper date?" I suggested.

"Yes, I suppose you could say it was – a blind date, like one arranged by a friend. The agency manager told me the client wanted to meet 'someone with your attributes', but as I didn't hear the conversation between them, for all I know the manager could have been lying through her teeth; he might have asked for any girl. That's before he was shown my photograph. It was a dinner date and...well, I'll come to that. He was staying at the Sofitel. I was told to meet him in the lobby. As he had an idea from the photo what I looked like I guess he was more likely to recognise me than me him. The agency gave me a description: it was full of that tall, dark and handsome stuff which I immediately put out of my mind because...well...that's what you would expect them to say, wouldn't you? I took my time dressing as I wanted to make an impression on him.

"Naturally, I got myself to the Sofitel exactly on time which I now realise was not the accepted thing to do. If it was a date I'd met before I would have had no qualms being late to a socially acceptable degree."

Cut to the chase, I thought, Dad, because all this preliminary banter, although to some extent interesting in itself, seemed to me to be a long way from where I wished Jessie's tale to be. I guess she picked up my impatience because she quickly moved on.

"I believe I looked stunning," she said. "Little black number as they say, thin shoulder straps, clinging short dress showing my curves. I was ready for anyone.

"I sat down in a lounge chair and cast my eyes around in an attempt to locate this date. I had barely turned my head when this man appeared out of nowhere and came striding up to me at a fast pace, bent over holding out his hand to shake mine and staring directly into my eyes with the boldest of green eyes. 'I'm Brad Cooper. Thank you for agreeing to join me for dinner,' he said. 'I'm Jessie,' I said, rising out of my seat, fighting to regain my breath which had seemed to slip away at his sudden appearance. Stupidly, I forgot to give him a false name. I hoped my real name would not complicate matters.

"Well, I won't bore you by relating all that happened because...it's not important now, is it?"

Dad, I must say I was a trifle disappointed with this ending to her story; maybe I wanted to experience some vicarious thrill by listening to every last detail of her date, as if I was a young schoolgirl pestering my best friend about how she felt when some new boyfriend kissed her. Don't be shocked, Dad, by what I am telling you. Of course, if I was alive and we were having a conversation at home or over the telephone, none of this tale Jessie told me would leave my lips. But later I will tell you some of the things Catherine and I got up to and the crazy things we did.

≈

George paused. I wondered whether he was turning his mind to the time when he was young. Certainly I was. There are some matters parents can never be told. Chloe had mentioned how close she and her mother were, but I reckoned that there must have been many things that she conveniently held close to her chest. It's a kind of natural law. Unspoken, a form of unwritten convention that is part of the process of growing up, adapting to the world. George smiled a knowing smile as if he had succeeded in picking up my waves of thought. I went over and refilled his glass of wine and gently patted him on the shoulder. Before I removed it he put his hand on mine and gave it a squeeze. I could see he was struggling with his emotions. Mine were skating on thin ice. I told him it was okay, I understood. But what could I understand? Was it his feelings as a parent who had lost a child in shocking circumstances? Was that it? As a parent I recognised that the death of a child was an event that no one could prepare for. George was a strong character; that was beyond doubt. But even he couldn't prevent his almost hysterical lamentations of grief at the funeral. Now, he accepted the fact that Chloe was dead. Nothing could change that but he was still struggling to come to terms with it, as anyone would. I asked him to continue.

≈

"No, I suppose it isn't," I said, "but you could give me a general outline, couldn't you, and tell me how you ended up here?"

"Sure, no problem doing that," she said, brightly.

"I settled into this escorting pretty easily; I took to it like a duck to water you could say. Just about every night I had a date so I was glad when my period came each month so I could grab a rest for a few days. It was exhausting after a while because every night I had to be on the top of my game, nicely dressed, carrying a bright and happy face with me and sparkling conversation to match. To be honest, I got sick of churning out my life story to every Tom, Dick and Harry that I came across. So I began to give out different versions of my life story to these men in an attempt to create some freshness, to make me appear a bright little spark giving off an exciting history. Because they did want to know, you realise. I reckon they did it to create a good impression. Or was it because they had some sort of class and, by instinct, knew exactly the right moves to make to draw out from me sufficient information to help both of us get through dinner or whatever without long periods of silence ruining the occasion? Eventually they all got round, in a roundabout fashion, to what they all wanted. Then I took charge of them and lead them off to wherever we had to go, after negotiating a price of course. So…I did this for a while…until I came here…" she suddenly concluded in a soft voice that trailed away, like the ending of a song.

"And how did you get to come here?" I asked her.

"The gatekeeper told me I was hit by a car."

"Really!" I exclaimed.

I was surprised, for I thought her death was sure to have come about by something to do with her job, like being stabbed to death or shot by an angry client, or an overdose of pills; not something much more mundane like a car accident. Sorry Dad, I hope you are not upset at my seemingly flippant treatment of her death, as I have just remembered you telling us about that kid you played cricket with being hit by an oncoming truck and your friend who was hit by a car when you were riding your bikes to another friend's place. It's just that, compared to her lifestyle, a death in a road accident seems to me the last thing I would have thought of, though James met his fate in a similar way.

"Yes, the gatekeeper said I was returning to my car in a hotel underground car park after finishing up one of my jobs and apparently I stepped into the path of a car coming up the ramp on to the street and got cleaned up, just like that, dead as a dodo…and so here I am."

She rose from the seat and walked a few steps away. She stopped and then slowly turned to face me.

"I have to go now," she murmured quietly and turned on her heels and quickly disappeared into the distance.

I was a little stunned because, I mean, why did she have to go? And where could she go? We were all here for eternity so I reckoned time was no consideration at all. The gatekeeper had indicated that time here was a totally different concept to earth time so I felt disappointed that our conversation had ended in such a manner. Then it occurred to me that Jessie might still be grieving the premature ending of her earth life and was finding it difficult to accept it. Even here we are still individuals.

I gathered myself together and remained where I was waiting to find out what would happen next.

≈

George finished reading but did not close his folder as he usually did. I suspected there was more that George had to say.

"Do you have another visit typed out for us George?" I asked him.

"Yes, there's more," he said.

"Let's grab something to eat and continue then," Debra said. She and Emily went off to the kitchen to bring back the finger food that she had prepared earlier.

When they were out of the room I asked George if he was okay. He smiled.

"It just saddens me that this Jessie was also so young. Okay, her lifestyle may have been questionable but should anyone die so young?"

"George, I am afraid it happens more than you would like to think: young babies, barely out of the womb, teenagers, all so young, all tragic cases. Death is part of being alive it's said. I know that's no comfort to you George being one of the many unlucky parents that has lost a child. It's easy for me to say and I'm not being flippant or tactless, you know that George, but... these unfortunate things happen. I'm sorry George."

George got up and went out the front door.

"Where's George gone?" Emily said as she returned carrying plates of food.

"He just stepped outside for a bit of fresh air," I said.

"He hasn't had one of his episodes again, has he?" Emily asked with a concerned look on her face.

"I don't know; he just needs a minute to himself. All this affects him you know."

"Yes, and I have to live with it," Emily replied sternly.

Debra went over to Emily and kissed her cheek and hugged her. No wonder they say it's harder for the ones left behind. I wondered whether the dead would agree.

We ate some sandwiches and drank tea while waiting for George to come back. He did after a few minutes and joined us as if nothing had happened.

"I'm a little shocked," Debra began. "That Jessie is certainly not someone I would want any child of mine to be mixed up with."

"Don't be too judgemental," George said. "Chloe is merely relating the story of someone that she happened to meet. Not everyone she meets will be to our liking."

"I realise that," Debra countered. "Nothing against Chloe; it's just that this Jessie comes from a different world than we are used to."

"Maybe," I said, "but I can understand her situation. Her upbringing wasn't necessarily the best, so who are we to judge?"

"I'm not judging, just commenting," Debra said sharply.

"I guess Chloe wants us to keep in mind that there are a variety of lifestyles in the afterlife as there are here. I mean, I'm sure she will encounter people outside her usual environment. Every person surely can't be a White Anglo-Saxon." Emily said.

"I've no doubt of that," George said. "I reckon Chloe is attempting to make me realise that all people of whatever colour or creed, are essentially equal. We are born equal and die equal. Unfortunately, equality often disappears in the long time between birth and death."

"And more than that," I jumped in, "Chloe wants her story to be spread around so eventually the whole world will come to realise that we should not engage in petty arguments nor castigate other people because of their religious or political views or lack of them. And the colour of one's skin should be irrelevant."

"Maybe Chas," Debra said, "but how come the world continues along its stupid path established centuries ago, countries and terrorist group's intent on killing each other? In the end some peace deal is done and lo and behold we're now best of friends. We used to hate the Japanese but ever since the war ended it seems to me we have willingly engaged in trade with them, ditto China, the former 'yellow peril'. Hundreds of years ago England and France fought wars practically all the time. Now, they are buddies. We hated the Germans in two world wars; now they are okay. So why start in the first place? Young men sent off to the other side of the world, lambs to the slaughter. Their sacrifice is eventually in vain, isn't it?"

"So you don't believe any war is justified?" George asked.

"Not really, but I admit, sometimes it is necessary to fight – if the other side doesn't listen to reason."

"Haven't we strayed from the point here," I said. "We are listening to George read out Chloe's story; we are not here to engage in philosophical discussions on the right and wrongs of war."

"Good point," George said. "Another time perhaps, but in any event, that was the end of that visit. I have some notes on the next visit. Do you want me to continue?"

"Of course!" Debra exclaimed. "But first let me get some more to eat and top up our drinks."

Debra having done so we settled back and waited for George to begin.

Chapter Eleven

DAD, TO ENSURE I DON'T BORE YOU TELLING YOU THE STORIES of people I have met here I will switch and tell you about two of my best friends I had on earth. The first one is the very close friendship I developed after I started working at the Lort Smith Animal Hospital. Even now I can't remember whether you actually met Catherine; Mum certainly did as she was often around at our house.

We met some four years ago. I was only a nurse but she was a fully qualified vet. At the time I was becoming a bit cheeky as my self-confidence was slowly developing and perhaps it was our shared sense of adventure which drew us together. This mutual adventurousness even extended to our sharing an attraction for a particular young Italian vet student with whom we both flirted outrageously. For some unexplained reason Catherine would always laugh at my naïve, but genuine questions regarding men and personal issues. She was older than me so what was more natural than to ask for her opinion on various matters? What really triggered our close friendship was the time we spent together working night service. She often burst out in uncontrollable laughter at my individual style in answering the phone. I would use a posh sounding voice as if I was a Queen of society, even answering mundane questions from our less desirable clients (for we did have some shockers) with cheerfulness. One incident I particularly recall. We had a Bull Mastiff named Hooch who required restraining to be examined. He must have taken some liking to me because he attempted to pin me down on the floor and have his way with me. This continued for some minutes whilst I, as politely as I could, asked Hooch to get off me. At first Catherine was useless; she was engulfed in a fit of laughter. Eventually, she enlisted the help of another nurse to remove Hooch but not before having a good laugh at my expense and calling others over to see what Hooch was attempting to do.

We had great fun playfully bickering with each other and I prided myself on the ability I had to steer and manoeuvre our 'arguments' to ensure our workmates overheard Catherine's sarcastic and cruel response to my 'innocent' taunts. Unaware of my previous cheeky comments, our workmates would chastise her saying 'Catherine, don't be so rude to Chloe'. I would then innocently gaze up with my big blue eyes and give her a cheeky smirk. Her reaction to my smirk clearly showed she would have loved to strangle me.

Dad, in case you are thinking that all we did was mess around I must remind you that working at Lort Smith could also be very difficult. I remember comforting Catherine when she became emotional after a confrontation with management. Difficult clients also made her very upset and I tried as hard as I could to understand her situation and get her to look at her problems with a positive outlook. Once she had a very bad headache so I picked her up at her home in my car and drove her to work to do an x-ray of a dog that she had promised the owner she would do.

We weren't the only mad ones though. At the canteen one lunch time we sat engrossed in silence as a nurse, obviously besotted with one of the vets, fed him with a spoon as though she was his mother and he was a baby. Catherine looked at me and I returned her amazed look. We both then simultaneously giggled and burst into laughter. Did I go bright red when the nurse suddenly looked our way and caught me laughing at her!

We went to Sydney once. Catherine's boyfriend and I were always arguing as to whether it was his or my turn to drive. He seemed to win every argument about driving so, with Catherine's help, we murdered songs from *The Sound of Music,* just to annoy him. On New Year's Eve we danced and sang our hearts out at an old English pub, polishing off a cheap bottle of port and flirting with some cute English backpackers and at the stroke of midnight cheered along with the rest of the boisterous crowd as fireworks lit up the sky. Slightly under the weather next morning we somehow made it to Catherine's family home for lunch where I had to endure her persistent demands that I play the piano for her parents. They seemed to be delighted with my playing but I felt very embarrassed being the centre of attraction.

Bondi Beach made both of us realise very starkly our shortcomings. Here we were with our pure white bodies parading up and down whilst surrounded by gorgeously tanned topless women. Jealousy is probably the most apt description of our inner most feelings.

We also enjoyed dancing. Just to be a tease one night I wore a very tight pair of jeans and as I danced with several boys who had moved in to surround me, I cheekily flicked my head from side to side, gyrated my shoulders around and sang happily away as if I didn't have a care in the world and I was on my own deserted island, oblivious of the crowd around me. An attractive Italian boy had me in a fizz one night until I found out that he was married. I gave Catherine an almighty earful when I got back to her.

You know my old blue Corolla, don't you Dad? Catherine and I had many laughs and cases of extreme embarrassment involving my car. Driving down the Eastern Freeway one night, the inside light began to flash on and off. We laughed ourselves silly because no-matter what we did we couldn't stop the flashing. Another time we were parked in front of a bar in Brunswick Street outside of which sat a group of boys, obviously drunk. Despite repeated attempts we just could not close the front passenger door. Catherine was inside pulling on the door whilst I leant my weight and attempted to push it closed. Those boys sure teased us no end as we pushed and pulled away, all to no avail until we finally got it to close. Needless to say we dissolved in hysterical laughter for many weeks afterwards as soon as one of us mentioned this little incident.

Catherine also stayed at our place on occasions. If she was studying I loved to invade her room and in a playful manner dance around whilst I quizzed her on the meaning of life and love. I played to the full, as if I was in a play, a role as a posh woman. I would prance around her imitating a socialite, insisting that I was posh. 'I live in a posh suburb, I went to a posh school,' I would tease her, and holding out my hand in a limp fashion, I would say: 'Yes, I am sooo posh!' She would collapse in hysterics at my charade of a socialite. As well as dance for her, she often forced me to play the piano whilst she lay on the couch, lost in the music. No matter that I often played the same pieces over and over again, she did not seem to mind at all and would lay there in a sublime manner as if her thoughts, contemptuous of the mundaneness of life, had elevated to a higher plane.

One night I was driving us home in her car as she had had far too much to drink. As usual, we were singing heartily to some song on the radio when we passed a police car. 'I've always wanted to go out with a policeman,' I crooned seductively. Seconds later the police car had turned around and was closing on us with its lights flashing and siren wailing very loudly. 'Oh my God!' I exclaimed in a panic. I'd had two glasses of wine and I was afraid I might be over .05. I was breathalysed and somehow wasn't over so we were sent on our way. We laughed uncontrollably, hysterically, all the way home.

Catherine sat house for people while they went on holidays and minded their pets. Often I would go and visit her. I loved to play with the animals and allow them to sit on my lap. After a hard day at work she would often be tired and grumpy, so she would allow me to look after them. One time she was staying at a home in Cheltenham looking after two dogs called Wilbur and Sampson. I spent the night there once. Catherine walked into my room in the morning and found me asleep sharing the pillow with Wilbur, a Jack Russell terrier. She was always telling me I would catch some horrible disease as I invariably slept with my cats and dogs at home, but I loved my animals and as I didn't have anyone to share my bed what better alternative than my cats and dogs who I adored? Dad, I remember you told me once that when you were young, your cat would often creep under the bedclothes and go to sleep at your feet, so I know you will understand. I absolutely loved staying with Catherine when she was house-sitting as it gave us an opportunity to relax away from the pressures of work and my study.

We loved going to parties. One I particularly remember was at Neil's place. Cars lined both sides of the court where he lived and there appeared to be no way we would be able to park anywhere close to his house. Both of us were dare-devils at heart and so we decided to try something out of the ordinary. We manoeuvred carefully between the parked cars, moving barely an inch at a time, giggling like the little girls we were until we reached Neil's driveway. We simply turned into it and parked practically outside the front door. Composing ourselves took a good five minutes as we continued to announce to ourselves in a grand and pompous manner that *we* had arrived. We allowed

Neil's mum to prattle on about her dogs and browsed over her treasured photos of Neil as a golden-haired boy. She also showed us a locket containing strands from his first haircut. When the time came to leave, Catherine decided she was not in a fit state to repeat her drive between parked cars and went off-road by driving along the nature strips of several neighbours. Not surprisingly, we were hardly able to control our laughter. We were very cheeky, Dad!

Catherine's Aunt Rosalie went through a period of hosting Tupperware parties. I often joined Catherine and her friends and family and listened politely to the spiel that her Aunt gave off. The problem was I felt compelled to buy something nearly every time as I thought it was unfair to her Aunt to go to the trouble of putting on a party without getting some form of return. I somehow overlooked the fact that I was under no obligation to buy but it was against my nature to see anyone's feelings hurt. Often Catherine would cringe at comments made by members of her family and I would have to give her a nudge or a gentle smile to remind her not to feel embarrassed by them. It didn't worry me what they did or said. I took it all in my stride.

Now that I have had time to reflect I can recall the last time we met before I died. I was on night service. Catherine had been on day service but had stayed back to 10 o'clock as she had an emergency to deal with. I had arrived at around 5 o'clock and I remember her mentioning how fresh I looked. I believe I had recently developed an air of confidence as I was about to move into my new role as a human nurse and subconsciously gave off a professional manner that all of the staff recognised and commented on. Catherine told me on several occasions how proud she was of me in moving away from Lort Smith and my imminent graduation as a human nurse. That night I gave her a huge surprise. I walked into the surgery dragging her reluctant boyfriend along to visit her before she went home. We had huge grins on our faces until he saw what she was doing with the dog she was operating on. Her boyfriend pulled a face and got out of there as fast as he could. That same night the daughter of the owner of Jackson, a dog that Catherine was house-sitting, dropped him off for Catherine to take home. While I waited for her to finish up I made a bed for Jackson behind the reception desk and sat with him. I hated putting animals in cages unless they were ill, so I sat with him, gently stroking him until Catherine came to collect him. I never imagined as she led Jackson out through the sliding exit door that I would never see her again.

Dad, you must appreciate that though having a loving family surrounding you is important, so is the love and friendship of a close friend. Catherine was that friend. I do hope that she is not despairing too much at my death. I want her to move on and live a full life, a fulfilling one, a life that is full of meaning and love for her fellow creatures, particularly the animals we tended together. I have been rather long-winded Dad, but I felt I had to because, as I said, although I may have mentioned her name to you, I don't believe you ever met her.

Not so with Stephanie. In our school days we were as close as could be. Attending the same schools, practically living in each other's skin, alternating from being at one house to the other meant that we were as close as two peas in that proverbial pod. I even went on a trip with her family to Hawaii; do you remember that Dad? I bought back a clock for you, made out of wood with a map of all the islands in the group set out. Do you still have that somewhere, Dad? Last time I saw it, it was on the side table near your front door. Keep it, Dad. And remember where it came from and that I gave it to you. I also vividly remember the time you joined us to celebrate my eighteenth birthday at that Thai restaurant near the corner of Union Road. At the time I was bereft of other friendships so I regarded Stephanie's presence with our family as essential to my mental health. I had an inferiority complex I suppose, and went through hell attempting to establish some degree of standing in my world. At the time she was one of my few rocks. Naturally, we began to drift apart when she got a boyfriend and then later became engaged and planned to be married. Do you remember the time I talked to you about the dress I bought to be her bridesmaid at her wedding? By then, although our friendship was still solid on the surface, various cracks were beginning to surface. That's all gone now and it doesn't matter anymore. It's a lesson, isn't it Dad? Life is too short to worry about the trifles of everyday life that surround us and somehow bog us down and corrupt our minds. Better don't you think to get on with life and pass over the things that in the end don't matter in the slightest? That's all I'll say about Stephanie, Dad, because you basically know our story. I'll get back now to telling you about the next person I met.

≈

George got up to stretch his legs. We had been drinking slowly but I think we all needed another glass of wine. George nodded when I asked him if he would have a drink. I don't keep much wine in stock as I have a tendency to grab a bottle every time we go out to dinner. I found a Pinot Noir and quickly returned so George could continue.

"I never met Catherine before Chloe died but of course I have met her since. Her love of Chloe is evident not only through the words Chloe used to describe their relationship but also in Catherine's attitude to her memory. It remains strong. Once, not too long after Chloe died, we had lunch together because I needed to talk to her of Chloe. The air was racked with so much emotion we invariably had to break off talking because the pain inside both of us was still overwhelming. Even now I crack up occasionally if those memories suffocate my mind. Chloe is right, don't you think? Life contains much that is beyond belief."

I didn't want to answer George with a jumble of banalities. I bustled around, handing him some nuts and topping up everyone's glass, searching for an adequate answer.

"It's complex, that's for sure," I feebly replied, dissatisfied with my answer.

George gave me a glance. "Yes, I suppose it is," he slowly got out.

Chapter Twelve

Between our meetings with George and Emily, Debra and I spent a considerable time poring over George's notes for he was kind enough to give me a copy of each visit. He believed it might help us in our analysis of Chloe's story. It became clear to us that Chloe had a two-fold purpose in speaking to George. First, she intended it to be a communication between father and daughter and secondly, to be an instrument by which he was to give the world proof of the existence of the afterlife.

I regarded the second as virtually impossible to achieve, for sceptics abound and the world is filled with people who only believe what is regarded as an impossible occurrence if they are personally involved and experience an event themselves. Merely hearing the story from George might not be sufficient for people to believe.

"I believe George," Debra said to me one day, "but I'm not sure how many others will. I mean, if we heard this story from someone other than George, would we be counted as believers?"

"Probably not," I answered. Whenever this proposition was put to me by Debra in any of our conversations I slid into a state of melancholy knowing that George would be regarded as a fabricator, a teller of fantasy, unable to deal with the tragic death of his daughter.

I wanted to regale others with the experience we were sharing with George but I had sworn that I would not until it was clear that Chloe's visits had concluded. None of us could forecast when that would be; for all we knew Chloe's story would continue for months, even years. And anyway, I had no wish to steal George's thunder. To my knowledge, Chloe communicated solely with George, and never with her mother, or any other person. At this stage, I believed it was a private affair between father and daughter. It was only because Chloe had indicated that George should eventually tell the world that he felt he was able to confide in me.

I admit I cleared my mind of virtually everything else from the moment George had brought me into his confidence. I had my job at the bank of course, but it took a back seat. I went through the motions, working assiduously as ever it seemed to my colleagues but secretly, in my conscience, I sought for answers to the conundrums she raised, the problems associated with determining what was right and what was wrong, not to mention the world's ills. However, some work colleagues did comment on my apparent preoccupation with something. If I appeared to be in a far-off place perhaps they thought I was turning over in my mind any one of a number of burning issues I normally had to deal with at work. At home with Debra, we tried to live a normal life but it was an impossible task. One or the other of us would raise some part of George's notes, forcing us to discuss it in depth.

Our time with George and Emily knew of no other subject. If there had been a visit, George would read out his notes to our enraptured ears. If Chloe had not appeared for a while we would wonder when the next visit would be. I regret to say we virtually abandoned our other friends, meeting some only intermittingly, only a sufficient number of times to give them no reason to believe we had deliberately cast them out from our circle of friends. Part of me wanted to keep in touch more than we did but my dominant side saw no immediate future in socialising to any extent with any couple other than George and Emily – for what could we possibly talk about to these other couples: Inane chatter regarding mutual friends, politics, the economy, work? All those matters that, once I was on the road heading home, I had no desire to talk about. Nothing else mattered except the next chapter from Chloe. I felt the four of us were joined together in a conspiracy to keep the visits secret until George said the word. Then news of the visits would be released to the world like a major discovery. I believed that nothing as important had happened for two thousand years – that's how much I was consumed by Chloe's story.

Our weekly turnabouts continued for a few weeks until George telephoned me early on a Friday morning and announced Chloe had visited him again. We were scheduled to meet at George's home on the Saturday night, but we agreed to bring it forward to the Friday night at my urging as I could not bear to wait another day.

This is what Chloe had to say about Craig.

≈

As humans on earth comprise many types of people, with different coloured skin and cultures differentiating one group from another; the same applies here as you would expect. So far I've told you about James from Ireland who drank himself to death and Jessie, the girl who went off the straight and narrow track. The next person I met you are probably more familiar with. He wasn't a lawyer, but a businessman, and I guess in your dealings at work you would have met a few clients like him.

I came across him sitting by himself on a seat along the path I had been wandering along after Jessie and I parted. I won't bother about the introductions, for what were they but a repetition of the same words, no-matter whom I met? There was one difference though; he was American, from the South he said. He told me that on earth he was black, an African-American he called himself. I couldn't tell here as we all were endowed with a pale whiteness. His name was Craig. I could tell he was older than me; he also seemed to be a rather tall man. I sat down beside him and he started to tell me his story.

"Yes ma'am, as I said, my momma called me Craig. You know, I never did like that name my momma gave me as I thought it, well, a bit prissy; can I say that?"

"A bit weak or sissy, we would say," I answered.

"Well ma'am, I think you hit that little old nail right smack bang on the head there."

I didn't believe I had said anything out of the ordinary so I merely smiled and waited until he was ready to continue. As an aside Dad, I found that he could talk without stopping for breath so perhaps the conversation I am about to relate is only a summary of the actual sentences that poured out of his mouth and not exactly what he said.

"Ma'am," he began again, "as we seem to have plenty of time here, and I seem to have been here for one heck of a time I must say right now, I'll just get on with tellin' you all about me and then we can do a swap sort of thing, and you can tell me all about your little old self, is that a bargain or what?"

That was fine with me because after speaking to the gatekeeper, then James and Jessie I was a little worn out with telling my story. Then I thought: why should I let that bother me, for what else was there to do here than pour out your life story and relate the final event that preceded your arrival in the Waiting Room? So I told him that was okay with me and asked him to start.

"I'll leave the end to last, which is probably the most natural thing to do, ma'am, because it's kinda hard to tell a story backwards I would imagine, as you might just get mixed up real bad and you wouldn't be able to understand one single little word of what I was a tellin' you, isn't that so right?"

I nodded in agreement.

"Other than my name I was kinda happy with my childhood. My folks were well off so we didn't have to worry about money or livin' from hand to mouth as many folks seem to do. My pa's pa had creamed up quite a deal on trading stocks and real estate, building this and that, then thumping up the price to make a killing when he sold so my pa never had a worry in the world; he just breezed through life as though it was standin' stock still. He grabbed my ma, the prettiest little thin' anyone ever laid eyes upon, and rushed off and married her 'fore any other of the locals ever had a chance to put in a bid for her. Yes ma'am, he was real smart doing that when he was only 18 and she was not too much younger than him. He musta been fertile as a horse, and ma too, because before five years were up, my ma had pushed out four little ones, just like that, one after the other, as though she was shellin' peas or somethin' like that, you get my meanin' ma'am?"

I think I did, although his way of speaking was a novelty to me; the benefit of watching American movies came in very handy.

"Well, ma'am, me and me little siblin's were as happy as Larry as they say. The last one out was a girl and she turned out a real tomboy because, I guess ma'am, she mucked round with us so much she just took on our ways until she growed up a bit an' knew for sure she wasn't like us fellas at all. Then she kinda went all prim and proper and pretended she was a lady but us brothers knew much better than her; to us she was just one of the gang. She said she was built different to us, but we wasn't so sure until one day in the woods near our place she showed me and the brothers what she meant. When she dropped her panties and there was nothin' there, well ma'am, you coulda chopped me down with an axe because until that very day I never saw no boy like that! She said don't tell ma and all of us promised and crossed our hearts and hoped we died before any one of us would let out such a secret. I thought, well who else knows about this sort of thin' cos none of the fellas at school had ever mentioned anythin' like this before, I can tell you that, ma'am.

"I reckon I was no more than nine or maybe ten so then I realised schoolin' was old-fashioned and way behind the times cos no teacher ever said one thing about this to me or anyone else to my knowledge. Maybe I had to get a lot older before I could be told these sorta things but it sure confused me I must tell you. Anyway, eventually I learned everythin' there was to know about being female cos one time on the way back from school, musta been when I was fourteen or so, this girl that kept smilin' at me and twistin' her hair around in her hand every time she spoke to me, was walkin' by my side and when we were goin' through this park in a part we called 'the forest' cos there were a lotta trees there and dense bushes, she grabbed my hand and dragged me into the bushes so no-one could see us. All of a sudden she undid her blouse and pushed my hand onto her little tits, sorry ma'am, perhaps I shouldn't use that kinda language here, breasts I mean ma'am, and started kissin' me all sloppy like over my face. Then she grabbed me down there ma'am, you know what I mean I am sure ma'am, and started movin' her hand up and down. Well, I never had a girl do that sorta thing to me before ma'am and it sure was a shock to me. Well ma'am, from that day onward I guess you could say I was rather learned about the female genda. I saw there was a big future and an excitin' one at that if you get my meanin' ma'am, so every girl I came across I tried to get learned in some new aspect, you know? Well, eventually everybody does, I suppose.

"One day my pa comes up to me and says, 'well boy, watcha gonna do for a livin'?' I said, 'Guess I don't know, pa.' And then he gives me this big talk on how much money his pa had made sellin' land and that sorta stuff, and how he had followed in his pa's footsteps and he had made a bag of money doing the same sort of thin' and how it would be a good thin' if I followed in *his* footsteps and learned from him how to sell all these houses and land that he did and how all you had to do was talk yourself blue in the face convincin' people that did you have a bargain for them and all that smoke and mirrors stuff. And I already had picked up that if you had a heap of money then pretty gals were sure to come sniffin' around to see if they could put their hand in your pocket and get somethin' for themselves as well, without workin' for it one little bit. So I told my pa that that was okay with me as I wanted to make a lotta money and live a comfortable life, not like those poor black and white critters that hung around doin' nothin' all day or if they had a job and just slaved away in a factory or some lousy diner out the back of nowhere with nothing but dust and a howlin' wind to keep them company.

"So, after all that, I went and worked with pa as some sorta 'prentice, learnin' on the job like. I got to dress up in a fancy suit and pa let me have this real smart Buik to drive around town in just to impress everyone and make them think I was important like and rich as anythin'. Pa musta learned me pretty quick cos after just a little while he started givin' me more to do and lettin' me take people out to check out a house and try and get them to sign up. The houses we had to sell were pretty big and the sellers always wanted to screw the last dime out of any buyer who came within a sniff of the place, and I tell you ma'am, I didn't mind that at all cos the more the buyer paid the more I got into my own pocket as commission. And ma'am, I sure tell you that there is nothin' better than gettin' a big fat amount paid to you just for gettin' some person who is gonna buy a house anyway to sign on the dotted line. I tell you, every time it happened I just wanted to dance a little jig in the office cos I was happy as a bee in clover; I sure was ma'am. And the best part, ma'am, was I could spend as much money as I wanted on entertainin' anyone I thought might be good for the business, you know like developers of big subdivisions of land or some attorney or other who I knew had clients who had money to burn and were lookin' out for a good investment. Bankers as well, cos they lent the money and sometimes it might happen that some young green couple would never have done this sorta thing before so what better opportunity than their friendly bank manager introduces them to someone like us who knew all about real estate and investment and would be able to help this young couple out by goin' outta our way with all the kindness and friendliness we could muster to help out to their benefit. Naturally it was to our benefit as well, for why would we do it otherwise, ma'am? Let me ask you that."

"No, I suppose not," I answered, rather meekly.

Dad, this was how he talked, non-stop, and words poured out of his mouth at great speed as if he was in a competition to determine who could speak the most words in a minute. It is a wonder I am able to repeat all that he said back to you, it really is. Yet he seemed a happy and friendly sort of fellow although I had at this stage heard only a fraction of his whole life story.

"I say I liked to entertain, well I sure did ma'am, but it sorta ruined me in a way. You know, goin' out nearly every day for lunch sure makes keepin' neat and tidy pretty difficult ma'am, it makes it real hard. And not only goin' out for lunch, but what I ate ma'am, that was the worst thin' of all. You know, us Americans like our food real good and you probably heard many stories of the fast food places that all started in the States, yes siree, ma'am, I just know you have. Fries, burgers, you name it, we just love to swallow them down – that's just for a usual lunch, ma'am. When I had my entertainin' shoes on it was no mere burger we feasted on, no ma'am. We found out the best place we could find and we entertained them real good with steaks, huge ones of course and plenty of beer and any kind of wine or spirits they wanted, martinis by the score too. No expense was spared ma'am, I must say. I'd just flash my Amex card at the end of the lunch and I wouldn't feel a thing. It was like not payin' at all. Just eat and drink all we wanted and then hand over that little bit of plastic. They sure come in handy, don't they ma'am?"

"I imagine they must," I got out, although I knew he didn't expect any answer.

"Yes ma'am, I just kept bookin' those lunches and dinners on the plastic as though there was no tomorrow, and ma'am, we enjoyed ourselves as if there was never goin' to be a tomorrow. Clients, friends, it was all the same to me. After a few months of this I started to notice somethin'. You can guess what that was ma'am, I expect. Well, I will tell you, ma'am," he continued without waiting for my response.

"I got bigger and bigger in the stomach, just like that; bigger and bigger, until I had to let my belt out a couple of notches, and then I had to buy a new range of shirts, and then I had to buy a new suit, and then everythin' else. I just grew and grew ma'am, like someone was blowin' me up, just like a balloon it seemed to me, ma'am. And I was drinkin' more and more and at the same time splurgin' on every sorta food you could think of. Then I noticed somethin' real strange, ma'am. You know I told you girls were hangin' around me cos I was loaded with money; well, I seemed to find it hard to make out now. At first I didn't have any idea at all, ma'am, why this should be so. My personality had not changed one little bit; I was still as friendly as a man could be. Then one day I looked in the mirror, and ma'am, I sure didn't like what I saw. I musta put on at least fifty pounds, ma'am, believe me, I could say with all honesty as I stand before you ma'am, I was a giant...and I didn't like it one bit. So I decided to get myself back in shape. Then I thought how was I goin' to do that? And when would I have the time? I was still workin' as hard as I ever had despite me lookin' like a grizzly bear. And there was no way I could cut back on my entertainin'; it just couldn't be done. By now I was looked upon as the best marketeer for miles around. It was my job to get clients in and do everythin' that had to be done to cement relationships, new or old. My pa was lookin' to slow down a bit as he was getting on and he had made his fortune so why would he want to keep his nose to the grindstone when he could get others to do all the work? That included me of course. I knew I had to keep the business goin' cos it was really a family firm like; it was up to me you know, to take over from my pa when he'd had enough. We also had a lotta good young people I was groomin' quite nicely to keep the business churnin' over. Anyway, I just had to cut down and get back in shape. First, I cut out the beer and wine, well not all of it of course; I had to have at least one glass at functions I was compelled to attend, just to be sociable. Martinis went right back south. I cut down, that's for sure. Then I started workin' out, you know ma'am, at the gym. Of course, I'd been a member for years but had hardly found a spare minute to go much before. But now I did. I worked out a few times a week, had a few swims, though I tell you ma'am, when I was swimmin' I coulda almost emptied the pool by just jumpin' in. Ha! Boy, did I look a real sight to see, decked out in my trunks, yes ma'am, a real sight to see, like a beached whale I was at the start. But eventually I got my figure back and then, lo and behold ma'am, I was gettin' those admirin' looks again. And then I met this cute young woman, 'call me Laura' she said; she was an attorney, ma'am. Lawyer, I think you would say, ma'am."

"That's right. My father is a lawyer," I said very proudly, thinking of you, Dad.

"Is that right? Well ma'am, that is one hell of a coincidence I must say!" he exclaimed with a degree of surprise.

"Yes, I suppose it is," I said.

"Yes ma'am, she was the cutest thing goin' around in our little town. Well, we started datin' and before long we were a regular item, you know. She kinda reformed me, ma'am. I didn't want to lose her, so I made sure I kept in shape and didn't go back to that old lifestyle I'd been leadin' before. Not as much eatin'; not as much drinkin'; a bit earlier to bed, you know ma'am, all those healthy thin's.

"Life was rollin' along like a regular bouncin' ball until one day when my pa just went right along and died, ma'am. Just keeled over and died, from a heart attack it was ma'am. I said to my ma, well, I guess I'm the head of the family now, bein' in the business and all. Yes siree, I was the chief now in charge of all those injuns'. Laura was a real help cos of her learnin' in the law. She helped me sort out the business cos after pa was dead and buried we discovered that the family business needed a bit of sortin' out cos, as Laura put it, it was a bit of a mess, all over the place in fact. Somethin' to do with family trusts and companies and hell, I just didn't know what she was talkin' 'bout at the start, but to give Laura her due, she got that company up and goin' again, she sure did, ma'am. Heck, I was so proud of that gal of mine, I just had to get up and marry her 'fore someone else popped the question of her. That was the happiest day of my life, ma'am, when her pa walked her up the aisle and plonked her right next to me in front of the preacher. I reckon I got out 'I do' as quick as lightnin' after the preacher asked me all those questions as to whether I took this woman and all those other things they are in the habit of asking which no one of us knows what in the hell they are talkin' 'bout cos they sound so unnatural like. And didn't she just look gorgeous in that long white gown she got 'specially made up for the day. It sure cost a heap of money, but ma'am, I got to tell you it was worth every penny that she spent cos she looked just like an angel. And ma'am, I've been here a little while now I guess and I must say I ain't seen no angels here at all."

"This is only the Waiting Room. I expect you have to get into the afterlife proper before you see an angel," I hazarded.

"Well, you could blow me down, ma'am. I never thought of that, I sure did not. Now you mention it as you just have, it sounds perfectly logical, it sure does. This ain't Heaven or the afterlife as you called it at all; no, you are so right."

"Tell me more about your wife. I hope she isn't here."

Dad, as soon as I said that I felt quite foolish because it was like I was saying, 'I hope your wife isn't dead, unlike you,' you know what I mean, Dad? But I never meant it to sound so brutal.

"No, thank God, she isn't here yet, at least I don't believe so," he said in a doleful tone, as if my mentioning his wife had triggered bad memories, not of his wife, but of his dying. I hadn't asked him at this stage how he had died as I wanted his life story to unravel piece by piece, as if I was reading a book from cover to cover, not skipping over the middle pages straight to the last page just to see what the ending was.

"My wife, yes siree, she sure was a real peach I gotta tell you. Her ma and pa weren't what you would call rich but they had lived pretty comfortable all through their lives and Laura turned out to be real smart, as well as a real good looker. She breezed through high school and college as if she wasn't even tryin'. You know, I'm not just sayin' this cos she was my wife but plenty of folks told me that you know, all those friends who went through law school with her and had actual experience you could say of how smart she was. And the way she talked ma'am, it was a real treat just to sit in front of the fire when we had people around with a drink in my hand while she took the floor so to speak and sallied forth on any topic you could name. Sometimes it was some case she was involved in, sometimes about the President and how he was ruinin' all our rights and killin' our boys all over the place by sendin' them off who knew where to fight some Muslims or other. Me, I never worried about that sort of stuff. I thought, heck, if our President says we gotta go fight some place so these awful damn terrorists didn't come back and crash another couple of planes into a buildin' in America, well that was okay with me. I mean to say, isn't that his job: To stop all those nasty and evil people comin' in to our country and doin' just awful things to us innocent Americans? That's what I reckon anyway. Now why Laura chose another point of view from me I can't say but I guess it's to do with her learnin'. I mean, she often had to go to court and defend some poor critter who maybe robbed a store cos he was high on drugs and needed some cash to buy more coke or hash, a real down and out sort of guy, black and white guys all alike so I guess she decided in her mind that maybe these goofs were not to blame for what they did you know, that maybe there was some other reason behind it all; their environment or somethin' like that she used to say. It ain't like she was poor herself; she sure weren't. I had loads of money and even when we got hitched together she was quite comfortable like. She kept on talkin' about underdogs or somethin' like that, which was strange for me to hear cos I sure do know about poor critters; but it's their own fault I often said to her. Then we would have a real argument about it and she would try and bamboozle me with fancy words and sentences that stretched out so far into the distance one could never see the end of them; they just kept pourin' outta her mouth for minute after minute until I lost track of exactly what she was sayin' so I would give up listenin' and let her ramble on, all the time pretendin' that I was takin' notice of her and what she was sayin', but ma'am, I weren't, my mind had closed. When finally she stopped and looked at me in a kinda way that seemed to say she was expectin' an answer I never knew what to say so I would just give her a smile and shrug my shoulders as if to say: 'What can I say to that?' She would give a shake of her pretty head at me and sorta scream out in exasperation. I don't know why she did that cos I ain't no attorney and I don't know how to answer like an attorney. Ain't that right, ma'am?"

He expected an answer this time.

"Yes, I suppose you weren't an attorney, but surely you don't need to have studied law in order to speak to people, especially to have a conversation with your wife, do you?"

He gave me a look of curiosity, contemplating what I had said.

"I never thought of it like that," he said, slowly, as if he was choosing his words very carefully.

A silence ensued for a few minutes. He looked to be deep in thought, contemplating what he would say next.

"You know ma'am," he began again with deliberation, "I did love Laura very much, despite our different points of view on some political topics. I suppose you could say it was like opposites attractin'. It was other things that made us fall in love. For one thing, as I said, she sure was the cutest thin' goin' around, and that's somethin' hard to go past. And at the time I reckon I was the handsomest guy in town and, bein' a bit cheeky and having an outgoin' sort of personality, I guess she was attracted to me. I don't know really..." he drifted off.

I felt a little sorry for him now, for this conversation recalled the past when he was with his wife, which was now all gone. I felt I had to say something to spark him up as he was certainly looking miserable. On earth we all go through this, don't you think, Dad? At one moment we are feeling on top of the world, happy with our lot, content with our situation; the next, we suddenly have a ton of troubles on our shoulders. Maybe it is a cutting remark made to us or perhaps our mind has drifted off into thinking mode and, the problem with thinking too much is that it can, out of the blue, bring on a bout of feeling low. I think that is universal, Dad. Some people can effectively camouflage their true feelings and always appear sparkling and bubbly in outlook. Others, like me and you too Dad, I think, wear our hearts on our sleeve and so when a little incident comes along and ruins our day, our blues last for many hours or days until the passage of time takes it away. Isn't that so, Dad? Most of us eventually recover and I guess it is only those medically determined to be clinically depressed who never snap out of it. For there is a difference you know. So, I had to get Craig back on track or our conversation was certain to peter out.

≈

George hung his head.

"I get depressed," he said dolefully.

I knew that, as George had already told us about the psychiatrist's report. Yet I didn't know how to respond without mouthing something hackneyed. I allowed the silence that followed to grow into a vacuum that not even the squeaking of a mouse could penetrate. I mean, grown men discussing depression? It was virtually unheard of. Perhaps best just to mention the word and leave it at that. That was usually enough. And moreover, this was in the presence of our wives as well. Men talk of football, cricket, and politics; anything but a subject that has anything to do with our emotions or state of mind. George was crying out for help but I felt useless, unable to reach out to his troubled soul and sooth it. I had to say something, but what?

"We all understand, George," I finally said, glancing at Debra and Emily to include them in my answer, "It's because of what happened to Chloe; it's perfectly understandable; it's okay...you are doing fine...even to get together time upon time and narrate Chloe's story...I feel very privileged, and I'm sure Debra and Emily do as well."

George turned his head in my direction. A smile began to peek out from behind his otherwise gloomy countenance, just like a breaking dawn.

"Thank you, Chas," he said.

I allowed him some time to his own thoughts before I asked him if he was ready to continue.

"Yes...I am," he said with a sigh of resignation, as if the state of living was getting too much for him. After a deep breath and a sip of wine he began again.

≈

"Did you and Laura get around to having children?" I asked him.

Immediately he brightened up and appeared interested in continuing.

"Well ma'am, thank you for askin', cos if anythin' made me and Laura happy was our kids. We were blessed by the Lord with two beautiful children, one of each so to speak."

"That's great!" I exclaimed by way of encouragement.

"Yes siree, those two little kids were a bundle of joy to both of us. Katie was the eldest. She woulda been about 15 or so and Jack about 12 or thereabouts when I...came here. Katie was the spittin' image of her ma, she sure was, with that same unblemished face and cutest of smiles. Now, she was an angel I can say without any doubt at all, ma'am. I ain't being bias, ma'am, no, not at all.

Everybody said so. I was her pa and it made me very proud I can tell you ma'am, when complete strangers would whisper to each other as we was walkin' past them some place 'how beautiful that little girl is'. That's what they would say, ma'am. They ain't had no promptin' from me. They just said it right off the top of their heads, like a reaction that they never had a chance in stoppin' coming out. I would keep walkin' with Katie and smile away at the world as though I had just been elected to some high office. On reflection now ma'am, I don't think even bein' elected President could come close to the happiness that I felt when somebody said some kind and pleasant words about Katie. Air would fill my lungs and I would walk along that sidewalk holdin' my head as high as I could without it being separated from the rest of my body. Ma'am, I sure was tickled pink as people say when they is happy as a bee in clover. And clever too she was, ma'am, shooting straight A's. Winnin' prize after prize at school, even now she is at high school, she just keeps on winnin' those prizes cos she can't help it, ma'am. I mean, can anyone who is as smart as smart can be, ever be stopped being top of the class? I don't think so ma'am. Can anyone stop that Lance Armstrong winnin' that Tour of France year after year? No siree, ma'am. I bet he will just keep on winnin' year after year if he wants to. What is it now, seven straight?"

Dad, you of course would have known the answer, but sport never being my forte I didn't have a clue, so I answered with a big shrug of my shoulders.

"No matter, you get my meanin'. And not only was Katie as brainy as anyone around, but she played any sport she took up as though she learned all this stuff while she was inside her ma, waitin' to come out and get on with livin'. Tall for her age she was, so basketball was a natural for her, plus tennis and runnin' track. I could go on for hours about her."

I had no doubt that he could. He could talk, Dad, I assure you and even his fleeting descriptions of his life were filled with sufficient information for me to feel totally aware of his situation.

"Tell me about Jack," I asked.

"Now Jack was a different kind of fish, ma'am. He was born I reckon to be contrary just for the sake of it. I'm not sayin' he's no good ma'am, no I could never say that, but he was like a piece of chalk and Katie was like a piece of cheese, if you get my meanin' ma'am."

I got his meaning Dad, very easily, as not only the words he used made one understand his kids hadn't come out of the same package, but his general demeanour ensured I knew what he was getting at. I told him I understood what he meant.

"Thank you ma'am for that," he said, though why he had to thank me I could not figure out as I was sure I hadn't done anything that would warrant me being thanked.

"At school, Jack was regarded as a bit of a rebel, ma'am. Often he played truant and I would have to yell at him a bit to try and explain why he had to go to school. 'Sure pa,' he tumbled out every time I had a chat with him. He'd keep on the straight and narrow for a while and then he would be off agin. Folks around town would see him wanderin' round the local drug store or kickin' stones into the water off the bridge across the river that ran through town. They'd call me and tell me he'd been seen again: 'Your boy's at it agin,' they'd say with a sigh ringin' through their voice. What could I say? Nothin' much I reckoned. Just tell 'em thanks and be waitin' at home for him at his usual time of comin' home if he had gone to school. For Jack had a slice of street cunnin' about him, even though puttin' pencil to paper might have tested him. He made sure he arrived home at the same time every day to give the 'pression he'd been to school. Normally Laura and I would still be workin' but Mama Cass would be home. She weren't that singer of course but we called her that cos she was built just like that Mama Cass used to look before she choked on that sandwich and died. She was black as the ace of spades, even blacker than me and Laura, but that didn't stop her bein' called Mama Cass. She sure was some keeper of the house I must tell you, ma'am. Every little thin' was spotless as a pin that had been licked clean within a hair's breadth of its life. You coulda eaten off that floor in the kitchen, you sure coulda, ma'am. As soon as Katie had popped out and Laura wanted to go back to her law books we picked up Mama Cass from an agency and, well we ain't had no breath of trouble from her the moment she heaved herself through the front door. But, back to Jack, 'fore I forget. His schoolin' weren't all that bad, ma'am. Hope I didn't give you the wrong 'pression but his grades were sorta average but 'pared to Katie they were way down south and Laura being competitive and all that, she always gave Jack a good goin' over with her tongue every time his grades came out. Katie scored straight A's of course, while poor Jack scrapped out C's with maybe a B if he tried a bit more in a particular class. He wasn't dumb; it was just that his mind seemed to be elsewhere and he never seemed to regard his schoolin' as important cos, as he said to me once, there were more things to have knowledge of than what the teachers taught him inside a classroom. I could see his point. Schoolin' is just a sorta preliminary thing you have to go through before you get to the real world. Maybe Jack's mind had already jumped from the schoolroom to the real world before the other kids could get there? Weekends, he wandered around the fields close by and up and down the trails that meandered through some woods handy to our house. He was a sorta nature boy cos he'd open up when he'd returned from his ramblin' and tell me about all the different types of critters he'd caught sight of. You know, birds and foxes and skunks and snakes, all those sorts of things. So after a while he started keepin' animals at home like rabbits and dogs and frogs. Katie and Laura, being females, no offence ma'am, were put off by these creatures, complainin' about the smell they did, so I had to put a limit on what Jack could brin' home. Least ways it kept him occupied with somethin' healthy. And Jack would keep to himself a lot, lockin' himself in his bedroom for hours on end if he hadn't gone scoutin' around outside. One day I peeked in when he was out and I saw this notebook open on his desk. I thought for once he'd been doing homework but it was only some poems or somethin' like that written out, not anythin' complete I imagine but jottin's of lines or a verse or somethin'. Whether they were real poems and he'd merely copied out some line or two he had memorized I couldn't say not being a poetry man myself. So I guessed young Jack had more to him than met the eye. I'd always loved him of course but when I saw all these lines of poetry written out I was a bit weepy and became a little bit more proud of him than I'd been before. It meant he'd somethin' inside of him and he wasn't gonna follow the crowd. So both my kids are sorta makin' their mark in different ways. Pity I won't be there with them."

He looked downcast when he finished speaking, his head bowed down between his legs with an outright sad countenance. What should I do now? I thought. Sneak away before he raised his head? I didn't consider that was the proper course to follow as I felt I had some form of moral obligation to lift him out of the doldrums he had clearly fallen into. I realised I had to get him to give me some insight into his happier times.

"Tell me about yourself now," I suggested, hoping that he would switch his story around and concentrate on the good times I was sure had rolled through his life.

"I believe I've already done that, ma'am," he answered, still in a doleful manner.

"Yes, you have told me something about your background, but you must have some sort of idea how you came to get here."

"I only know what that gatekeeper, was that his name, ma'am, told me."

"Well, of course," I responded, "but did anything major happen to you leading up to the time you…died?"

"Now that you bring it up I recall that havin' lived a life as healthy as I could, includin' doing some 10k runs and a short triathlon, for some reason I started to lose weight. My energy levels dropped to a real low level. At the beginnin' ma'am, I reckoned I had come down with that chronic fatigue syndrome, cos I just couldn't raise a gallop, ma'am. I couldn't even get in the car and drive to work. Ma'am, it soon reached the stage where I didn't want to even get out of bed. So I would just sleep all day, and even after doing all that, ma'am, I would still be tired as a dead rat. Doctors I don't care too much to see, so I put off goin' for long as possible. Laura nagged at me like a good wife should to get off my backside and get down the clinic and see what in the world was ailin' me. They say a drippin' tap will drive even the strongest man out of his mind if each little drip taps away on a man's forehead, so like that never endin' drippin', Laura's carpin' wore me away. So I gets up and get Laura to drive me down to see the doctor I ain't laid eyes on in years, ever since the day Jack had to be cut outta his ma cos he just didn't want to come out I suppose cos he might have been enjoyin' all that sleepin' in there. Well, this doctor gives me the run over and does all these tests which I can't make any sense of at all, proddin' here and pokin' there, like a real stickybeak he was, wantin' to know this, askin' me to tell him that. Then he gets me to have a scan of all my body. So the big climax comes a few days after when he calls me and Laura back in. Immediate I lay eyes on him I knew somethin' had gone wrong cos he sure didn't look too happy,

I can tell you that ma'am, yes siree. 'You got cancer,' he came right out with. Well ma'am, you coulda knocked me down with a feather when those words sunk into my head, ma'am. Me and Laura just looked at each other without a word bein' said. Two gapin' mouths I suppose the doc saw, gapin' in pure disbelief. I had to hold meself together ma'am, cos I went a bit wobbly in the knees and thought I might just tumble outta that chair and hit the floor like a sack of flour or somethin' heavy like that. Eventually I recovered and we got the doc to tell us everythin'. I can't repeat it here, not cos I don't want, but cos I can't remember the entire details ma'am, cos it was a few months before I..."

"So you died of cancer?"

"Hell no, ma'am," he forcefully replied. "No ma'am, the gatekeeper told me I had a heart attack."

"So what happened to the cancer?" I asked him.

"Well ma'am, I ain't got a clue about that now. He said, that is the doc, ma'am, I had to have some chemotherapy to get rid of the cancer. And I went for this treatment, every day for a while and then weekly for some other time till the doc says it ain't gettin' any worse. I was sure glad to hear that ma'am for I tell you I didn't look forward to dyin', not at that particular stage of my life, or any individual stage for that matter ma'am. So I asked the doc, 'Doc, so this treatment is gettin' rid of this cancer?' And then he said: 'No, it just isn't getting any better'. Well ma'am, you coulda knocked me down with the baby of that feather when he told me that. I mean, I'd being goin' through all this treatment, stuff pourin' into my body and all that sorta thing, and here he goes and tells me that it ain't made no difference, not one little bit. So I thinks to meself, why in the hell did I have to go through all this, ma'am? It ain't much fun ma'am, having this cancer treatment and if it don't make no difference ma'am, why should I do it?"

I had no answer to that, Dad. I was studying to be a nurse, but I wasn't a doctor and so couldn't give him a medical opinion. Anyway, it was too late now. I thought of grandfather who had non-Hodgkin's lymphoma. Dad, remember that at a conference with the doctor in hospital you were told that grandfather would only last three months if he didn't undertake chemotherapy and you all decided to give it a go but the result was that he died in three months anyway, even after undertaking the treatment. Seems the same thing happened to Craig. I mentioned grandfather's case to him and he agreed that there must be occasions when an accepted medical procedure or treatment is not the best medicine. But that still didn't explain how he had his heart attack. I pressed him further.

"Ma'am, it sure is very strange, that's all I can say. I reckoned I had got meself clear of heart attack territory what with all that runnin' and swimmin' and cyclin' I was doin' for those triathlons. I read all these books about exercise extendin' your life and all that sorta thing. I recall readin' a couple of books about this guy called Jim Fixx and how runnin' had saved his life, but ain't it real funny ma'am, this Jim Fixx died himself; what from, ma'am? A heart attack, at the same age as his pa who weren't a runner! So I guess it don't make a bit of difference, does it ma'am?"

"No, that's strange," I replied. Dad, I seem to recall that I was aware of this story, and how you brushed it off at the time as a genetic disorder because his father had died at the same age, 42 I think it was. Or maybe I am thinking of that joke that the meaning of life is 42? Recalling how he died brought me quickly back to reality. I was here, in this Waiting Room, along with millions and millions of others, wandering around...for what? Well, it was for judgement on our life. That was it. God merely had to mark our card and hand it down to us and that would be it, for ever. I suddenly felt scared because like most people I crave acceptance, to be thought of favourably. I wondered whether I had lived my life as I should have. I believed I had but, then again, it was not up to me. I felt like a party in a court case, waiting for the Judge's verdict. I had put my side of the story; the other person had put his, and it was now merely a question of waiting. The gatekeeper had explained that I would have an opportunity to put my case to God but this prospect filled me with horror. He had seemed to imply that I had nothing to worry about, but I still carried doubts around with me. And being here, listening to these stories stressed me out, not for me so much but for the people I had met, especially James and Jessie. Then I thought that no matter how much anxiousness surrounded me or any of the people I had met, there was no way our lives on earth could be rearranged; the facts could not be altered; history could not be rewritten. We had laid our cards on the table by the way we had conducted ourselves on earth and no amount of fancy words before God could really alter the verdict. Whether a person who truthfully expressed remorse could sway God I had no idea. We just had to wait.

I felt that Craig had gone as far as he could. He had a spent look about him so I muttered goodbye to which he merely gave a grunt, and slowly rose off the seat and continued my travels along the path.

<hr>

George closed his folder. His eyes went to each of us in turn, waiting for a response.

"He was certainly a character," I opened with.

"Yes," echoed Debra, "so different from the others."

"Particularly in the way he spoke," Emily said.

"You got the accent and spelling down very well George," Debra said, glancing at his notes. "How could you do that?"

"I don't know. It just rolled out exactly in the tone Chloe used. Normally it would be hard to imagine anyone remembering so much verbatim, but as I have mentioned to you guys previously, I seem to have the ability to do so."

He left it there, unwilling to have us believe that some magical power had been delivered to him...by a higher force. I hadn't a clue as to how he was able to do it. All I knew was that he could. A sceptic would certainly raise this point as an impossibility leading to the conclusion that George may have been faking this whole scenario, putting this afterlife thing forward as part of a giant hoax.

Certainly I believed Chloe's conversation with Craig had not taken the reason for her communications with her father any further. Of course it was an interesting tale of a typical American hailing from the South, but nothing more than any of us had heard before on any one of the plethora of invasive American TV shows. I hesitated to express this opinion out loud. It was not that I thought George may have missed something. I did not think he had. The others may have felt that too as our conversation seemed to lack its usual sparkle. Whether unknowingly we were all tired I couldn't say. Perhaps the women also had their reservations as to the real relevance of this conversation. I'm not criticising Chloe, far from it. But Craig's story did not enlighten us any further. For all we knew the conversation may have been the kind that could have taken place just about anywhere except of course for the odd comment or two on death and the gatekeeper.

The last few minutes of the conversation showed Chloe maintaining her anxiousness while waiting for her fate to be decided. She mentioned she felt like she was in a court case waiting for the Judge's verdict. That feeling surely was also felt by George in his role as a lawyer. I had never been involved in a court case but plenty of times in my business career I had felt a clutch of nerves in my stomach as I contemplated some deep problem which I had had to brief the boss on. An executive always wonders whether he or she will cop it in the neck for some minor infringement of protocol regarding corporate governance.

And if there was an afterlife and we would be judged on our conduct on earth what would be the impact on our lives: A brutal rearrangement of how we acted or a shrug of the shoulders to indicate ambivalence? A refusal to change because – I'll deal with that when I get there?

As we made our way home Debra remained unusually silent. I realised she too was contemplating all sorts of matters. I had my personal beliefs; Debra was entitled to have hers. Perhaps two cones of silence had enveloped us ensuring we could not articulate our inner-most thoughts to each other. There would be another time and another place for that. It was clear we had not heard Chloe's complete story. I needed to hear it in its entirety before I could pass final judgment on the unfolding story.

Chapter Thirteen

VISITS DID NOT FOLLOW ON ONE AFTER THE OTHER REGULARLY, in accordance with a preordained timetable, unlike a train schedule. Far from it; often weeks went by before Chloe came back to George. As far as I can recall, she gave no explanation for the gaps in her visits. Then again, as Chloe often said, time and again, afterlife time was not the same as earth time; it may be that from her viewpoint there was no undue delay.

I knew George would have told us if Chloe come back for it surely would have been contained in his notes. It was like when you read a gripping novel in bed at night; you don't want to put it down and go to sleep; you are too engrossed in the story as you whip through one page after another; you feel compelled to keep reading until, against your will, sleep finally conquers you.

Waiting for George to tell me he had another chapter to read out meant life was lived on a knife edge. I suffered from anxiousness and anxiety while I waited for his call. Debra too had become entranced and pestered me constantly for news. I also understand she spoke to Emily virtually every day, craving news of Chloe's return. I wondered how other people would have felt, waiting like we were, on tenterhooks for George to say the word.

I could pad George's telling of Chloe's story out by inserting bits of our social life together in between the readings. But what we did in between paled into insignificance when compared with Chloe's story. Her stories of James, Jessie, and Craig were interesting in themselves but they had another aspect when one took cognisance of where these conversations took place. Reciting what George did at work or at night when he was home or the cases he was involved in may have also been interesting in parts, but so what! Compared to Chloe's story these insertions would be boring, mundane and quite pointless. I challenge anyone to assert that there is any comparison. It's like chalk and cheese.

A week or so after George's reading of Chloe's conversation with Craig I had to go to Sydney for work. Imagine my chagrin when George called my mobile early Friday morning to announce another visit and Chloe's meeting with April. I was completing my business on the Friday afternoon but I was compelled to stay the weekend for a company executive retreat. I had no hope of getting back before Sunday. I realised the others would want to meet before then.

"I can't come back until at least late Sunday afternoon," I told George.

"Gee Chas, I can't wait that long, neither can Emily and I'm sure Debra will be the same. Emily knows of Chloe's visit because she woke up when I was at the computer. I guess by now she will have called Debra. You know them, more anxious than we are!"

I had to agree with George. Our wives were voracious in their desire to be informed immediately of each visit.

"Look George," I said, "why don't you three get together and I'll call after I finish dinner and I'll listen on the phone while you read. That way, at least I will hear it tonight."

"That's a great idea, Chas. My landline is capable of conducting a conference call so that'll be perfect. I'll call Emily now and arrange it."

So that is how I heard the next reading. I finished dinner with my colleagues as soon as I could and raced back to the hotel while they went out drinking. George answered when I called his home and after settling our wives down, he read out the next chapter.

≈

The view before me was unreal. It had a sense of being a scene from a film with green, rolling hills one finds in many places in the world. But the distance that stretched away to the horizon gave me the impression that there was no end to this place; that it continued so far it was beyond human comprehension, much like the extent of the universe. Whenever I caught a glimpse of someone, they never appeared to be within reach; there always seemed to be an unbridgeable gap between me and them. Then I thought to myself: why had I then come into contact with James, Jessie and Craig? Why not people from a culture other than a Western one? Perhaps I was being directed, as if I was a puppet, only to those people to whom I was meant to speak? Perhaps I was meant to learn a lesson from their stories? I had no answer. Being here, I contemplated that eventually all that was presently a mystery would be revealed, but I couldn't at this stage grasp the reason for what was taking place around me. I drifted along as if in a dream, being lead on to I didn't know where.

Suddenly, at a slight bend in the path I was walking on I came face to face with a woman. She had appeared as if from nowhere and stood still, blocking the path. I reckoned she was older than me, but by how much I could not say.

"Hello," she said. "Would you like to talk to me?"

"Of course," I replied, happy to have someone else to converse with.

Nearby, there was another seat. I hadn't noticed it prior to laying eyes on this woman. Why did a seat suddenly appear when I needed one? I dismissed the thought from my mind as I was on the verge of speaking with this woman and I needed to have a clear head.

By now I knew what to do. After I introduced myself, I raced over my life history as quickly as I could as I wanted to get to the bottom of this woman's story. Somehow I remember you telling me Dad, that the secret of being regarded as a good conversationalist was to get the other person to talk about themselves because most people enjoy telling their own story, caring only for themselves and their own importance. And when the two of you parted, the other person would be in a happy frame of mind because they had virtually talked non-stop primarily about themselves. So this is what April told me:

"My name is April. Why my parents named me after a month of the year I haven't a clue. Perhaps they wanted to be different. At school it caused me no end of headaches because I became the butt of many a joke in the schoolyard, especially when it was actually the month of April. I won't repeat them to you now but I guess you can imagine how inane they were. One stupid one was: 'Go home and take a shower, April.' You told me you came from Melbourne. Coincidentally, I was also born in Victoria, in Geelong, but my father was an investment consultant and, when I was still at primary school we moved to Manly, in Sydney, because my father received a big promotion. Initially I loved Sydney and the harbour because I enjoyed travelling on the ferry from Manly to Circular Quay, especially when the sea was rough and the waves chopped around the boat and crashed over the bow as we plunged through the swell. And it was clear that Manly was a trendy place to be seen in. My parents were relatively well off so I wanted for nothing. I got through secondary school without too much trouble and, as soon as I turned 18, I got my licence and found a super looking green MG to cruise around the streets of Sydney and the trendy suburbs. I was certainly the centre of attraction, I can tell you, but I played off the boys one by one because none of them truly interested me at that stage. I flitted from one to the other as if I was a butterfly and I suppose I was, treating them rather cruelly at times I recall. But I'll skip over the rest of my younger days because these days most girls live their lives uniformly with each other; only the names and places change. At school, thoughts of being a journalist crossed my mind and I realised that there was not much time remaining to grow up. My school coached me pretty effectively because I breezed into uni without too much trouble. I was determined to work hard to get a cadetship after I got a degree but it didn't pan out like that in the end. I got mixed up in the wrong crowd and...well, I messed around too much and flunked out. Naturally, my parents were aghast and nearly disowned me for they were highly embarrassed for some reason even now I find it difficult to fathom. I mean, it was me that failed, not them, so I should have been the one to feel disappointed and downcast, not them. I was pissed off too. Not with anyone else, but with myself. I mean, all the people I hung around with got through so I should have been able to socialise as much as I needed to but still do sufficient to pass. So that was that."

"What did you do then?" I asked

"I got married," she said.

Boy, was I surprised when she said that, Dad. I mean it's very unusual for girls to get married at a young age these days, unlike back in your day when it was quite normal. That's just a statement of fact, Dad; it is not intended to be a put down. Society changes over time and nowadays there are more career options for young women than getting married.

"Married, just like that?" I asked her.

"Well, not immediately," she answered with a smile. "Strange you may think it to rush off and do something rash like that, but

I thought if I couldn't get through uni then I better find some back-up to support my desired lifestyle. I had no wish to be left on the shelf in my thirties because I had delayed getting married in an attempt to show my independence. I didn't get married to become a slave, far from it, but I calculated it as a form of business decision to assist my future."

"Was it just for 'business' you got married or was there any love involved?" I asked her, concerned that her story would show her to be a calculating, money scheming female.

"For love, of course! It's just that I made a conscious decision to fasten up the process and deliberately went out and put myself in a position to do it. This was the 'business' part of it. Anyway, it was a guy I had known for some time, so it was easy for me to manoeuvre him into the right frame of mind. He was five years older than me, so it wasn't so bad for him was how I viewed it. We dated for a while and...I trapped him a bit because I got pregnant and, out of duty or honour, he agreed to marry me."

"How old were you?" I asked her.

"Just turned 20, I think."

"What did your husband do?"

"He was an architect, or he was going to be because I think he had just got his first job with some big firm in the city. Anyway, his father worked in a finance company as some sort of executive so the family were like my parents, pretty well off."

"What did your parents think of you getting married when you were pregnant and all that?"

"At first they spat chips and endlessly lectured me, but after the baby was born they came around and became proud as punch grandparents, showing off pictures of my little baby girl to everyone they came within cooee of."

"And what's her name?"

"I had been given a name I wasn't too keen on so I had to

make sure her name wasn't regarded as stupid, so we called her Emma."

"That's a pretty and popular name," I said.

Dad, as I recall, you or Mum once told me 'Emma' was one of the names you were considering to call me before I was born, so when April told me her daughter's name was Emma I immediately looked upon it as a good name.

"Yes, I think so. My husband had a grandmother whose middle name was Emma so we agreed to call our baby Emma after her. Life for a few years went swimmingly. I remained at home bringing up my baby. There was no need for me to work as Sandy, that's my husband, was on a good package. We bought an old house and renovated it to our liking. I believed that life could not be any better. Sandy was the perfect husband. When he was home he would take his turn changing the baby, doing some household chores and generally being supportive. Then after a year or so he got a promotion and his work habits changed dramatically. His firm were tendering for some huge projects overseas and he was often required to travel for a week or so at a time, to America and to Asia. Even when he was home he seldom poked his head in the door before 8 o'clock. Saturdays, he either went into the office or marooned himself in his study going over his plans. Sundays too were often taken up with socialising with his colleagues. You know what I mean, I'm sure. He would be with his boss and workmates in one corner whilst we poor hapless wives bounced babies up and down on our knees and talked baby talk not only to our kids but with each other as well. I needed something more than gibberish about baby habits or recipes, the usual type of thing you find in the women's magazines. And a few of them were TV junkies and would go over last week's episode of some soap opera or discuss *Big Brother* and who they thought would be evicted. I never watched those ridiculous reality shows.

Usually I read a book while waiting for him to come home or else I was ensuring that Emma was settled or dinner was on track, for the new rules of the house entirely revolved around Sandy and his work. As he was about to leave the office he would ring me and tell me his arrival time. I therefore had to calculate cooking down to the last second as dinner had to be on the table within a minute of his getting home because he would be famished after a long day. If for some reason it wasn't, the usual laments of a male would pour forth. How he was earning all this money to support me and Emma; how he worked long hours; how I had nothing else to do except look after the baby and prepare meals so why couldn't I have dinner ready the minute he walked in the door? What could I say in return? That I had been cleaning up all day after *our* baby and there was more to working at home, cleaning up, washing and cooking than met the eye? Oh, I could and did so on occasions, but what would happen? He would tear into me and say how ungrateful I was, how he was keeping me in luxury and, when he was really mad at me, he would throw in the fact that he was forced to marry me and I had trapped him and all that sort of thing. When he said that, my blood would boil over. We would trade insults all night and wouldn't speak for days and days. All I had in my life was Emma and some contact with the women in our circle of friends. Come to think of it, these confrontations would come not too long before his next overseas trip. Anyway, for all that, over time we began to drift apart. He had his work and I had the baby. How was I to get out of this rut I found myself bogged down in? I continually asked myself this question. I decided I had to get out of the house and find myself a new circle of friends; some women who weren't merely the baggage or appendages of Sandy types from his work. But Emma was still young; I think she was not yet three. Various plans eventually began to hatch in my mind.

"But I felt cornered. I didn't want to run back home to my parents; that would have been a backward step. I had to physically separate; there was no way I could have a separation under the one roof, as some couples do. I knew for a fact that we couldn't operate on a level civil enough for it to work out. I also had to consider Emma. She was still young and I had no intention of subjecting her to the sound of constant bickering and raised voices. I therefore decided that I had no other alternative than to leave home. I had some money tucked away for a rainy day and I guess this was a perfect occasion for me to dip into those funds. So I secretly rented a unit south of town as I didn't want to live too close to our home. I needed to find my own space without him pestering me. I know I must sound like a bit of a fish-wife, not appreciating all the things Sandy had done for us but for my own peace of mind and my own sanity I had to be away from him, at least on a temporary basis. I had no idea if this was to be a permanent arrangement. Of course, I would have preferred it if our relationship hadn't sunk to such a low level, but I certainly wasn't going to bow down before him and accept meekly what he wanted to give me, as if I was a dog and once in a while to placate me he would throw bits of meat my way. No, I had to establish a new life. I had flunked out of uni, which I now regretted very much, so I was even more determined not to stuff up my immediate future. And I needed to create a peaceful environment in which Emma could grow up. I know people say that at least if I had stayed she would have had a father in the house. I acknowledge that. Of course, that would be nearly everyone's preference, but often things don't work out that way.

"When he was at work one day, Emma and I shifted out. Other women may have also stripped the house bare, but I couldn't do that. My intention was to live with Emma in a world created entirely by me and without any bind to the house we had shared with Sandy. I didn't want to be staring at the furniture, reminiscing about the old days. So I went and bought a complete new set of everything. All I took was our clothes. I left a note for him on the kitchen table and walked out to commence a new life. I had no idea what the future held for me, but I told myself to be strong. I think I was, but at night when I was alone it was easy to panic and question whether I had done the right thing. Tears flow easily in these circumstances and I can tell you Chloe that many a night I rocked my Emma to sleep with tears flowing down my face. Despite Sandy's protestations to me when he rang my mobile, I refused to give in and return home. He was totally astounded by what I had done and could not understand why I would want to leave our beautiful home. But that was the point. He was so short sighted that he could not see the widening cracks in our relationship which were tearing us apart. All was rosy in his world because he was living a life which, according to him, was perfect. I begged to differ. It takes two to tango and that is fine with me but he seemed to be dancing solo.

"Eventually I was set up in my new home. I was forced to tell him where I lived as he demanded access, although that faded away as quickly as his initial enthusiasm had bloomed. After his original surge of interest following Emma's birth it had all been left to me so it was very enlightening indeed to hear his tales of woe of feeding Emma, bathing her and getting her clothes on. Weekend access lasted barely two or three times as Friday night to Sunday afternoon with Emma interfered with his work. His overseas trips continued, so during those times he never laid his eyes on Emma. Eventually, he wound back access from the whole weekend to a single afternoon, usually on Saturday. I think his social life increased substantially after I left because I was no longer the millstone around his neck. Initially, the usual group of mothers that I had been involved with was all I had for comfort, but some of these friendships went by the board because a few of them no longer had the inclination to mix socially with a single parent with a youngster in tow; we no longer had much in common. They were universally happily married. I was an unhappy single mother. I was the odd one out. I was in a quandary because my life appeared to be going backwards."

≈

Dad, here April paused in her story. Her life seemed stuck, going nowhere. I truly felt sorry for her as to me she appeared to be a very genuine person. Separation is, I suspect, not the first choice that couples make when a relationship hits hard times. I had only to recall you and Mum to realise that. I waited while she sat very still and quiet, staring at her feet, contemplating the next part of her story.

≈

"I had to work," she suddenly commenced again. "Emma was still very young, and to prevent me going insane staying at home on my own with her, I had to get out into the community, and find new people to interact with. I needed to work. I wracked my brains wondering what I could do. I had no training. What could I do? I needed something, anything at all. Eventually I landed this job in an old people's home. I couldn't be a carer because I didn't have any certificates or had undertaken any courses so I was merely a sort of dogsbody, serving meals, cleaning up after the old people who'd spilled food or just made a general mess, helping out in the kitchen and laundry as best as I could. I lasted a while but in the end it wore me down because I reckoned the home was like a half way house to the grave. Not too sick to be in hospital but incapable of being looked after in their own home by their children; a place to be sent to and spend your time withering away. A giant step towards a lonely death was how I regarded it once I became familiar with how things worked. I was young and it depressed me no end to think that one day in the future I might be a patient in one of these places. What dignity could one maintain when your bowels went haywire or you were so far gone mentally that you had no idea of anything? After a while I decided I wanted to live a life without this sort of thing hanging about my neck, strangling the life out of me."

"What did you decide to do?" I asked her.

"I resigned and went back to looking after Emma. While I was working she had been looked after at a child-care centre. She was fine with other babies and young kids surrounding her all day. But it didn't take too long for us to get used to each other again, I mean, being together all day. Oh, I think I must be boring you, Chloe, with all this sort of stuff!" she suddenly exclaimed.

"No, not really," I reassured her.

≈

Dad, I had nothing else to do. If April wanted to give me her life story verbatim, then why should I complain? It was not as though I had anywhere to rush off to, and I had an eternity to get through, didn't I? Even if I came across every person who had died there would still be plenty of time to hear billions of life stories was how I looked at it. Yes, I thought, even if it was becoming slightly repetitive, why should I be concerned? And Dad, maybe you too are becoming a little bored with this but I'm merely attempting to give you some idea of the various people I came across while I was waiting for the gatekeeper to come back.

≈

"That's good, because the last thing I would want to do is bore you," April began again, smiling at me.

"No, it's very interesting," I replied.

"Anyway, I'll skip a bit because for years after my separation I lived from one job to another, as I couldn't settle down. I was fidgety, permanently restless, and unable to concentrate for long periods. Even when I reached thirty I was no better. Some men had come and gone. Emma was the stumbling block, not from my point of view mind, but from the guys I got mixed up with. A young child never seemed to fit into their plans so they never fitted into mine. Sandy had gone off and got married again to some blond model so he wasn't interested in taking Emma permanently and I wasn't enthused by the prospect of Emma's teenage years being spent in the company of some bimbo who surely was living a lifestyle at odds with the way I had been bringing her up. It was not as though Sandy ever asked for custody. He clearly wasn't interested as it would have ruined his social life with his little charmer of a wife who knew everyone there was to know socially and so was able to drag him along and do what she had to do to keep him entranced. He had access whenever he wanted but I made sure that Emma didn't stay too long with them as I was aware that young children often succumb to temptation and fall victim to the illusory world that I was certain engulfed Sandy and his child bride. Did I not laugh myself silly when I heard that he had made her pregnant and it was going to be twins? The smirk remained spread across my face for weeks on end from the day Emma returned from a visit and spilled the beans. Yet, I was happy for Sandy if that was the life he wanted to live. And Emma would have two half-sisters or brothers she could become interested in playing with in the future if that was her choice."

She stopped again, collecting her thoughts, perhaps reliving her experiences at that particular period of her life, contemplating what might have been. Her story was beginning to drag out a little and I needed to know now how she died. This was the most interesting part of all my conversations Dad, asking each person how they got to the Waiting Room. I had realised by now that it was the gatekeeper himself who broke the news to each person as they stepped through the door at the end of the tunnel. And I realised too that each one of us had his or her personal tunnel to travel along before reaching the white door. When I recall what I have told you, Dad, it seems so incomprehensible, doesn't it? But Dad, everything that I am telling you now is the truth. I understand that you may not be able to grasp the reality of it. You probably can't because you are not here with me and we all know of the saying that 'seeing is believing', but now that you have heard what I say you must stop waiting to see before you believe. I longed to know how April died because she looked young and I could not imagine that she had lived to a ripe old age like your grandmother. Here, all inhibitions vanish, and so I asked her straight out how she had died.

"I had gone to Bondi Beach early in the morning one Saturday late in the summer. It was a weekend when Emma, for a change, was at her father's house. Even at such an early hour it was very hot and hundreds, if not thousands, of people had already invaded the beach, surfing, swimming in the shallows or lazing around on towels and under umbrellas on the sand. A wind had whipped up out of the blue and the waves were getting up and breaking all along the length of the beach. I went out into the water and body-surfed the waves back to shore for what I guessed was about half an hour. The sun was merciless by this stage, beating down relentlessly. There was a strong undertow but I didn't want to leave the water and sunbake as I burn very easily. Waves crashed over me continually as the wind drove them towards the beach. I began to become a trifle apprehensive as the undertow seemed to drag me further out towards the open sea with each successive surge. I was contemplating getting out but I decided on one last wave. That turned out to be a really big mistake. As I finished the wave I was dumped and the undertow grabbed me and dragged me under the water. I began to struggle which I know now was a silly thing to do. Instead of just going with the outward flow of the current, I fought like mad because I had a vision of being swept out of the sight of the life-guards and being attacked by a shark a mile off shore where nobody could save me. As I struggled I began to swallow water and this was my undoing. Everything went black. I must have lost consciousness under water for I can't remember another thing until I came here and the gatekeeper told me I had drowned."

April stopped speaking with a suddenness that made me give a little start. She was a very good talker I can say without hesitation. Now, she was lost for words. Her eyes seemed to be fixed on some unseen object far away on the horizon. But, even though I believed I had only been here a relatively short time, I understood perfectly well what was racing through her mind. It would have been thoughts of her daughter. Like me, she had no opportunity for that last goodbye. That is the shock, Dad. To come here and realise that the loved ones we have left behind have had no chance to whisper their most loving, intimate and tender thoughts as a final word. Yet I felt satisfied, happy that I had heard April's story and knew she was reliving her last moments on earth and, just as I was, feeling upset that her loved ones were suffering at her premature parting.

≈

"That's the end," George suddenly announced. No one spoke as we attempted to digest this latest episode. George finally broke the impasse.

"Chas, what do you think of the names, Emma and Chloe?" he asked.

"Emma is a soft and pretty name but Chloe is also very popular," I said.

"What's in a name anyway?" he asked rhetorically. From my hotel room in Sydney I pictured him apostrophising the wall, as if he was in conversation with some ghost. I let his remark pass. I was a long way away and so I held my tongue. I preferred that there weren't any unnecessary interruptions to George's readings or his commentary on what he had completed reading out. In any event, insertions or asides in the narrative were all George's doing. We were merely a conduit for him to unload this weight which appeared to be crushing his psyche, his very soul. I was willing to listen to him for hours without a single stoppage if necessary. I am sure Debra and Emily felt the same.

Another period of silence made its way down the telephone line. Their faces weren't before me so it was difficult for me to interpret the mood in the lounge room a thousand kilometres away.

"When she mentioned my separation from Michelle, that touched me to the quick," George said. Other than a long marriage with Chloe's mother, until he met and married Emily, George's subsequent relationships were shorter and stormier. I had gained the impression over the subsequent years that he was constantly under a great deal of stress in those relationships. Deep down I believed that George sincerely regretted the break up with Michelle and for some unaccountable reason was never able to learn by his mistakes. I wondered how Emily felt at the mention of Michelle; bringing up previous relationships can be a testing time for some people. She must have let it slide away because I did not hear her speak.

I heard some muted voice so I had to speak loudly to make myself heard.

"What did you say, George?" I asked.

"Chloe is right...the worst aspect of her sudden death, and that of April too, is that no one had an opportunity to say those precious words...of goodbye," George said in a loud voice, returning to this constant theme. It sounded to me as if an agonising look of pain had spread over his face, and actual physical pain was at that very moment being inflicted on him by some unseen force.

"Yes...that would be quite brutal," I said.

"And isn't that's what life is all about, George?" I heard Debra ask him. "None of us know the time or the place of our passing; that is the true mystery of it all."

"I agree, we cannot all be blessed with a death bed farewell as the movies seem to favour," Emily put in.

"But...poor Chloe," George began again, "she was lying there for hours, in bed, dead, until her mother eventually realised she was not asleep."

What could anyone say to that? I silently shook my head. I couldn't say a single word. Neither Debra nor Emily spoke. My mind began to wander as if it was in a vacuum. It seemed my brain had frozen, taken time out, suspending for the moment my thinking process.

George went on, jumping from one thought to another. "Oh, I talked to her while she was lying peacefully in her coffin the night before the funeral. That was some comfort, but of course, poor Chloe could not respond. That is the saddest part of this catastrophe."

"I have to get a drink of water George, back in a minute," I yelled out down the line. I did need a glass of water as my throat seemed to feel parched but in reality it was to allow myself a minute or so to pull myself together and wipe away the tears welling in my eyes. When I returned to the phone I could hear mutterings between Debra and Emily.

"Debra is going now, Chas," George said.

I heard her yell out goodbye. "Goodbye," I replied. "Speak soon, George," I said and hung up the phone. I opened the door of the mini-bar and made a swift attack on its contents that eventually sent me into a long, uninterrupted sleep.

Chapter Fourteen

When Debra picked me up at the airport I immediately asked her for her reaction to George's behaviour on Friday night.

"To me, he appeared very affected by not having the opportunity to say goodbye," I put in while waiting for her answer.

"Yes, he seems to be constantly pre-occupied with this notion as though he could reluctantly accept her death but not the prelude to it," Debra replied.

"I might as well have been on the moon," I said referring to my being away listening to George's reading, "but I also had that impression."

"And when he started talking about Chloe lying in her coffin...and not being able to talk back to him, well, to me, it was bordering on an illness of some description, abject depression perhaps, that he needed help with."

"I certainly heard it as a father in deep distress. Whether it was such that needed treatment I'm not qualified to say, but it certainly sounded like it," I replied.

I truly believed Chloe's visits were a comfort to George and were helping him overcome his grief despite his being traumatised by the suddenness of her death. No-one I had ever heard of had had such a privilege. People involved in an accident apparently resulting in death and then returning to the living from the after-life can be read about...but this? From George's perspective it may have been all very well to receive communications from

Chloe, but his angst was that he could not respond to her pin-pointed questioning of him.

"As I told George at the time, having the opportunity to say goodbye is rare, particularly in the case of accidents or other sudden deaths," Debra said.

I agreed with her but otherwise kept my counsel. We drove for a long way in silence. Doubtless, each of our minds was attempting to come to grips with George's reaction to Chloe's conversation with April. It was as though this concentration on the moments prior to death and a lack of a final goodbye led to a surge, a tremendous resurgence in George's grief. Lying in her coffin with George bending over, perhaps lovingly stroking her cold hands and touching that unmoving face, that unbreathing body; perhaps George's replay of what happened in that room where her coffin stood silently the night before her funeral had caused George to have some kind of turn, some episode, some reaction to it, that even more than two years after her death George was still struggling to cope with. He had also told me that Michelle had placed a note to Chloe in her coffin as a way of dealing with her grief.

Debra parked in our garage. We both sat there, staring into the future, wondering what would come of all this. I had no doubt that Michelle and George had both been damaged, psychologically damaged to a degree that would forever alter their lives and even George's relationship with Emily.

I telephoned George as soon as I put my case down.

"I had another visit last night," he said without bothering to say hello.

That surprised me; usually the visits were much more spread out.

"Tomorrow night, over here at our place George; you guys come over here," I barked out as if I was a military commander reinforcing my orders to the officers for the coming battle. George must have detected the urgency, the stridency in my voice for he readily agreed.

That night, although I was dead tired from my trip away, I could not sleep, eventually getting out of bed in the early hours of the morning. I made myself a cup of tea and sat quietly in the lounge room turning my thoughts to the evening of the day that was almost upon us.

I was very busy Monday during the day and had little opportunity to turn my mind to the coming chapter of Chloe's story. I could have worked on for a few more hours but I got myself away before six for a change and rushed home. I told Debra not to organise a big dinner; instead she rustled up finger food and drinks.

I gave George a bear hug when he and Emily arrived as if I had not seen him in ages. Emily received her customary kiss on the cheek. Formalities out of the way we sat down in our usual places and eagerly waited George's reading.

Without any words of introduction he began.

≈

Dad, I will tell you one final story. To me, this is probably the saddest case of all. She was a young woman who died at the same age as me. Her name is Clarissa. Here is what she told me.

≈

"Unlike most people who come here, I believe I am different, for I knew I was coming, well in advance. You on the other hand found yourself here suddenly. Although I didn't understand by what mechanism I would arrive here I took it as an article of faith that I would get to Heaven. Well, I know I'm not in Heaven yet but I fully believe that I will be soon. Long before my illness, I often went to church with my parents and generally lived a good life and mixed with the right crowd. And when I was told the bad news, that cancer had invaded my body, for some unexplainable reason I took this news calmly. My faith, a titch over ambivalent until then, firmed dramatically from the very moment I was told. I believe God spoke to me although it would be hard for me to be precise as to when or how this took place. All I can say is that although my body was being ravaged by cancer, I enjoyed an inner peace and I looked forward to my death. I had accepted it. There was no use ranting and raving that it was unfair like many people seem to do. I was past that. Drugs were poured into me, but I had a deep suspicion it would prove useless and so after a while, when I knew there was no possibility of remission, I told the doctors to stop the treatment. They were amazed and said I was giving up on life too easily. I laughed out loud when the doctor told me this because I saw death as a part of living. People aren't afraid to live, so shouldn't they also be prepared to die? That sort of question may spook some people but they are the types who don't have a positive attitude."

Dad, in my opinion she was a most beautiful woman. Not from a physical aspect, but more from the spiritual side. I suppose it is hard for people to believe this woman was so uncomplaining. She told me her cancer was her own fault. Isn't that a refreshing attitude, Dad? When so many people tend to live their lives putting the blame on the rest of humanity for their misfortune, it certainly was a welcome change to come across a person such as Clarissa. I only wish I could have met her on earth. She told me she had developed a severe case of melanoma, skin cancer. In my nursing course we learned there were three major types of skin cancer. The first is melanoma, the most serious type which unfortunately Clarissa had. There are two less serious types - basal cell carcinoma (BCC) and squamous cell carcinoma (SCC).

BCC is the most common and usually does not spread. SCC can spread to other parts such as lymph glands, lung or liver. She too lived in Australia, mostly in Queensland, and it was agonising to hear her explain to me how this all happened. In her teens she was a beach addict, always down at the water's edge with her friends swimming and sunbathing. Her object was to get the deepest tan of all her friends. She told me that by the end of each summer she would be practically black. I'll let her tell the rest of her story now.

"Boys would wolf-whistle at me all the time when I was well tanned so I guess I believed that the best way to attract boys was to have the best tan around. Even in winter when the sun wasn't as strong as in summer, I still worked on my tan. Sunny days would find me on the beach. Overcast and dull days I would use the absence of sun as an opportunity to go to a solarium and have a session of sunbaking. And if there was no sun for a week then I would be down at the solarium every day, working on the tan, pumping rays into my body, all for the purpose of attracting boys. I realise now that was an extremely foolish thing to do, but sometimes you don't think of the consequences of your actions, only the benefits that can be gained. And when I looked at my tanned body in the mirror I was proud that I had the necessary discipline to stick to my plan. My parents nagged at me when they saw me almost turning black but like most teenagers I ignored them because I thought I knew best.

"As my teenage years drew to a close, I had to have a job. Eventually, I got one as a waitress in a café down at the beach. It had an outdoor area which I loved because I could get some sun even while working. I would deliberately linger at tables giving the impression that I was doing so because I was friendly and loved talking to customers but in reality it was for the purpose of maintaining my tan. My hair, once on the fair side of brown now tended towards blonde because of my exposure to the sun and, to tell you the truth, as a result of a few bottles of peroxide as well. It must have had some effect because I was never short of boyfriends. My life then was all about fun. Parties at night when I wasn't working a late shift in the café, and the beach at weekends during the day together with visits to a solarium as often as possible made up my life. Come to think of it now, I really didn't mind working in the evening as it meant a late start and so on hot days I would sunbath all morning until I had to start work.

"I had no interest in study. As soon as I could, I left school, much to my parents' disappointment. Oh yes, I finished Year 11 after a couple of attempts but I only scrapped a bare pass the second time due to my complete lack of interest. My teachers would urge me to knuckle down as they said I had brains but didn't use them. Well, that wasn't telling me anything I wasn't already aware of. I knew I had a brain but I didn't care to use it as my mind was occupied by my desire to fill up my life with having a good time which I equated with having fun at parties, drinking, smoking cigarettes and other stuff, attracting boys and generally having a good time. After I left high school, I decided to get out and explore the country. Not trekking out into the back blocks or on trails through the mountains. No, I wanted to be at least half civilised about it all. So I planned a trip around Australia with a few friends. As soon as I got my driving licence I bought this second-hand kombi van dirt cheap, loaded some camping gear in and took off with my boyfriend and a girlfriend and some guy she hardly knew who had long hair tied up neatly in a ponytail. We intended to do a big circle around the coast following the highway, making sure we stopped off at towns that had good beaches and cheap camping grounds. We planned to be away for months. Sometimes we lingered for weeks at a time at a place with a sparkling beach soaking up the sun. I was on the beach for hours at a time and never had to go near a solarium as I was able to get more than enough natural sun. My skin was a dark brown. I never took precautions as I considered I had made my body immune to damage even if I thought about it, which I probably didn't. I was in love with my boyfriend so I was happy as a lark at this time of my life. Surfing and hanging around the beach, partying at night when we could find a town with some night life. Other nights we just made up our own little party and got drunk and popped some pills to make us even happier than we naturally were. My boyfriend had brought along tons of various types of drugs and so we all indulged as much as we wanted to. Where he got them from I didn't know but he seemed to have an endless supply. So you can see Chloe that my life was one long party which I thought would last for ever.

"But it didn't. One day we were all lying on the beach when my girlfriend noticed I had some moles on my back. They were dark brown, almost black, spots no bigger than a five cent piece. She said they looked dangerous and I should get them checked out by a doctor. I brushed off her concerns by assuring her she was being a bit of a drama queen and as I was barely in my early twenties what had I to worry about. 'It might be cancer,' she said rather seriously. 'How can it be cancer? I'm too young to get cancer,' I told her. 'I think you can get cancer at any age,' she said. Her serious attitude annoyed me because all of us were having a good time and I didn't want anything spoiling our trip. So I shrugged my shoulders but to keep her happy I said I would go to see a doctor though originally I had no intention of doing so."

Dad, I could have taken over her story and recited it myself; it was so obvious what she was going to say. But Clarissa surprised me.

"Just to please my girlfriend however, I called into the next medical clinic we came to; in Broome I think it was. Anyway, I went to see this doctor, a friendly enough sort of guy, younger than I imagined a doctor would be, with a rugged appearance and a neat little beard. He examined me all over pretty thoroughly which I didn't really mind because he turned cuter and cuter by the minute and he had a very gentle touch. He hardly spoke as he went about his business; he was being professional and very thorough. After he finished he had an expression of deep concern on his face. 'I think you may have skin cancer,' he said in a matter of fact manner. No long-winded prologue regarding the theoretical aspects of cancer; no, he just came straight out with it. I was astounded because being so young I had never imagined it could happen to me. 'It can occur at any age,' he said. That may have been the absolute truth but it was no comfort to me at the time. Whether other people also had some form of cancer did not concern me. I was only concerned with myself. I think that was a natural reaction. Don't you think so, Chloe?" she asked.

What could I say? It was very obvious. Of course it is natural to have regard only for yourself in those circumstances. It's human nature. Then a horrible thought crossed my mind. Clarissa had told me that she believed that the doctor she saw was professional and thorough enough to make a correct diagnosis. That of course is how it should be. Dad, by now you will know of the incident that took place not long before I died. We never told you but I am sure Mum would have mentioned it to you by now. I remember that Mum wrote a note which I took to the doctor and showed him. Mum said I was overcome by some sort of turn when I was on the phone and was completely paralysed, frozen to the spot, unable to move or even speak. And yet I now recall that the doctor merely prescribed Voltaren tablets for stress. That's what my doctor said I was suffering from. Stress caused by my exams at uni which were coming up. And yet the gatekeeper told me I had suffered a fit as a result of my having a long-standing brain tumour. It doesn't jell, does it Dad? By now you may have a better answer as to what happened to me, but how can I doubt the gatekeeper? If anyone would know it would be him. He must be, what is it called Dad, omnipotent is it? Or is it omniscient? Sorry Dad, you know I've never been too good at English, and I am certain you of all people will know what I mean, you are so clever, or so you used to tell us! So my heart jumped when Clarissa was telling me this because a doubt suddenly crept into my mind as to whether the doctor I saw made a blunder, a real big one. I shivered internally as I thought that perhaps it was a bungling by the doctor in his diagnosis that caused me to die? Certainly it was too late now. I was dead and nothing was going to change that. I mean, my physical body had passed away but in a twinkling my spirit had come into being which, Dad, you now know is true because you are listening to me and if it wasn't true I wouldn't have been able to speak to you, would I now? I'll get back to Clarissa now.

≈

"It's before the Coroner now," George said.

He hadn't told me that before. George had told me of the autopsy results but he had left it at that. The medical terminology for Chloe's death on her death certificate was 'Pleomorphic Xanthoanstrocytom'. Some very rare brain tumour George had told me. But this was the first time he had mentioned the Coroner being involved.

"Yes, there's going to be an inquest some time soon. I wrote to the Coroner and asked for the matter to be investigated. I had read in a medical text book that a seizure is a symptom of a brain tumour. I had to do something, for Chloe's sake," George said. "The Coroner asked some specialist to investigate and my lawyer told me his opinion was that the note indicated a seizure and that Chloe should have been sent away for a scan to ascertain if she had a tumour."

"And if he decides that, what next?" I asked.

"Well, first of all, the Coroner in the case is a woman. We'll wait and see what the Coroner says before we decide what to do."

"Does this mean you might sue the doctor?" I asked anxiously.

"Maybe," George conceded. "I've been to see a medical negligence lawyer at another firm," he added. "She thinks we have a good case because the psychiatrist I was required to see said I was suffering from a Major Depressive Disorder in partial remission. I told you before I was depressed...and now it's been confirmed."

A silence reigned for a few minutes. I imagined George's mind was at this very moment feverishly ticking away with the various permutations which would arise following the Coroner's decision. I could detect his anxiousness; his wanting this episode in his life to be finally behind him, if that was at all possible. He was a lawyer but he was so personally involved he had to get independent advice. That was natural I thought. How could George act for himself and his family in a case like this? Impossible, I believed. And my belief in George as a man increased when he told us about the psychiatrist's opinion. He didn't have to tell us that. It was his private business but I guessed telling us was some form of release, a cathartic act.

George resumed his reading.

"Yes, I think that is perfectly natural," I said.

"I thought you would agree, Chloe. Well, he said I had to immediately go and see a specialist to get his opinion confirmed as I would have to start treatment as soon as possible or I was a goner. He didn't use those exact words but that was his meaning.

I had no chance of beating this unless I went at it pretty hard. He gave me a referral to a specialist in Perth which as you know is miles away from Broome; in my condition he said I had to go to the best specialist he knew of. So we started driving to Perth. There were four of us and we all took turns. Naturally I considered the trip cancelled and for my sake my friends agreed that we just had to get to that specialist as soon as we could.

"Within a few days or so we had arrived in Perth. The specialist I was referred to had private rooms in St Georges Terrace and as soon as we found a cheap hotel we rang and made an appointment. The doctor had apparently already sent his notes to the specialist so he knew I was coming, and therefore I got in to see him immediately. His diagnosis was very blunt. I had skin cancer on my back and around my neck and spots on my arms and legs. Without any hesitation he told me he had to operate straight away. The specialist told me he had to excise each lesion from the skin. There were a lot and once he confirmed I had melanoma he did larger excisions on each spot. But it was too late for him to stop the spread. I was in hospital for a while as I wasn't able to travel. I let my friends leave because they had no real obligation to stay. I even forced my boyfriend to go home because he had to work and...well, I thought no-one would want a cancer riddled person as a mate. My parents came over as soon as I called them from Perth. We'd had our problems so I hadn't bothered to ring from Broome because I wanted my cancer to be confirmed before I let them know about it. I'm very hazy about what happened next because it is some time ago now. I underwent some more operations to remove cancerous spots as they surfaced and had doses of chemotherapy. That's all I know. You must remember, Chloe, this cancer turned my life upside down and inside out. My mind was somewhere else than where it should have been. I'd given up the drugs because...well,

I had so many legal drugs running around inside of me that I had no stomach or was in any position to do illegal stuff. Naturally, I couldn't work and my boyfriend had disappeared by the time I returned home. I mean, I wasn't a cripple, was I now? And even if I was, if he was a true boyfriend he would have stuck it out a bit more, don't you think?"

I did think so and I told her so. Her boyfriend sounded to me like a bit of a rat but what can one expect from some people? Her speech became somewhat slower at this stage as if she was deliberately skipping over years in her life because it was too painful to speak about. I became confused myself because even though I was a student nurse and understood medical terminology relating to cancer, her story became disjointed and she appeared to be confused as to her treatment. I worked out that she was pronounced terminal a year or so before she actually died but she delved into meditation and changed her diet in an endeavour to rid her body of the cancer that was eating away at her. Medicos might not approve of the self-treatment she gave herself but there are many cases where adopting a different lifestyle has arrested a cancer and even sent a patient into remission which may last for years. Ian Gawler, who lost a leg to cancer, is one person you most likely have heard about, Dad. He got into meditation and completely reformed his diet. So it can happen. I'll let her complete her story now, Dad.

"I started to lead a solitary life. I was too sick to work and I had no desire to force my friends to confront a dying woman. If a friend did happen to come to the house, ever present at the back of my mind was the ugly thought that this friend, who on the surface was quite cheerfully chatting away about the most inane of topics such as the weather, might have actually been wondering when I was going to die, most likely praying that I wouldn't drop dead in front of them. So I never chased after any of my friends.

And even the closest of them finally resorted to ringing me, as if they did not want to see my body, afraid that the cancer might have reduced me to a skeleton. As I explained, I attempted to reduce my anxiety level by practising meditation for hours each day. I did feel more contented and at peace with myself, but I still had negative thoughts that I was merely delaying the inevitable and that I would die an agonising death in the not too distant future. I also read books to gain guidance as to the best methods to adopt to give me some more time. I believe all this turning in on myself definitely helped because for a short period I believed total remission was not far away. But every time I went to see my doctor for an examination and undertook more tests I would be greeted by a shake of the head; there was no discernible improvement. Often it didn't get any worse and, although this was encouraging, it did not approach the goal I had set myself of recovering fully. So, not too long ago I took a sudden turn for the worse and had to be admitted to hospital. Out went the unconventional treatments I had been having and, once again, in marched the regime of western medicine that doctors are familiar with. Chemotherapy doses overpowered me and I was left utterly depleted. As my pain increased the doctors ordered morphine to be administered. It slightly reduced the pain but left me very sleepy. All I wanted to do was close my eyes and drift off to sleep. Eventually, this must have happened because I suddenly found myself here having to rely on the gatekeeper to inform me of the details of my death. Is that what happened to you, Chloe?" she asked me.

"Yes, I dreamed I was moving at rapid speed along a tunnel where everything was white until I came to a white door."

"Yes, that's right," she said excitedly. "That was exactly what I went through."

"Maybe every person goes through that experience," I wondered out loud.

"It certainly seems like it," she answered.

Dad, our conversation then drifted away as it appeared there was nothing either of us had to add. Her smile of goodbye lingered as I continued to sit on the rock, contemplating who next might cross my path.

≈

George's slow closing of his folder announced the conclusion of that episode.

"Poor girl," Debra said.

We nodded our heads in agreement.

"So young, like Chloe," I said. Chloe's story was excruciatingly sad for other than her short interlude when she spoke of Catherine and Stephanie, each episode ended with a death. But how could it be otherwise? She was describing conversations with people who had died.

"Life is so fragile," George cut in, interrupting my private thoughts.

"These women she met, all comparatively young, but..."

"Yes George," I said, "that's the saddest part of all, and yet," I hesitantly added, "this Clarissa contributed to her own death, not caring for herself, unlike Chloe who was completely innocent of blame."

"Isn't it the point, that no-matter how Chloe died, or whose fault it was, or whether it was anybody's fault at all, she is no longer with us," Emily said.

"And she died before me," George said.

I knew this was chewing on his conscience. It is unnatural to have to bury your own child. That's not the accepted order of things.

"This woman, Clarissa, she was seeking popularity and instant approval by craving a tanned look. And look where it got her," I said.

"From what Chloe was saying, she may have had a high degree of confidence which might have made her feel she was immune to the danger of too much sun. The young seem to have this attitude, don't they?" George asked.

"Men might, but it's a rash generalisation to diagnose all women as having this devil-may-care attitude. Chloe was never like that, was she George?" Debra asked.

"No, not in the least. Certainly, her confidence was growing as she matured with age. I understand from Michelle she mixed with the people she worked with and her fellow students at uni, but I would never count her as being reckless in her behaviour."

"You are saying that this Clarissa was reckless?" Emily asked him.

"Well, to a certain extent. Constantly seeking out the sun and heading for a solarium on a cloudy day might be seen to be going a trifle too far. Natural sun is fine but haven't we been warned for many years not to lie around in the heat of the day?"

"Of course George," Debra said, "but many youngsters never heed these warnings. They regard them as an example of adults ruling their lives."

"Yes, I agree with that," George said, nodding his head.

We remained silent, sipping our drinks to camouflage our hesitancy to speak. These sessions with George wore me out due to the intensity of George's reading and our animated discussion afterwards. My thoughts were concentrated on Chloe's words. I never knew what was coming and I therefore couldn't anticipate George's reaction. Some days he did not appear to be affected as much as on others. I asked him once why he put himself through this ordeal, a kind of public reading which would daunt most of us. He was content to bare his daughter's private communication to him, her father, to us. It was cathartic, he said. For when he was listening to Chloe speak to him while he was asleep and when he was transcribing it on his computer he actually believed Chloe was still alive, bound to knock on his front door and appear in front of him in earthly form. He, of course, realised it would never happen but at those times his mind was in a different sphere of existence, somewhere between the earth and the afterlife.

"How many more times will Chloe come back?" I asked George.

He shrugged his shoulders. "I haven't any idea," he said. "I don't expect it will continue for ever though. I expect she will come to some conclusion and tell me why she is visiting me. Unfortunately, there is nothing I can say in return. I just have to wait. But however long it takes I'll do my duty and transcribe her words. It's the least I can do for her."

Solemness shrouded us, as if a cloak had been thrown over the four of us to still any extant ebullience in our mood. As I have indicated, none of our sessions had any tinge of frivolity attached to them.

Debra darted into the kitchen and came back with more food. I grabbed a sandwich to prevent me from speaking in the same way we sometimes reach out for a security blanket when we are hit by some trouble. Emily stroked George's arm. Debra and I exchanged glances without a word.

"Would you like a cup of tea, George?" Debra finally asked.

"Yes thanks."

"I think we all could do with one," Emily said.

I followed Debra into the kitchen to help with the cups and saucers. No words were exchanged; there was no need. We were both aware of George's state of mind.

Often there are times when there is no need to repeat what has been said before.

Chapter Fifteen

Life returned to normal for a few weeks. George seemed to be in court most days; the bank made sure I earned my fulsome salary. I left home before the sun rose; I arrived home late, greeted by streetlights glaring in the black night. Debra maintained the house in her efficient style; our kids even dropped in for a chat once in a while. A few times we were privileged to babysit Andy's daughter. She certainly took after her grandmother: at least that's what Debra said. Andy had named her Chloe. George had smiled like a full moon when I told him.

Our world continued, but Chloe's absence and her presence in the afterlife hung behind all our activities. Her existence, her being, lurked behind the façade we erected to hide our secret from the many people we were required to deal with in our busy lives. The secret remained engrained within our hearts and minds. I hadn't breathed a word to my children nor had George mentioned it to anyone. We felt that it was best to wait for some time before George informed Michelle of Chloe's visits. George certainly had changed for the better I believe since the visits began though he still was liable to fall victim to teary episodes after an appearance by Chloe. Her visits, although welcome, brought back to him the bitterness of her loss.

Of course, the day did come when Chloe came back. Afterwards, I was visibly affected by what she told her father but for now George can take up the story. Chloe returned on a Saturday night and on the Sunday we met at George's for a barbeque lunch. George began to read.

≈

I was lost deep in thought when I heard a familiar voice and I realised the gatekeeper was standing before me. I was a little spooked when he suddenly appeared because he seemed to have materialised out of nowhere. Then I recollected where I was, and who he was. I told myself not to be silly.

"Hello, Chloe," he said in the sweetest of voices one could imagine.

"Hello," I stammered, unsure of what else I should say at this juncture, apprehensive that my time had come to speak to God. And Dad, what else could I be but petrified, for my long-term future depended on this interview I was about to undertake. The gatekeeper had no need to remind me; I instantly recalled our conversation as soon as he appeared before me. He had told me he was going to see God. Now he had returned.

"Are you ready?" he asked, holding out his hand towards me, as if he wanted to guide me somewhere.

"Yes, I suppose there is no time like the present," I got out which I now realise was a trifle foolish because I had already come to the conclusion that here time is of no special consequence. Time was the past, present and future all neatly bound up together. I'd had lengthy conversations with James, Jessie, Craig, April and Clarissa as well as the gatekeeper and yet it seemed that they were over in the twinkling of an eye whereas on earth if I conversed with so many people consecutively, exhaustion would have overtaken me by the end. Here I felt as if I had not expended any energy at all and was still feeling as fresh as I was when the door had been opened.

"Then follow me," he said.

I immediately noticed that for some reason I once again could not see very far into the distance. When I was wandering around on my own and in the midst of my conversations, I could see way off to the far horizon. Not so now. I knew the gatekeeper had some power to do these sorts of things to my sight so I was not afraid, more curious I suppose. I stayed close behind him as I did not want to get lost. As I followed him my mind was racing, thinking about God. What was I going to say to Him? How was I to address Him? Just call him God? Perhaps the gatekeeper would tell me.

Suddenly, catching me completely by surprise I could fathom out that a path, about the size of a footpath on earth in width, lay before me.

"Chloe," the gatekeeper said, coming to a halt. Suddenly, I was able to see further along the length of the path into the distance. "Please go ahead. Do not be afraid. You are in safe hands. Keep to the path and soon you will be met by someone who will lead you to God." Before I had an opportunity to ask a question he had disappeared from sight, as mysteriously as he had appeared. I was alone. I looked ahead of me and, tentatively, took my first steps forward towards my goal.

I continued along the path, slowly, as if I was a snail. I must admit that I was beginning to feel extremely nervous, even a little scared. The path seemed to narrow or perhaps it was my eyesight narrowing again. The path meandered in one direction and then another, like a path that wound its way through a dense forest. I thought it strange that here, a path would need to wind around so much. It was not as if we were on earth and the path had been made by workers hacking away with machetes in a forest and over the years a track had been worn by the constant tramp of feet. Here there were no imprints at all. When I looked down I expected to see some evidence that other people had previously walked along this path; people who had died before me and had passed this way on their journey to meet God. Then I thought that perhaps every person had their own path allocated to them. I mean, Dad, if there was a God, and there was such a place as the afterlife, then of course it stood to reason that anything could be arranged. God had only to wish it and, bingo, there it was. If He wanted every individual to walk along their own path then he would merely have to click His fingers, so to speak, and it would come to pass. My mind was wandering Dad, for nothing else but these kinds of strange thoughts entered my mind.

Suddenly, I heard a noise like thunder from a coming storm. I heard my name being called; it seemed to be echoing around me. Once again a fear, a severe paralysing fear took hold of me. I stopped dead in my tracks, afraid to move. I wanted to avoid the risk of missing hearing or seeing something.

"Chloe, can you hear me," this voice boomed out of nowhere. It seemed to surround me, as if I was in a cinema and loud speakers in every corner were blasting away.

"Yes, I am Chloe," I answered, literally trembling, afraid to speak too loudly in case that was not the correct procedure. "Who are you?" I added apprehensively, for I believed this was God speaking to me.

"I am the Spirit," the voice said, this time at a more understandable level.

"Oh," I answered with a jerk in my voice. "I thought you were God," I quickly put to him.

"That's understandable, but I am not God."

"What happens now?" I asked.

"I will escort you a little further on along this path."

"To God?" I asked.

"Yes, I am to escort you to the place where you meet up with God."

"Could you please answer me one question?" I asked.

"Certainly Chloe, what is your question?"

"Does everyone come along this path from the Waiting Room to meet God?"

"Yes, they do, Chloe. Every person must come along this very path to be judged by God."

"But I have not seen anyone else along the path; nor have I seen any evidence that this path has been used by the millions and millions of other people who have died before me. Why is this?"

"This is a mystery known only to God. Your eyes are in a special state. Therefore, you cannot see the people ahead of you on the path, and you cannot see the many people stretched out behind you who have entered the path after you. Time, and distance, is of no consequence here as you may have gathered by now and so you have no real idea how long, by earth time, you have been in the Waiting Room, speaking with other people or indeed how long you have been coming along this path. The gatekeeper escorted you to the path and you commenced walking along, thinking your own private thoughts, wondering what was going to happen to you. By your earthly concept of time you might believe that this has only taken a very short while but it may be that it has really been an aeon of earth time."

Dad, I had indeed lost track of time so what the Spirit said to me made sense. Indeed, it made more sense when I realised that I had not been hungry or thirsty from the moment I had emerged through the white door and found the gatekeeper standing there. Clearly, this was a different world, a spirit world, and what I knew and believed on earth was vastly different here. Then I asked myself – who was the gatekeeper that had greeted me? Surely not some common helper, some angel taking his turn opening the door to greet the dead as they arrived?

"Who is the gatekeeper?" I suddenly addressed this Spirit, attempting to peer into the nothingness that surrounded me. Just silence; a black hole silence I had never before experienced. I hoped that I hadn't made a fool of myself by asking some terribly dumb question. I waited for an answer; for I knew there would be one eventually.

"Sorry, Chloe," the voice boomed again. "I was under the impression you may have guessed by now."

"Well, he told me he was the gatekeeper and so I assumed that was the name he had been given and thought no more about it until this very moment."

"That's a very sensible answer, Chloe."

"Sorry, no, I didn't even hazard a guess."

"Well, then, I'll tell you."

Another lengthy silence ensured I was fully concentrating on his answer.

"The gatekeeper is just like me, a helper; one of many helpers, a servant of God."

"A helper? A servant you say?"

"Yes, that is right, Chloe. The gatekeeper is a helper. You have met the gatekeeper, and now you have come into contact with me. All that remains is to come face to face with God and your journey will be complete. Let us continue your journey along the path. Follow my voice and keep to the path and we will shortly arrive at our destination."

My eyesight had improved a little more and I could make out more clearly the direction of the path. The Spirit now and again spoke to me as I walked my way along the winding path, ensuring I kept going in the right direction. All this time I had not caught sight of him and I soon realised why. He was the Spirit and as spirits have no bodily form they cannot be seen. And even though I was now in the spirit world and had no bodily form myself, I realised that some spirits take on even a greater spirit form than us 'normal' spirits, if that makes any sense, Dad.

Suddenly, a white wall appeared in front of me, blocking the path. Approaching, through a sort of thick haze that clung to the borders of the path I saw the outline of what looked like a door. I had a sudden sensation; even though I had no physical body, a shiver ran up and down my back; I felt alone. I was alone, for when I asked the Spirit if he was still there, in the void, my question was met by a deathly silence. I put two and two together and concluded that this door led to God; God was waiting for me behind that door. Déjà vu; behind the other white door that confronted me was the gatekeeper. Now, another white door blocked my path. And I knew who was waiting for me on the other side of the door. All I had to do was open it and God would be there. I shivered with anticipation, but for a time, I don't know how long, I was stuck where I stood. I could not move. What I was about to see had bound me up; it was as if I was frozen solid, unable to command myself to move. Somehow I did eventually get my act together and went up and touched the door, for unlike the other door, there was no knob or handle. It slid open as soon as I had touched it; I slowly passed through. I could see nothing. The white mist had closed in and seemed to be clinging to me. There was no path winding its way into the distance. Shortly, a huge wall of noise shook me. It seemed to surround me. The blackness that surrounded me began to fade as the sound reached its crescendo. Above me, I made out a figure seated as if on a high platform or like a judge in a courtroom, holding out his arms as if it was a sign of welcoming, like the many images I had seen on the stained-glass windows in church. I didn't have to ask who this person was. It was God.

Dad, how can I describe God's appearance to you? Words that I use cannot accurately depict the scene that was before me. In general terms, he looked exactly like the gatekeeper. However, God took on a wiser, more mature appearance. I could tell this from my first glance. Certainly I understood the presence of a knowing countenance; one that easily demonstrated perfect knowledge and wisdom. So who else could this figure be, but God?

"Come closer my child," God said to me. I moved a step forward but I couldn't open my mouth to respond. I could merely stare with reverence, wonder and perhaps bewilderment that, even though I knew where I was and that I had encountered the gatekeeper, the Spirit and now, it seemed, God, it was all too incomprehensible for me to fully understand. During my life on earth, religious people had talked about getting to Heaven and being with God for ever more; now that I was on the verge of gaining entry to the afterlife, it was still a shock. It was like when you have to stop and pinch yourself to believe a story which sounds as if it has come out of left-field. I could not believe this was happening. Was I still in the middle of a long dream or was I, as the gatekeeper had reassured me I was, dead, in the spirit world?

I took another pace forward and began my conversation with God.

"You met the gatekeeper," God commenced.

"Yes, I did. He introduced himself to me as the gatekeeper."

"Yes, that's correct. My gatekeeper has reported your conversation to me so it will not be necessary to fully traverse the same ground. As you realise, it is now my task to decide whether you should be admitted to Heaven."

"Yes, I understand. But may I ask one question?"

"Certainly, my child, you may ask any question."

"I just would like to know...what I should call you... I mean, when we are speaking to each other. Talking with other people I meet here is easy...perhaps I can refer to you as God because... well, you are God."

"Well Chloe, my Christian children always refer to me as God in spoken and written form so you may call me God. Other religions do not use the word 'God' directly. For example, my Muslim children call me Allah as do Arab Christians, but they are in reality referring to me."

Dad, all this time I was speaking with God I could not see what was behind Him. I presumed it was Heaven, but I could not be certain. I asked God where Heaven was.

"A reasonable question," God answered. "Of course you cannot see it at the present because you have not as yet been admitted and it is not considered proper for you to see the place until you are permitted to."

At this point I froze because God's answer could have been an indication that I mightn't be admitted. I became worried and apprehensive as to my future. It was sounding bleak.

"That doesn't sound very optimistic," I ventured.

"Not at all my child," God responded. "It was merely a statement of fact. There is no need to read anything bad into it, but I can assure you that there is a place close by that some of the religions on earth call Heaven."

To me, that could have meant anything at all. Close by here might not mean the same as on earth. Then I recalled where I was because it was so easy to forget; many things here had their comparisons on earth. Spirit form vaguely resembled human form and my conversations with the people I had met took the same form as on earth, except we were all dead, of course, and it was our own individual spirits that were speaking to each other.

The decision of whether or not to admit me was that of

God alone. I wondered whether I had led a good life, sufficient to warrant a passage straight into the afterlife. My inferiority complex may have been at work in the spirit world as it invariably was on earth. That was me, wasn't it Dad? Always putting others ahead of me, whether they truly deserved it or not. Then I thought: what is a good life? How is it calculated? The number of good deeds performed throughout a lifetime? Was it a question of quantity or quality? A short life like mine surely meant that the number of good deeds would not have been as many as in a regular biblical life of three score and ten. I believed there was some degree of quality attached to my good deeds which surely must have counted in my favour. There was my care of animals both at home and also at the Lort Smith Animal Hospital. Surely this was deserving of some merit. What about the absence of evil thoughts towards other people? Like you, Dad, I too always gave people the benefit of the doubt and regarded every person favourably until some incident forced me to change my mind. On balance, I might have scored well on this point. My self-deprecation could have lead to my periods of depression and general loneliness that from time to time racked me. Dad, you might believe I am exaggerating here, but I'm not. Remember the time I rang you and you asked how I was, and I told you I was lonely? I am sorry; I am starting to forget what I told you earlier. And Dad, I am speaking to you a long time after the events actually took place so please forgive me if I repeat myself.

"Chloe, do you recall the Ten Commandments that were handed down to my servant Moses?"

"Yes, I believe I do," I answered fairly honestly because as you know Dad, I was brought up a Catholic though I must confess to you Dad, I don't know whether I, or anybody else for that matter, are able to swear on the Bible that they have never broken a single Commandment.

"Do you believe you have always adhered to every one of my Commandments?" God asked.

This confused me. I had never been married but…you know I had a boyfriend not too long ago, Dad …and as you know I had… stayed at his place a few times. So what was I to answer? I knew I had to be honest; I really did, for once again I had to remind myself where I was and who was I speaking with. Of course, God would know if I wasn't telling the truth. This was a test, much like in the Bible where Jesus was tempted by the Devil to jump off the mountain and float safely to earth, merely to prove his power. Is that right, Dad? Was that one of the temptations of Jesus? I'm sure you know, Dad. It's the sort of question that you would know the answer to, perhaps one of those Trivial Pursuit types of questions.

≈

George broke off his reading.

"At this point I had to remind myself that what I was experiencing was…so unnatural, that to be perfectly frank, I suppose it is easy to find it impossible to believe. That is why I have told no one except you," George said, looking at each of us in turn. "Chloe was putting all these questions to me…and I had no idea of how I could possibly answer them."

"Perhaps she doesn't want an answer from you, but is merely posing these questions in an endeavour to force you to think about certain matters," I said, for to me, as Chloe herself kept on expressing, the whole situation was virtually incomprehensible. Disbelief just had to be suspended, and I was doing so, at least until the conclusion of Chloe's visits which I hoped were now not too far away. And yet I did believe…

"That is why I am telling you these things, Chas. I knew you would understand."

"I don't know whether you can say I understand," I said, stopping short from giving a longer answer because, to be truthful, I did not know what else I could say.

George smiled, wiped his brow with his handkerchief, and steadied himself before he continued.

≈

"All except one," I answered, afraid to hear God's reaction.

"And which one would that be, my child?" God asked with a smile.

"I suppose you already know," I answered; I was afraid of saying out loud what I hoped was concealed in my mind.

"Yes, we do know Chloe. It's about your boyfriend. Did not my gatekeeper tell you that God was all knowing?"

"Yes, he did."

"Then there is nothing more to say on that point, is there? Some of my children have a very bad attitude with respect to this. I am displeased greatly. However, one day in the future these children of mine will act with more knowledge and understanding."

I bowed my head to concede the point. I did not know exactly what he was referring to when he spoke of some of his children. Perhaps it was the custom some countries had of stoning women to death for adultery He was referring to, but I had no desire to labour the point.

"I see that you appreciate that you have done wrong, but you are forgiven, my child. Of much more importance is that on earth you did not commit murder, you did not steal, you never gave false evidence, you loved your mother and father, and you loved your neighbour as much as you loved yourself, perhaps even more, as your nursing of both animals and humans amply demonstrates."

I felt relieved on hearing these words. It was as if my deeds were being applauded, but I never felt I was doing anything special when I had animals or humans under my care. To me, that was a natural thing to do, as necessary as breathing or eating and drinking.

"So you see Chloe, you have generally adhered to the law set out in the Commandments. Are there any others that you feel you may not have fully complied with, not deliberately, but by omission?"

I remained silent for a moment, attempting to gather together a suitable answer.

"Which Commandment would you be thinking of?" I ventured.

"When he was on earth my Son said that the first and greatest commandment was to 'Love the Lord your God with all your heart and with all your soul and with all your mind.'"

I swallowed because I knew what God was getting at. Dad, I was never the greatest churchgoer, was I? I accompanied Mum when she insisted on it, like at Easter or to midnight mass at Christmas. But Dad, did you set a good example? I don't want to criticise you or Mum, but as neither of you went regularly I didn't believe it was expected that I should frequent Church more than you or Mum. I felt as if I was in a bit of a bind because God had me pinned on this one.

"I'm sorry," I said. "Of course I believed, but perhaps I was too concerned with living from day to day, helping my sick animals or patients, to bother too much about...Anyway, I would like to stress that I believed that if I helped a sick animal or patient in a hospital, that counted as a demonstration of love of mankind, and love of you, as much as merely rolling up to church."

"My child, you have spoken well. Good deeds certainly show

a humanitarian aspect, demonstrated by many stories in the religious writings of which you are aware."

"Do you mean the story of the Good Samaritan?" I asked.

"Yes, that is a well known story," God replied. "Yet it is only one of many, is it not?"

Here I was a bit stuck, Dad. I had heard of the deeds of Jesus, but I could not recall any others at the moment, and of course I knew nothing about the good deeds of Mohammad or leaders of other religions. I had a vague notion that Jesus used parables to illustrate a theme or viewpoint and, here I was, speaking with God, and I did not realise that He would concentrate so much on various stories from ancient times. I imagined this conversation with God would be about me, my own acts and deeds on earth. I had no idea that I would be quizzed on parts of the Bible. I needed to turn the conversation around and talk about myself and my hoped for entry into the afterlife. Of course, now I was here, now that I knew that what humanity had been told for two thousand years was in fact correct: there was a God and there was a place called Heaven, I was determined to be admitted. Otherwise, everything I had done on earth would have gone to waste. I did not want to be sent away from the Waiting Room for a long spell in another place. But God's words had soothed my concerns to some extent and He appeared to be on my side; the only question being my love of Him and my demonstration of that love.

"Yes, there are many stories in the Bible that the priests told us about in church as well as my religious teachers at school," I said, hoping this generalised statement would satisfy Him.

There was a silence. I expected God to answer but He didn't.

Finally, I broke the silence by asking whether He wanted me to talk about myself, and tell him things that were important for His assessment of me.

"There is no need for that my child. I already am aware of your conduct on earth. Let us talk of other, more worldly matters. I find such a discussion can be fruitful."

I didn't understand what He meant but I didn't want to appear to give that impression so instead of asking for an explanation I remained silent for a moment.

"I suggest you ask me various questions and I will give you the answers. I am aware that on earth many people question my very existence, demanding proof in the form of demonstrations of my power. Isn't it said that 'seeing is believing'? But I believe I have already done that. I sent my Son to spread my Word. Over the years some people have chosen to believe, others have rejected me outright because, in their eyes, they see no evidence of my existence. They discount the clear evidence I gave them as sufficient proof. I sent my Son to save them; to give them the opportunity to become believers in me. The believers will be saved; the others may not. So, my child, ask of me what you will for I am ready to frankly answer any query you may have."

"One question that is asked on earth," I said, "is, if there is a God, why does He not intervene in world affairs to stop various evil situations, such as war, and genocide carried out within nations. Or do something to prevent poverty and diseases in the poor countries that kill people, especially young children?"

I asked this, Dad, knowing full well that I had discussed this with the gatekeeper, but I wanted to hear God's answer.

"We know of this eternal lament; other people before you have asked the very same question. I understand my gatekeeper may have had this conversation with you upon your arrival here. Let me try and answer this question, because I concede it is a vexing one.

"Man inhabits the earth but for a short time. He is given the opportunity to act in accordance with his own desire, his own inclination. Life is a choice fundamentally between good and evil, though many people do not look at it in such a stark delineation; they perceive of life as containing various shades of black and white, more of a grey hue, of good and bad. As I previously indicated, I sent my Son to spread the Word, to announce to people by His preaching of the existence of this place where people who carry out their duties as servants of God, and who perform good deeds, have the prospect of achieving everlasting life. The problem for my children is that leading a life that will warrant entry into Heaven is not easy. One has to make choices and unfortunately many people find it too difficult to make the correct one. They are tempted away from a good life by the temporary attainment of some material satisfaction which eventually will be gone with the wind. Such a life is illusory. It is short term gratification, but at what cost? It is no panacea for the problems that living brings, whether it is within the family, at school or at work with colleagues. Man has been taught which way is the correct way. It is up to each individual person to decide what road they wish to walk along. And, when they die, they come here to be judged. Man is an individual; he has a brain for thinking, and the ability to analyse situations and then decide what course to adopt. What would then be the purpose of life, if I was to constantly interfere with life on earth? There would be none. It is like a test, an examination if you like, of every person. They must make the decision. They have a soul; they have a capacity to work out what course to pursue. And now you know that is true because you are here, with me, in your spirit form. Your body is no more. Your mortal remains are gone."

"Only if I am admitted to...," I interrupted quickly.

God gave off a smile.

"Yes, my child; you are perfectly correct. That is my decision of course."

"I have always had doubts about myself," I said. "I turned inward in the belief that I was inadequate and that other people were more deserving of reward than me. Other people seemed so alert to the world; so street wise I thought I had no chance of competing with them. Is that a fault in my character?" I tentatively asked.

"Some people do have a propensity to turn inward, but many others direct their thoughts outwards, towards self-interest rather than towards the welfare of those less fortunate than themselves. They are concerned with what can be obtained for their own benefit, what they can achieve for themselves, and neglect or disregard those people who would be able to achieve something worthwhile if they received a helping hand. But my child, I can certainly say that, in this regard, there is no fault in your character. Your activities during your life openly demonstrated your concern for others. You at first were lost. But you changed; you found yourself. Some people may say you matured. This is true. You were growing older and your experience of life gave you more confidence. Yet, I say that your decision to work with animals and study to get a diploma to enable you to do so, showed us here that you had decided to think of those creatures unable to help themselves, poor, sick and abandoned animals. Your devotion was well known, hence the large attendance at your funeral of your friends from the Lort Smith Animal Hospital."

Dad, is this true? Here I had no awareness of time, and yet God led me to understand that my funeral had already been held. Oh, how I wish I could have been able to say goodbye to everybody, but I didn't have this opportunity. The moment we die we are cut off from the living. Our body remains to be disposed of while our spirit finds its way here. I was stunned by God's reference to my funeral, for it once again reminded me that I had died, and was cut off from you and Mum and all my family and friends. I felt a deep sadness overtake me and my mind wandered over what had happened to me. How long I did this for I am unaware. All I know is that when I looked up I found God waiting for me to return from my reflections and resume our conversation.

≈

"Most of the people at the funeral I did not know," George said. "People from the Animal Hospital, her lecturers and fellow students from the University; people who loved Chloe as a friend, as a colleague; all came along to farewell her."

His voice died out. He excused himself and hurried out of the room. Oh, what anguish George must have been feeling! If I had been in his shoes what would I have felt; how would I have acted? He was incredibly strong to hold so much pain inside but I knew that every now and then it had to break out; it just had to or the man would surely have gone totally insane. We waited patiently for his return and his story to continue.

Eventually he returned and began reading again.

≈

"And your decision to become a human nurse was a gigantic step, my child. It showed you loved people because you wanted to help those who could not help themselves; those who are dependent on others every minute of the day; those who require constant attention to stay alive. You will have read that love of people is akin to a love of God; and so it is. On earth my Son showed people that helping those less fortunate, and people who are of a different gender, race, colour or religion gives me the most pleasure. Those people not only show their humanitarian side but demonstrate their love of God, even if it is done vicariously, as it is done in my name. It is therefore to your credit that you undertook studies to become a nurse."

"If that is so; if it is considered such a good thing for me to do, why did I have to die, when I was on the verge of commencing work as a nurse?" I asked. Dad, I was puzzled by this. If people such as doctors, nurses and all those wonderful people working overseas in projects that assist those poverty stricken people in Africa and elsewhere are undertaking good acts, why do some have to die before they should? Now I was here I had automatically turned my mind in that direction as I know many people on earth have put forward the very same question to religious leaders. I was at least fortunate to the extent that I could ask a direct question on this very point.

"My child, this question is linked to the previous point we were discussing; why don't I interfere and stop illness and disease and conflict between nations? Mankind was told they were formed in my image as you now can see. The human race consists of generation upon generation of all descriptions, of different colours and varying cultures and languages. The human race has branched out widely, in many separate directions from the time when everyone's ancestors first inhabited the earth. Man was formed and its existence has continued exclusively by the union of a man and a woman. In doing so it is not possible over a lengthy period of time to ensure that in every case each piece of the animal specimen called Man is formed perfectly, without error or fault. If it was, no one would die.

"The creation of my children, over time, through the generations means that from time to time various things go wrong. As a student nurse you will have realised that the human body is a complex organism and is made up of many linked parts. I created Mankind but I did so as I said, not on the basis of physical perfection, without fault, but with inbuilt deficiencies if you like that come out from time to time in certain individuals. In your case, my child, you developed a brain tumour that lay undetected. You had a history of migraine headaches, yet no one thought of giving you a head scan. I ask: why not? Symptoms showed themselves over many years and the seizure you had a week before your death should have triggered your doctor's mind, based on his training, to send you off for a scan. If he had, you might have been saved. You see, life puts humans to the test. Every single day all of my children are put in a position where they have to make decisions. Not just life and death decisions as in your case, but common place ones that make each person decide whether to undertake an act of kindness or one that I consider unkind or bad; an act of evil you might say. I am sorry that you feel aggrieved by your death; it is certainly a shock to almost everyone who comes here. All deaths are a combination of factors. The personal conduct of the deceased may be the sole contributing factor. Deliberate intervention by another may contribute as does an omission to undertake an act that could save someone. Yours is of the latter kind. Your medical history clearly is of such a nature that it is clear you died by omission."

"I had no idea of this," I said.

"That's true, my child. You had concerns, and that is why your Mother urged you to make an appointment to see your regular doctor, an appointment you unfortunately could not keep."

"Yes, I recall I was to see her on a Monday; but when did I die?" I asked, unaware of the day.

"It was the previous Friday morning, my child."

I hung my head. Dad, I knew nothing of this as I told you. I also realise that eventually you became fully apprised of the circumstances surrounding my death. I do not know how much earth time has passed since my bodily death. It could be one week though that is unlikely as I was told my funeral had taken place; it might be one month or one year for all I know. But what I do know is that you are still living on earth and able to listen to my speaking to you in your sleep. And Dad, don't ask me how a spirit can speak to you in the middle of the night. The fact that I am here is a miracle in itself, isn't it? As the spirit world exists, my being able to speak to you doesn't seem so hard, does it? At least I am happy that you and Mum found out what happened. God only told me I had a rare brain tumour. Resignation settled itself upon me; I was dead, and that was that.

≈

"Poor Chloe," George whispered.

I felt myself swallow. I too whispered "Poor Chloe" but more to myself.

"She never knew what happened to her, did she?" George asked me, as if I was some one who knew the answer to every imponderable question.

"It doesn't appear so, George," I answered softly. Frankly, I was stumped as to what I could say in these circumstances. How does one answer these types of questions, ones that fly straight to the meaning of life itself? How could I, or anyone for that matter, console someone like George who had experienced a loss of a magnitude that cannot be calculated? I couldn't bring myself to try. For me, it was sufficient that he respected me and Debra as friends and allowed us to hear his daughter's story of her death and journey to the afterlife; and yet, the story was more than that. I came to see it as a record of her life and all its triumphs and disasters. And her conversations with the people she met; it showed me, and I think it demonstrated to George that many stories make up the human experience; each of us has our own tale to tell. I am certain that Chloe also spoke to people of other cultures and gained knowledge of how they lived. Further, I believe this to be what life is about – to get through it as best one can knowing that yes, on some days you might act amiss of the mark but on others you could do things and say things that would bring joy and happiness to another human being. That was the purpose and meaning of life.

I explained my theory to George. He listened intently. "I think you may just be right, Chas," he said with a slight smile on his face, for he understood now that I too had come to believe, as he had. That was his original purpose in coming to see me: to see if I too could believe. His ordeal appeared to be approaching the finish so I asked him to keep going. He breathed out a heavy sigh and like a marathon runner plodding on to the finish he took up reading once again.

≈

I was determined to continue the conversation so I asked God whose fault it was that some people looked exclusively after their own interests while others' turned their heads in the direction of service of the unfortunates of the world.

"It is Man's fault, my child. As I have said many times, and it has been repeated in the teachings of religious people, a person's journey through life can be compared to a man walking along a road. He comes to a fork. There are two roads he can continue his journey along; one is the bad way, a life of desolation and destruction of self; the other is the good way, my way; the road to the afterlife. Each individual is given the ability to choose which road he or she wishes to travel along. The Christian teachings are well known; they were set out two thousand earth years ago and every person is aware of those teachings. Other religious teachers and other religions have also said the same thing as well, though often in a different form. It is also known that to disregard these teachings is done so at your own peril for that is part of the teachings. As was set forth in the teachings, the road to the afterlife is exclusively reserved for those who are pure of heart, pure in thought and pure in action."

"So why do people reject the good road?" I asked. "Are they lazy?"

God gave me a long look as if He was searching for the right explanation.

"You could say some people are lazy, my child. On earth some people say that life was not meant to be easy, while others attempt to live the easy life because to adopt the right way of living, to reject evil and embrace goodness, requires a great deal of hard work. But when a person has seen the light, has fully transformed their life by accepting the good life then, to such a person, life is in fact very easy. It requires a great deal of work and as with physical endeavour there are many benefits to be obtained. What is more beneficial, more beautiful my child, than everlasting life? When seen in this context, why wouldn't a person choose the right way to live, the correct way to interact with their fellow man?"

"Isn't it a question of faith?" I asked. "People may want to live the good life, but many cannot see why they should. In their minds, there is no proof of your existence, so they cannot believe; they have no faith and belief that there is a life after death."

"I agree; some people have so little faith. I ask you my child, doesn't the mere existence of the world and all the other worlds that Man has discovered and all that is in it point to some plan, some design that demonstrates there is a meaning behind it? Or do people imagine life on earth came about as a result of some accident? Just to gaze into the heavens should fill the hearts and minds of all people with awe and amazement. The stars sprinkled about the night sky, beaming their light from far away, a mass of light flooding back to bathe the earth; isn't this a miracle?

Poets know it; they sense the majesty glowing above them. The presence of untold beauty presented every night surely must move my people; they are not built of stone. I have created my people with imagination, with the ability to think, to analyse and yet, there are those among my people who question the existence of this place because of lack of what: scientific evidence? And yet it was I who created the physical world as well as the heavens. Isn't this sufficient evidence, adequate proof of the existence of a parallel world, one that exists in the spirit form? If a world of earth and grass and forests and desert plains and rivers and seas and mountains can be created by me, I ask you one simple question, my child: then surely I can create a spirit world where my people, who have believed in their Creator, can live for evermore? All that is required is faith. This is why I sent my Son to earth: to give the varying races and peoples of the world the opportunity to obtain knowledge of me and have faith to allow them to enter the kingdom of Heaven. And other religions too especially among our Muslim, Buddhist and Hindu friends have seen my light shine on them. Because of their different cultures established over time they have practices of love of me that Christians regard as wrong. But to me they are not wrong for they believe in me and their journey after death to the afterlife to be with me. Whether it is called Paradise or Heaven or simply the afterlife is not important; it is the same place, here with me and other people who lived a good life."

"I know what you say is perfectly correct. Yet for all the writings in the Bible, some people say that all this, I mean Jesus on earth, occurred so long ago that no real, positive evidence exists today that Jesus was indeed your Son. I understand that many scholars say there is probably enough evidence that a person called Jesus actually walked on earth, but still, some cannot draw the conclusion that this evidence proves that Jesus was the Son of God. I know you said that only faith is required, but today people are not as ignorant as those who lived two thousand years ago. There is greater knowledge of a scientific nature and, to be honest, many people are just plain sceptical. They cannot believe in something that they say cannot be proved."

"Yes my child, there are non-believers because they are sceptics; they have no faith. But examine these lives. They have no faith in my existence, in my Son and in this place. Their belief is that life is extinguished immediately they die. Their body is buried and that is the end of them. On the other hand, in their own lives, they do have some faith. They have faith in their own ability to undertake myriad tasks they may set themselves. Those that consider themselves having an intellectual bent have faith they can obtain high academic qualifications; those of a sporting nature have faith in themselves to believe they can achieve the highest possible position obtainable in their chosen endeavour; those that want to climb the highest mountains do so through their faith in their ability to overcome pain and great physical barriers. Why is that degree of faith accepted, and yet there is no belief that my world here does exist? Faith in physical ability leads to rewards of a material nature. A sporting event is won; academic qualifications are awarded; the English Channel is swum; a high mountain peak is scaled; leadership of a nation is bestowed. People who achieve such goals had faith, a belief in their own self bordering on fanaticism, and they were ultimately awarded by victory. So, my child, cannot the same be said of those of religious faith? They too will find their reward. But no reward will be found on earth, my child. No, it will be found here, with me and all the believers in me; with those who have the faith, utter belief and conviction."

"I accept all that. All I am attempting to say is that many

people on earth require physical evidence before they will believe anything. They need to see it with their own eyes."

Dad, God became silent and I waited patiently for the conversation to resume as I had an eerie feeling that my future was now to be revealed to me. A sense of gloom settled over me. My short life had now been reduced to a waiting period of silence. I couldn't hear a sound. I imagine outer space was like the deathly silence that entombed me at this moment. I could have been in outer space for all I knew. I had been lead to the very door of the afterlife but still I had no concept of where I was in comparison to the earth, though I believed I saw our sun and earth after I arrived. But where was I compared to them? Tales of Heaven being 'up there' flooded my mind. Perhaps my mind was being tricked into accepting a situation which was not real. I had no idea. I just waited. Then God broke the silence.

"My child, do you have anything further to add before judgement is passed on you?"

Dad, I almost let out a blood curdling scream of terror. Never in my whole life had I ever felt the horror I felt at this very moment. It is difficult to explain to you because I am certain no human on earth could ever have had that sensation of incredible horror and abject fear coursing through their veins that I was now experiencing. A description such as a panic attack to describe this spasm, this fit of terror, would go nowhere near accurately describing it. That is the nearest I can come. Struck down as if I was deaf and dumb, which I suppose in my case could not be considered inappropriate; I attempted to say something, anything.

"I find it difficult to find the words," I finally began, stumbling over each word as if the very power of speech had been but newly acquired.

"I never have been one to push my own barrow as it is said

on earth. I have been very shy in bragging about anything I have ever been involved with. Some things I undertook, such as my schooling, I am embarrassed to say, I did not perform as well as I could have. Other pursuits, such as my ballet and piano, I believe I did fairly well. Altogether, I was pleased with my development of these skills. My career, after somewhat of a wonky start, was coming on well...until I died. But, in the end, all I can say is that I did my best in all aspects of my life. I know I was not perfect, and whether I fulfil the criteria required to enter Heaven is not my decision. I can only present myself here as I am doing at this moment and wait for your verdict. I do know that I cared about my animals and the people I nursed in the hospitals when I undertook the clinical part of my studies. To me, tendering sick and helpless animals and people was not merely a job I had to do because I had no other. No, it would be completely wrong to say that. I sincerely believed that I was meant to undertake these tasks. Now that I am here I can see that perhaps you wanted me to do these tasks for you and that in helping as I did I was helping you. I admit my church-going was probably not as consistent as it might, but...I guess that is how life panned out for me. Basically, all I can say is that I did my best. I leave it in your hands."

Perhaps a more skilful speaker could have droned on for much longer giving extensive examples of all the good acts they had undertaken, but you know me Dad; never much of a talker. And what more could I do other than to briefly summarise my good deeds? God was all-knowing so He knew more about my own deeds than I probably did myself. If that was the case, what was the use of attempting to hoodwink God into believing that I was a better person than I really was? No amount of grandstanding on my part could camouflage any part of my history whether such a part was good or bad. I recognised that I had to accept God's opinion of me, whatever it turned out to be. There was no point in arguing with His decision, whatever it was. I steadied myself and looked proudly and with a degree of boldness perhaps in God's direction and waited for the verdict, as if I was a prisoner in the dock waiting, trembling inside, for the head juror to read out the jury's verdict.

Suddenly, the silence evaporated away. I heard a noise, like the faint sound coming from an orchestra as it begins to warm up its instruments. It began very softly but loud enough to be distinguished from the deathly silence that had surrounded me. The sound grew louder, like singing, perhaps from a choir in the background somewhere. I could not pick out any actual singing; it was more like a humming sound, like back up singers perhaps, you know Dad, a group or individuals singing harmony or maybe even Buddhist monks chanting. All of a sudden, the sound from this choir grew in intensity, until it burst in an extended crescendo; it continued for what seemed like ages. I just stood there, unable to move; overwhelmed by the beautiful noise, for it was a sound of pure beauty, more magnificent than a choir singing Mozart on earth; it was truly a heavenly choir. Yet I could see nobody. God was standing there with his arms extended in a welcoming gesture. To me, that signified nothing much as He had adopted that pose quite often when He was speaking to me, to emphasise a point He was making. Without warning or indication, the noise stopped. Once again there was silence. God walked towards me. He came so close to me I was able to more clearly see His features. An outlook of contentment and happiness emanated from His face which, in every pore, was full of love and peace and understanding. He stretched out His hand and placed it on my head. I felt this sensation of a surge running through my body. It is impossible to describe to you Dad, it really is, but my spirit body seemed to fill to the brim with some substance that cleansed me from the inside, as if it was removing from me all my false human thoughts and filling me with pure thoughts of love and contentment. Immediately, I felt I was in a place and in a state of unbounded joy that no state of happiness on earth could be compared. I felt totally cleansed; I felt like a different person. Then God spoke.

"My child, called Chloe, I call you to the Kingdom of Heaven."

With those words, He turned and walked along a pathway. By some instinct I followed, and as I did so my eyes seemed to clear and I saw before me a most wondrous sight. There were no pearly gates as everyone on earth imagines but there was a door flanked by walls that stretched a very long way upwards. God knocked and stood aside for me. I waited, unsure of why God would step aside for me. He pointed the way. I peered inside. Crowds of people, dressed alike, all in much like hooded robes, were lined up on both sides of the path which continued through the door and further into Heaven. The beautiful choir recommenced and God indicated I should now enter the door. I walked through it very slowly and stood just inside, a little apprehensive. Someone who looked like the Jesus I knew from paintings on earth appeared at my side, and smiled the most beatific of smiles.

"Welcome to Heaven, Chloe," was all he said.

I was too amazed to speak; too emotional; but happy and, for the very first time in a very long time, at peace with myself.

When I was young I think I had once read in the book of Revelation that all would be judged on the last day. Yet, this was not so. I had been judged now and had been admitted to the afterlife. I believe you may expect me to tell you more about it, am I right Dad? Well, I would but no words can express adequately in any meaningful sense the wonder of this place. So you must wait until you too arrive here, Dad. Anyway, haven't I given enough description of what has happened since my death to make you believe in the existence of this place; given you faith to live your life knowing that one day you will join me here? I believe so.

Well, Dad, what more can I say? Words now fail me, which you surely find difficult to believe given the number of times I have spoken to you. I have given you some insight into God, not to mention the people I met in the Waiting Room. I have met many others in addition to the people I have told you about; people from other nations and cultures. I could tell you their stories but I feel I have already spoken to you for long enough. But just remember, the tales of all people that I have met are similar to the ones I have related. People are all the same Dad, just remember that. Indians, Chinese, Europeans, South Americans, I met people from all these different parts of the world and I can tell you they share a common humanity with those of us who lived in a Western country and therefore each one of them should be treated equally on earth. Life is too short, (and don't I know that), for indulging in petty arguments over the way in which different cultures live their lives. God gave me permission to speak to you. He provided the means for me to do so. I have told you that faith is the only essential ingredient that you require in your life from now on. Believe in what I say, Dad. You must. I am terribly sorry that I left you and Mum so suddenly but you know it was out of my control. Live a good life in the future and try not to torture yourself that I have permanently gone. I have left you in bodily form, but my spirit lives on, not only here but also on earth. It is constantly around you and thoughts of me will surely be triggered from time to time. Think good thoughts; remember the good times; cling to your memories and I will survive in your heart until your flame is extinguished and you and Mum can join me here, reunited at last. Goodbye Dad. God bless you. You were the best Dad I could ever have had. And one last thing I need to tell you, Dad. I have also spoken to Mum, my friend and soul mate, and came to her in her sleep, just as I have with you. My words to her were not the same as yours of course as I have discussed our mother and daughter relationship and I have also used the opportunity to tell her of the lives of people other than James and the others I told you about. You may wish to speak to her one day about my visits to you as I am certain she will want to tell you her stories. And though you and Mum have not been together for many years please maintain your friendship. This is my wish. Until we meet again,

Love you Dad, Chloe.

Chapter Sixteen

"As soon as Chloe spoke those final words, 'Love You Dad, Chloe', I woke up with a start," George burst out, "as if a glass of water had been thrown directly into my face. My eyes were wide open. I looked around the darkened room. This was her final visit. I was certain of that now. This was her saying goodbye. I rushed to my computer and furiously typed out this final episode. There was no hesitation; the words flowed as if she was standing over my shoulder dictating. I had no need to pause and reflect on her actual words; I remembered every single one of them. I was on an emotional high but it could not deflect me from my need to transcribe this final chapter.

"After her first visit, questions had flooded my mind. Should I tell someone? I didn't want to be regarded as a nut case, saying I had been spoken to by my daughter from the afterlife. Originally, I committed myself to remain silent. I had no desire to be seen as needing help as if I was suffering hallucinations or under some sort of delusion. But eventually I relented and allowed you, Chas, to share her story, and then Debra and Emily. And I am glad that Chloe has also contacted her mother as they had a very close relationship. I am now certain that one day Chloe and I will be together again. Well, it is knowledge more than the faith usually ascribed to people of a religious bent. It is much more than that. I have it on direct authority. I believe I have the proof that people are looking for. Until now no-one else has found it. I have found it and this softens the pain I have in losing Chloe.

"I know I will not have any further communication from her. But I do not need any. Her words are now committed to print in my notebook and when my mind wanders off the track I will be able to refresh my memory of them to make me remember the good times we had together.

"Traces of my Chloe's existence on earth remain of course and those mementos are coveted from morning until night. Photos of her; a postcard from Paris, the clock she bought in Hawaii and other little knick-knacks. Chloe's words remain embedded in my heart and soul. It is my own special security blanket which I will unashamedly cling to for my remaining days."

George excused himself and left the room and went off in the direction of the kitchen.

"Well, that's the end, it seems," I remarked to Debra and Emily.

Neither of them spoke. I had a great deal of trouble controlling my emotions; tears welled in my eyes. Unashamedly, I allowed these tears to trickle down my face. Debra smiled and put her arm around my shoulders. Emily dabbed her eyes with a tissue.

"What do we do now?" Debra asked.

"That's in George's domain," I responded. "It's up to him whether he keeps Chloe's account of the afterlife to himself, and us of course, or whether he believes there is a benefit in spreading the story around. Perhaps he will go and speak to Michelle."

"How can a great story such as this be kept under lock and key?" Debra asked.

"I don't know. It's entirely up to George...and Michelle it seems now."

Without George in the room we appeared to be floundering,

incapable of decisive action. We waited his return with a degree of apprehension. We didn't have to wait too long.

George returned looking composed again. He resumed his seat.

"That seems to be the end, George. What do we do now?" I asked.

He smiled. "I'm glad in one way for Chloe's story to have finished. Now a new stage in my life can begin. Once the Coroner has made her decision it will be over. But for now I will read her story again to remind myself..."

He faltered. Dark thoughts of her sudden death still haunted him. It was one thing to know that Chloe was in the afterlife. It was another to have to cope with her physical loss, her absence from his presence, her inability to share with him his life on earth. Religious people might say he should have been ecstatically happy to have proof of the afterlife, but the human fragility of feeling loss is difficult to overcome.

George gathered himself together; his teary countenance vanished and he smiled to reassure us that he was alright. But nothing could convince me that he was not extremely distressed.

"George, I understand you are feeling upset still, but look at the situation from Chloe's point of view. She has communicated with you because she would have been well aware of your sense of loss when she died. This was her way of saying that you should not overly concern yourself with her death. You now know she is in a safe place, waiting for you."

George nodded.

"And because of where she is," I continued, "she wanted to make you and the rest of us fully consider how we live our lives. To make clear we should not be concerned or subsumed with the material aspects of life but with the spiritual and humanitarian; of showing compassion and understanding of our fellow human beings and empathy with the unfortunates of this world. Remember the stories she told you to demonstrate that people live vastly different lives. And she mentioned the spirits from other nations and cultures she also met and reminded us that we are all equal. Some of us act badly at times; on other occasions we do good things, but after death we are all equal; we end up in the afterlife. She is giving you a light to show to others, to allow them to see the path they should follow. Yes, now you must pass on the story to others; you cannot limit this knowledge to us, your best friends. You should also exchange stories with Michelle. You must be strong and release this secret you have only shared with us so far. Her story deserves to be told by you and Michelle."

"But this last episode, how will people take it? They'll pass it off as the ravings of a lunatic," George lamented.

"Not if they believe everything that came before," Debra remarked.

"Debra's right; it's a package, believe all or disbelieve all," I said.

"Yes, but it's so fantastic isn't it; meeting the Spirit, coming face to face with God, all that noise, choirs and stuff; who will believe it?" George pleaded.

"Remember what Chloe said darling," Emily cut in. "All you need is faith. You can prove that Chloe came to you from the afterlife, but she reminded you that you had to have a belief that all she told you will come to pass. The sceptics will not believe you in any event so don't worry about them. All you can do is tell what happened to you. Those that don't want to believe, won't."

"But how should I proceed?" George asked, seeking guidance.

I racked my brain for an answer. Only George can do it I thought. Other than Michelle, who would believe any of us if we spoke out? No one! This was a case where the assistance of an acolyte was not required. It was up to George and Michelle, if she could overcome her emotions, to go out into the community and spread Chloe's story far and wide. I thought George had the ability to do so. But before George did that I needed to know the answer to one question.

"George, let me ask you one question."

"What is it Chas?"

"You have Chloe's story, fully complete, in your folder. Apart from telling you where she was, what do you think is the message Chloe wants you to pass on to the people you tell?"

"I've had that question constantly on my mind Chas ever since the first visit. Yes, of course she wanted me to know there is an afterlife where we would meet again. I took from her long descriptions of the conversations with the people she met the message that we all live different lives and so each one of us has an individual story to tell, but that, in the end we are all equal because we all die. And because of that it is pointless to carry on despising other people, hating other races, disregarding the worthiness of other religions and nations. We need to live as one with the rest of humanity and erase discord between people and, I suppose what it boils down to is love everyone you come across because they too are a specific individual just like you. You are me and I am you and basically we inhabit this world together as we will in the afterlife that is to come."

George suddenly got up and paced around the living room as if he was contemplating what he was to say next. He didn't speak at all though; he just helped himself to a glass of wine from the bottle that had stood forlornly on the buffet. George was no genius but I felt that it would have been like interrupting the work of a Monet or Dickens to have stepped on the ruminations that were whirling around inside his mind. I indicated by my eyes to Debra and Emily not to interfere with his thought process. We sat in silence for what seemed like ten minutes, but was most likely barely a minute, waiting for George to say something. He was clutching his folder tightly as if he did not want to let anyone read it.

Eventually he sat down. "Well Chas," he began, "let's get to work on telling Chloe's story."

www.ingramcontent.com/pod-product-compliance
Lightning Source LLC
Chambersburg PA
CBHW061519020726
47502CB00006B/2145